FLIGHT OF THE FEATHERED SERPENT

Dana Alexander

ISBN-13: 978-1733300568 (paperback)

First edition ISBN: 978-0692792780 | 2016
Flight of the Feathered Serpent, Arizona
Printed in the United States of America

Cover design by Bespoke Book Covers

For the muse.

1

The top of my head slammed into the wall of the ship, jolting me awake. The wooden bed I was lying on creaked in defiance at the sudden halt in movement. Rubbing the spot that took the hardest blow, I glanced to the ornate carvings on the ceiling and lowered my gaze to the only porthole. The same intricate detail encircled the window. The colors of the sky were a brush stroke of gray and pale orange. *Land.* We'd arrived on the Yucatan Peninsula.

I rose from my semi-comfortable nest, straightened my clothing, and strapped my sword in place. Shouts of orders being given, followed by the sounds of running footsteps, fell below deck. A slight tingling sensation warmed at my left shoulder and ran the length of my arm.

"I feel you," I whispered, angling my head to the side. "Will you show yourself?" I reached a hand toward the man I'd come to know as Cerys but felt nothing as my fingers penetrated his image. The dream I'd awoken from so abruptly was one with detail of my bonding to the spirit in front of me. "Are you responsible for that vision of us?"

"Not this time. Your dreams are memories of other experiences, other places you have been. I wanted to be here when it was returned to you."

"How could you be sure it would?"

"Having a direct connection with the entity guiding your course, I'm privy to information released to you."

My gaze floated around the tiny quarters in search of my boots.

I was still getting accustomed to the recent knowledge that Cerys had all the information required to guide Kevin, the human form of his spirit and my love. For each human, there existed a higher level of being to guide them. The closest science had to proving such a theory was that of a parallel universe. It would take more years than I had on Earth to see the formula connecting spirits to the human experience come to light. While Cerys aided Kevin, I had yet to encounter my equal or even the memory of her. The only information I had was that her name, Arwyn, also belonged to me in realms far from Earth.

My memories had been withheld by the Alliance, a governing order that handed down the direction of the Soltari—an entity that set the rule of law for creation and its progression in the realms. They did this by voting on certain factors pertaining to the immortals and their ability to complete a mission. The Alliance believed my memories would give rise to emotions that might interfere with recovering the keys, risking the future of the humans who had opened the path for Tarsamon's consuming shadows. Kevin was sworn to secrecy to be able to join me in this life. The problem was the emotional connection existed, anyway, between Cerys, Kevin, and myself without any history to anchor it to.

I glanced up at Cerys. "I don't agree with the Alliance's decision. I fought for them to give me those memories, our history together." A seed of resentment had been planted when I'd learned it had been a vote that would alter my life. I wanted more than anything to understand the deep connection I shared with a man I'd only known a few short months. All I had were flash images revealing a life from long ago, and the need to know felt like a relentless itch I couldn't scratch.

"They've seen the clarity in your argument to not deny you, us, of what was shared."

I nodded. *Maybe.*

"And you've proven your ability by obtaining the first key."

"I hope you're right."

When I'd last seen Kevin a little more than a week ago, I'd almost interrupted his request to alter his agreement with the Soltari to protect me. The penalty for going against the Order or failing the mission was a permanent breaking of that connection forged so long ago. That grated on my nerves. A punishment for failure by an entity that had guided my existence and a belief system I fought for.

For Kevin, there was too much pain in my not knowing our past. Combined with my stubborn nature, it had caused tension to grow between us as he tried to protect me in the manner he believed was best, which often meant keeping track of my every move. I was too independent a soul for that sort of care. What occurred to me on our voyage across the sea was that what I wanted most, though I loved him, was distance. I'd have to find a reasonable common ground.

"Are you not pleased to have the memory of us?" Cerys asked, interrupting further thought on the matter.

"Of course I am." I pressed a smile across my lips, avoiding the intense stare I felt from him as I slipped the dagger in place.

A flash of the vivid dream blinked across my vision. Since waking from it, there at least existed an answer for our connection—a bond that transcended life. The tenderness we'd shared touched the core of my soul and frightened me. I'd spent my life blocking intimate relationships and close feelings for the vulnerability that came with them. No, I needed to keep the wall in place that numbed my feelings and kept me focused on my task to recover the last two keys.

With a decision made, I lifted my gaze to Cerys again. "They're waiting," I said, referring to the team that traveled with me. "I wish we had more time."

Cerys smiled and nodded once. I slid on my boots and glanced up. *What would it be like to have both Cerys and Kevin in the same room? Is that even possible?*

Warm tingles slipped down the length of my arm again. As I reached the door, I turned to see Cerys fading from view. I headed up the narrow staircase toward the deck.

A blanket of humidity fell over me. A fine mist surrounded the ship and beads of moisture began to form on my skin. I scanned the coastline and the dense trees and foliage we would cover. Making a trek through the jungle would require stamina in an environment I had little familiarity with. Even though I had pulled my hair into a sleek ponytail, the intensity of the warm air made it feel as though I was wearing it long and heavy. I had shucked my heavier garments for a pair of shorts and sleeveless top with a bit of stretch for comfort and movement only to find it sticking like a second skin. I doubted any material in this steam bath would be comfortable. I shifted my gaze upward to watch a sunset of deep yellows and pinks. White clouds were strewn across in an illuminated haze. My eyes drifted to the beach and a mountain below the colored sky. Several elves raced to lower the mainsail, while others finished tying off the bow.

They had initiated this voyage on a ship, undetectable by the human eye and, more importantly, by the evil that sought to interfere with our mission. But it was a temporary veil of protection to get us to the Yucatan and the location of the guardian of the second key. It wouldn't take long for Tarsamon and the dark shadows to track our energy path to this jungle, as they had done at the gateway at River Teith in Scotland. Darkness hunted light. As another level of guard, Lady Mara, a woman of no more than five feet tall and with a wrinkle for every hour of time that had passed, had a talent for creating certain unique tools not provided by the skilled elves. She had given me a ring to help hide my energy from the dark forces that chased us. Along with the gift was the limitation that the protection was temporary, but she hadn't said for how long.

Why didn't the Soltari place the keys in realms where we might be able to hide our energy? Such a place has to exist. The physical world was difficult to maneuver in, heavier, making it harder to move without being noticed.

As I stared across the landscape, the difficulties encountered on the last mission floated back to me, as well as the man with a lot of information who had turned against our team, joining with Tarsamon. C-05 had died once. Or so I'd thought. As a shapeshifter, he'd brushed against the energy of another man, assuming a new image—a spiked haircut set above an overly thin, angular face. But instead of the cool white strands of hair I was used to, they were now the color of soot, to match the darker shade of the soul he was transforming into. His eyes were what I couldn't forget. Gray steel that burned into my own, willing me to give up the key to him. He'd be back in one form or another, unless, of course, Tarsamon had lost patience with his first failed effort to get the key.

"Sara." Eldor, the leader of the elves, stood a few yards away. He lifted his chin in my direction. With the flick of a few fingers, he invited me to follow him as he ducked down a stairwell across from where I stood. As I came around, I saw the door to a cabin closing and entered.

Eldor's appearance was immaculate, with perfectly groomed long chestnut-colored hair resting behind his shoulders. His face was without a single line or wrinkle, despite his age of nearly four hundred years.

"I could take a bath on the deck just standing there," I said, realizing the scent of my skin and hair was becoming more fragrant the longer I was outside. *Easy to track for a hunter.*

He smiled, hearing the thought. "You may be," he replied. "And so I want you to have this." He lifted two blades tucked in sheaths, not much larger than my hands. "They're to be worn on your back. And before you ask, you're not only trained in swordsmanship but in all bladed weapons," he said, reminding me of yet another memory I didn't have.

"But I've never practiced with these in Ardan," I replied, taking the package and feeding my arms through the shoulder straps.

Ardan was the home of all immortals. A place where every soul resided, unless they chose to venture to other realms, and where those of us who were tasked with keeping the balance of good and evil could practice our skills.

"Shouldn't I recall some of the training?" I reached over my shoulder to pull one of the blades.

"You will when the time calls for you to use it," he replied. "The knowledge is present. While your skills at manipulating energy to protect you are useful, it doesn't hurt to have a few additional tools at the ready."

I pulled the blade through the air in a sweeping X fashion. The movement felt natural enough, as though I had done so many times. "What about the members of the team?"

Eldor and his fleet of elves were precision weaponry craftsmen, developing our blades, and expert fighters who had aided us when nearly consumed by Tarsamon's army of dark shadows and faceless demons a few weeks earlier.

"They've been provided for as well."

A knock on the cabin door redirected my attention.

"Come in, Kevin," Eldor said. I flashed a smile at Kevin that went unreturned.

"The ship is secured and Mac is ready to depart to the village with the team to locate the guardian of the key." A slight shine of perspiration glowed over his face and I felt him fight to not meet my gaze. He hadn't said more than a few words since our departure from Scotland. Like me, I sensed from him a desire to maintain a distance between us.

So that's how he's going to play it. Good, I need the distance anyway to concentrate.

Kevin's eyes met mine at the thought before returning to Eldor.

No complex emotions. Need to focus.

It would take me a little time to set aside the bond that we had begun to create since reconnecting in this world. But if Kevin thought he'd be able to focus on the mission that much more because of the space he was creating, he wasn't fooling me. Had he forgotten that I shared the same ability as he to feel what others felt and to hear the truths of their thoughts? His ability to block me was either weakening or I was becoming stronger at getting through. And he was most certainly in a battle with himself over his decision. His eyes confirmed that much. How long could he fight the good fight?

"We were just finishing up here," I said.

"I'll let him know." He turned to leave, closing the door behind him without another glance.

Cold.

"Be patient with him, Sara," Eldor said, giving my shoulder a slight squeeze. "He must find the best way to fulfill his obligation to the Soltari and the Alliance and not lose you in the process."

"I know. But patience doesn't make things any easier between us." I tugged once on the strap at my shoulder. "Thanks again."

"You love him, whether easy or not."

It wasn't a question, and yet I still felt obligated to confirm the statement. "Yes. And we both know that can get us killed with one wrong judgment call."

Eldor placed a light kiss on my cheek a second before I turned to leave.

I joined the six other members of the team, waiting for the two boats maneuvering closer to take us to shore. As I stepped into one of them, I felt something more in the balmy air than humidity, drawing my attention as though a rancid aroma floated on the current. I hadn't detected the shift in the energy earlier as I'd gazed over the landscape. I sharpened my senses but couldn't tune in to it. Kevin looked at me with the same knowing. *Stay with Ceanag.* I heard his thought and let my eyes linger on him before letting them drift to the team with their own connections to each other.

Aria had formed an alliance with Matt that seemed as old as the one Kevin and I shared. And despite Elise's attempts to thwart Juno's attention, they, too, were connected in some way I had yet to uncover.

Ceanag (KEN-uhk) MacCristal, better known to us as Mac, and guardian of the first key, was tasked with leading us to the guardian of the second key and journey with us until all three were obtained. Although we were guided by Mac, I also carried knowledge that would lead me to each one. If I needed to follow a different path than the one intended, there would be little I could do to deny that urge.

I hiked with the others through the damp and rocky terrain. Numerous fallen trees lay on our self-made path, along with hundreds upon thousands of sprouts of new foliage. We were headed into the depths of the jungle, far beyond any well-worn tourist routes, and across a landscape resembling destruction following a storm. Debris was scattered all about the ground. A bird whistled from above, signaling tranquility and calling my immediate assessment a lie. Above us towered mature trees and plants, shading us from the heat of the sun under canopies of leafy green arms clasped together. While the additional shade provided some relief from the heat, it would be more difficult for us to see anything or anyone who might be stalking. I would need to keep my senses sharply tuned.

As if he felt the same ominous sensation in the air, Kevin's next steps brought him closer to where I hiked, choosing to follow through with guarding me and withdrawing his previous affections. If that's what he needed to do, so be it. I respected the decision and had developed enough of a toughened shell to withstand the nagging loss of him while he focused on his duty.

Still, being close to him was wearing on my defenses, those I'd spent thirty-one years molding. My nerves tightened at the tension not eased with the silence between us.

When I first met Kevin, a feeling so strong had pulled me to him, making it impossible to ignore. Now, the desire to respect his decision and the proximity conflicted, making me want him when I couldn't have him. When I shouldn't have him. Duty came first. And for a split second, I wished he'd stay out of my immediate view. *Can't he walk behind me?* I didn't make any effort to block my thoughts from being read by him. And I knew he heard every unspoken word. I glanced to him without turning my head. But he made no effort to step behind me, staying within an arm's length and well within sight.

Adding to the tension was the growing sensation that all was not as calm as it appeared. *We're on a path to meet the guardian. Could it be something's wrong with this particular person who will lead us to the key?* I knew nothing of him or her. But I couldn't imagine someone so important, who had spent their lifetime preparing for the possibility of this mission, having an evil side. *No. It's not the guardian.* I sharpened my senses and hiked a few more paces before my gaze lifted to the edges of a wall extending above the trees a short distance ahead. I moved between the trees to see it was a temple. Mac, Aria, and

Elise kept hiking, edging around the steps, pushing long, hanging branches aside. I glared at its rough gray-washed stones until it bothered me enough to stop and tune in to the extreme sensations radiating from within. Matt and Juno stopped, too, and like a train coming to a halt, so did the others.

"We need to keep going," Mac said, turning to see why no one was following him.

I wasn't leaving until my curiosity was satisfied.

"She senses something," I heard Elise whisper to him from a few paces ahead of me.

"I've got to go in," I said. An unexplainable force was guiding me to enter.

"If it's the gateway—" Mac began.

"It's not," I interrupted and moved to go up the steps.

Kevin reached for my arm, holding me back. "Wait until we check it out."

I held my gaze with his and then let my eyes drop to his hand as it fell away. He shook his head as I turned to follow Matt and Juno up the steps.

The sunlight streamed through the broken roof, lighting long streaks of red racing down the temple walls. The pungent scent of rust broke through the musty aroma and seared my nostrils, leaving a bitter taste in my throat. *A fresh kill.* And not just a kill, a message. But for whom?

I froze in stunned silence. Every sensation of the recently taken victim, or a few, prickled my skin. Whispers could be heard growing louder. Spirits filled the room, trying to speak of what felt to me like the injustice of being robbed of life. It was another language, though, and one of which I had no knowledge. But the feelings of anger inside these walls pierced the stillness, delivering a promise of retribution. As an empath, I carried the burden of being able to feel all the emotions of those living, and apparently those deceased, doubling the intensity of any situation by having to sort my feelings from someone else's.

"Holy shit." Juno's words shook me from my trance.

"It wasn't long ago that whoever wreaked havoc in here left," Matt said. "Look." He pointed to a corner of the wall where light reflected a drop of blood chasing another on a path toward the floor, with the bright red color indicating oxygenated blood. My eyes trailed down the walls to the sandy stone floor to see the puddles. I felt my stomach lurch into my throat and swallowed hard.

"Where are the bodies that belong to this blood?" Aria asked. "A kill this messy would leave something more behind." She took a couple of steps to peer around one of the corners to her left. "Nothing there."

"Animal sacrifices?" Elise suggested, her tone resonating with hope for anything other than a human sacrifice. Each of us carried preternatural abilities and could sense the energy of a human over an animal.

"Not in a hundred years," Mac said under his breath.

Needing a good dose of fresh air, I bolted from the temple and down the steps. An image of Mary Ann, my loving adoptive mother, flashed across my vision. How safe was she? The shadows had already begun to make a presence back home in New York, as they methodically consumed the energy of the weaker, angrier humans, like a small child succubus, growing as it starved the humans of their life force. Mary Ann had dreamed of the very images our team had started fighting before we'd left.

I was bent over, resting my hands on my knees, unsure if the contents of my stomach were going to reappear, when I heard footsteps behind me. I angled my head to see over my shoulder and turned away, taking in another deep breath.

"You okay?" Kevin asked.

"Yeah. The stench was overpowering." As a psychiatrist, I'd trained as a medical doctor and had no qualms about the smell of blood, formaldehyde, and other aromas of the body. The humidity, however, made the scent of blood linger heavier in the air. I sucked in deep breaths as though I were drowning in them, just to cleanse the scent of rust from my nostrils and throat. *Lemon and sugar. Lemon and sugar.* I repeated the phrase that had kept me from hurling in the past. But it was the thought of what had happened in there that was more troubling than the smell.

"Our guardian of the key"—Juno's voice paused behind us—"is still alive."

I turned to see everyone exiting.

"Then you've seen the meeting we are to have with the guardian?" I asked, turning my attention back to Juno. He and Matt carried a second sight to see coming events.

"I have."

"Let's hope you're right," Mac said.

"I usually am."

Elise gave a blatant *ugh* sound as she brushed past Juno. He smiled. Though he was probably right, all of us had learned that our otherworldly abilities ran the risk of being untrustworthy while on the search for a key. At least they had in Scotland.

Elise had another issue with Juno. Since we were first introduced to each other in this world, Juno had loved to antagonize. And Elise was a prime target for him. It was also his way of getting her attention, by being playful and annoying.

I glanced at Matt for confirmation of Juno's vision.

"Our guide is waiting," Matt said.

"Then we dinna want to waste any more time here," Mac said, in that Scottish lilt that somehow softened any uncomfortable topic of conversation. "We've got to keep moving. There is nothing to do here." He stepped past me into the jungle.

Mac was right. We couldn't do anything about what might have been lost or taken in that temple. There sure as hell wasn't any evidence outside the building to give us a clue. All we knew was that the blood was human. And yet I couldn't escape the feeling that whatever had happened was a message I was meant to see. But what was it? A warning with the intent to have me abandon the quest for the second key? It would take a lot more than blood on a few old walls to frighten me. As I pulled my hands from my knees and turned to follow Mac, I stopped. I could have sworn I saw a movement. I stared at the stone window edge of the temple and caught the last quarter of what looked like a snake slithering inside the corner. My stomach lurched once more at the thought of what it would find on its downward trek.

If Tarsamon already completed his quest to consume the lives on Earth, would I know? Can he move that fast? I haven't passed through any portal taking me to another realm. As far as I'm aware, I'm still in the modern-day Yucatan jungle, where human existence remains probable, for now.

2

I felt the ticktock of time racing away from us. The dark forces that hunted us wouldn't remain still while we pushed on with the quest, not when their world was threatened more with each key found. We had to move faster, but there was nothing I knew of that could get us to the second key any quicker. And with C-05 working in conjunction with the darker forces of Tarsamon, that meant he had blabbed about his knowledge of the locations we would expect to find each key. C-05 had shared such information in exchange for his life, after he'd been caught in the territory of Ardan that Tarsamon claimed for his own, after being excommunicated from the Alliance. Tarsamon knowing the location coupled with the dark shadows' and faceless demons' ability to track energy trails meant the danger we would soon find ourselves in couldn't be too far behind us. We needed to remain focused, stay on track to keep this quest moving at a swift and efficient pace.

We emerged from the jungle on a dirt path that had long been cleared of the numerous trees and saplings. Within minutes we could see a small village ahead. The place appeared deserted, with the exception of four muscular men wearing nothing but loincloths who approached at a casual pace with spears in hand. *Guards of the village?* As we drew closer, we could see their faces were painted sky-blue with a shade of black extending from one temple, across the eyes and bridge of the nose, to the other temple. Mac reached an arm across, indicating to wait. The rest of the team followed his direction as he stepped forward to speak with them. We were careful not to draw any weapons and seem more threatening than we must have appeared with our ample supply of blades. The vibe I was getting from them was one of extreme caution anyway. Were they aware of what had happened in the temple? Did they know who had caused all of that bloodshed? If so, there were no thoughts of the like running through their heads, at least none that I could read.

We listened as several words were exchanged before two men walked behind us and the remaining two flanked the sides of our group. Mac pressed forward as we followed, until we entered the main village area. A group of children could be heard playing a short distance from us, but things seemed unusually quiet for what should be a busy village. No one was out tending to any cooking, weaving, or sewing. As we looked closer, all that could be seen were other men, like those who approached us, standing guard on the perimeter of the village and lush forest. We waited while the man closest to Kevin took Mac into one of the huts.

A few minutes later, Mac emerged and called me to go with him. Kevin approached, too, but Mac shook his head.

"Not now," he said.

Kevin nodded once and waited just outside the entrance.

As I stepped inside, I expected to see a man, but instead a woman with round, dark, hypnotizing eyes drew me into the hut farther. Her smooth black hair hung long behind her back and she sat with her legs crossed, looking up at me with a soft smile. I instinctively knew she was the guardian of the second key. She was older than I, perhaps midforties, I guessed. *What strengths does she have that will carry her through this dangerous mission?* Mac was an avid swordsman, like any of us on the team. But I couldn't see that skill in this woman, not from her petite frame.

"Sara, this is Topetine, the guardian."

I nodded in greeting.

"Please, sit," she said. Though I spoke four languages, the

traditional Achi or K'ichi' (Quiche) of the Maya was not one of them, and I was pleased she had chosen to speak English. "Show me your hand, Light Carrier. Though I need little proof to see that you are the one chosen to hold the power of the keys. It shows in your eyes." I presented my right hand with the silver band that identified me as the one chosen to hold the power found in the keys. "Ah, yes," she said. "Just as it was foretold." The lettering on the silver ring, bonded to my finger since I'd received it, began to light at her touch as it had when I met with the knights in Randun, a realm my team and I had crossed into on our trip to Doune Castle in Scotland for the first key. My gaze drifted from the ring to her eyes in time to see a flash of yellow run through them. A closer look revealed they appeared like that of a...cat?

"Your eyes do not deceive you, nor does the intuition that leads you," she said.

"You're a shapeshifter," I said. It was meant as a question but fell from my lips as a confident statement. I wasn't picking up on her ability to shift despite seeing the flash of cat eyes in the dark brown pools that studied me.

"Jaguar," she confirmed.

So that's the strength I detected.

"We'll leave upon sunrise to locate the gateway."

I nodded. "I have to ask. Do you know what happened in the temple outside your village?" My eyes narrowed in concentration as I awaited her answer. Mac sat quietly beside me.

"I know what you have seen. That, my dear, was no sacrifice, but a distraction to delay you. And let me caution you that as a Light Carrier in a most mystical place, you will see things others will not."

The snake? The metallic scent of blood had convinced me I had not imagined the gory details. Besides, the other members of my team had seen the effects left upon the walls, too.

"The answer you seek is that Tarsamon has escalated his approach into this world. He can't slaughter all, because he needs the energy of the humans. But he can take out enough to frighten you, cause you to make a mistake, perhaps?"

"To take me off course," I replied in a whisper. With C-05's previous research and knowledge of where to find the guardian, he could easily have interrupted my path. The corners of Topetine's lips turned up into a smile.

"Look," she said. She reached behind her and picked up a bowl containing a powdery white substance. She pinched a small amount, rubbed it between her hands, and blew the residue into a white cloud toward me. The powder hung like smoke between us as an image formed of a serpent with feathers attached. "*Kukulkan*," she whispered.

Reading her thoughts, I was provided insight that this image was a revered deity to the Mayan people. The serpent floated through the sky carrying what looked like the sun in its mouth. The image changed, showing a pool of blood, then a pool of blood at my feet in the temple. The dust fell to the mat we were sitting on.

"You are guided by the feathered serpent as you enter the world where the key is hidden. Trust your instincts at all times, especially here."

"Where are the people of your village?" I asked. "Are they safe?"

"Yes. Many are in hiding. The old tales we have held dear have foretold of your arrival." She patted my folded hands. "Some of the villagers are not so frightened, but most want to be sure all is safe before they come out.

"You and your friends may stay in the huts behind this one. Join us for a meal this evening, won't you? You'll see the fires."

"Yes. Thank you." I stood to leave. As I exited the hut, I nearly bumped into Kevin and it annoyed me further that I couldn't have any time without his close watch. I huffed past him, seeking room to breathe.

"You were right," I said to Juno. "The guardian lives." I grabbed my pack and faced the other members of the team.

"We're to stay the night in the huts behind that one." I angled my head over my shoulder. "We'll leave at sunrise to find the gateway. We've been asked to join the guardian, Topetine, for a meal tonight." Everyone grabbed what belongings they had unloaded from their shoulders and headed toward the huts.

"I need your satellite phone," I said to Juno.

"On one condition." I searched his eyes. "Make up with him already, will you?" Juno said, referring to Kevin. "His focus is not aligned."

"I'm afraid I can't affect his focus." Kevin strolled outside Topetine's hut, in conversation with Mac. "He's chosen to be distanced."

"Here," he said, handing me the phone. "Try something, will you? I've got to make nice with Elise, since it looks like a few of us will be bunking together."

I cast an eye at the huts. *Three huts, seven people. Great.*

I found an empty cabin, set my pack on the ground, and began dialing to get Mary Ann. My adoptive mother was the only person I genuinely trusted. The last time I spoke with her, she explained her fear about the dreams she'd been having. How the dark shadows were clinging to humans, dragging each person down emotionally, then physically to encourage rage between them. With little energy left to live, all of it being taken by the evil that had entered the world, all that existed was the growing animosity that fed the darkness of Tarsamon's minions. A fight for survival was at hand. The only answer to make sure the humans won was the keys.

I needed to know if Mary Ann was okay. It had been nearly a full month since I was supposed to call her back. So much had happened since then. My team and I had rushed out of New York with demon shadows in hot pursuit as we raced to the gateway in Scotland, then another distant world, and I'd nearly lost my life and the lives of my team due to my stubbornness. I still hadn't forgiven myself for it. The risk I'd taken still felt like a fresh wound. And here I was in the Yucatan ready to head through another gateway and face God knew what. This might be my last chance to check on Mary Ann. Ring five, six and finally she picked up.

"Mary Ann?"

"Oh, my God, Sara. I've been so worried about you."

"I'm all right. Remember, I said I'd be traveling? Are you okay?"

"Yes, fine. But I'm having a little trouble hearing you. Where in the world are you?"

"I'm in the Yucatan. This was the only chance I had to call and I don't have much time to talk. How are things there?"

"Ah, I don't want to discuss it. Lots of fighting in the streets. Remember that Rodney King incident in California ages ago? Like that," she said, not waiting for me to answer. "Haven't you been able to catch any news?"

"I'm tucked away in the jungle. Not much reaches us here. What about the dreams we talked about? The shadows?"

"Oh, yeah. Still having those nightmares. More often, too." By the inflection in her tone, she was shouting and yet it was difficult to hear her. *Good. They remain only nightmares.* "Listen to me, carefully. If things get worse, go to my house. No one will try to harm you there."

"Sara..." She paused. "I hate to tell you this but your house was ransacked. I went by after I hadn't heard from you and your gates were wide open. Looks like gangs broke in and trashed the estate. And one of your guards...the police found him. He was struggling to breathe."

No surprise after having demons crawling all over it, trying to find me. Juno had remained with the other members of the team to fight off the last of the shadows, allowing Kevin and me to escape. Juno said the dark shadows had disappeared when their target, me, abandoned them. I assumed the security guards had been overtaken by the shadows, at least that's what had happened to one of them. I had watched, unable to help Paul in the mad rush to escape, as he was pressed against a wall and a shadow slid into his body to consume him. By the sound of Mary Ann's voice, chaos had hit. Who knew if I even had a security team anymore?

"Is he alive?"

"He's on a ventilator. The police want to speak with you to get more information. I called them from your house. They came over and searched the premises, asking if I knew what might be missing. With all the vintage collectibles you had, I couldn't give them much information. I locked up the house so there isn't further damage. The gates are closed, too. But I think the police put a lock of their own on the gates."

Easily broken into.

"I'm sorry, I should've called you the next day like I promised. I was unable."

"At least I know you're okay. It's a terrible mess, though."

"Don't worry about the house. Are the dogs okay?" My two young Dobermans, Ares and Kona, were usually in the company of the primary security guard that lived on the premises, but I hadn't seen him or the dogs when I'd made the hasty departure.

"Yes. I found them wandering in the yard alone, loaded them into my SUV, and took them home with me. What's going on? When will you be back?"

"I don't have time to explain and not over the phone. I'm safe and with the friends I mentioned. I'll be back as soon as I can." I felt someone at the door. "I've got to go. I'll try to reach you again when I can."

"Is Kevin with you?"

"Yes. I'll call you the next chance I get."

"What's wrong?"

"Nothing to worry about. Trust me."

"I do. But I don't like the sound in your voice."

"It's just a little"—I hesitated and glanced at the entrance—"irritation. It'll pass. I've got to run. I love you."

"Love you, too, honey. Call soon. Better yet, get back here so I *know* you're okay."

"As soon as I can. Promise."

I didn't have time or the privacy to explain more to Mary Ann. I didn't think the shadows would hurt Mary Ann because she didn't pose a threat to the dark side's existence. Only I did. And I didn't need to upset the one person who'd ever cared about me with that reality. I blew out a breath, relieved she was all right.

I opened the front door and peered outside. There was a small patio with a couple of sun-rotted chairs on the opposite side of the louvered doors. They didn't look as if they could hold more than the weight of a small child. And yet I took a seat, hoping it would hold me, while my mind went back to Kevin. I didn't want to pay my dues to Juno for the use of his phone just yet. If Kevin wanted to talk, I would.

But for now, it felt better to let him do what he wanted and keep the distance. I leaned into what was left of the flattened cushions and stretched my legs out in front of me, crossing them at the ankles.

Juno was right. The tension between Kevin and me was growing and I didn't see how I could resolve it. Having been hardheaded about the passage that might carry us out of the fight we'd returned to in Scotland, I'd taken the blame for the dark forces capturing me. Kevin, on the other hand, blamed himself for not protecting me better. How long was he going to blame himself? Kevin had narrowly rescued me from C-05 in Tarsamon's lair, bringing with him a few members of our team. The move to free me in a world of evil was incredibly brave, and risky, too. But as far as he was concerned, I never would have been taken if he had stayed with me. Blaming himself was a waste of time. Our team had been met by the fiercest army of dark shadows we could've imagined upon our reentrance to Doune. There had been no way to avoid the showdown after we'd been surprised and outnumbered, even with the help of the elves.

"What's done is done," I said to myself and tilted my head back to close my eyes. "The rest will work itself out somehow."

Kevin wasn't the only one with a duty to stay focused, and I didn't need the roller coaster of ups and downs in an emotional relationship distracting me from the quest, not with things as dangerous as they are. There's no telling how long it would be before C-05 or Tarsamon would find us. But since C-05 had a handle on our location, I guessed it wouldn't be long before he did. The evidence of his knowledge, all of his research, had been scattered across a private room in a downtown NY office building basement before we set out on this mission. The Yucatan was one of the locations pinned on the enormous map I had seconds to view before having to leave abruptly. If I was sure of one thing, it was that C-05 knew where to find me, maybe not the exact spot per se, but that wouldn't take him long to find with the ability to track my energy better than a US Marshal chasing after an escaped felon.

Kevin would do what he thought was best and I'd respect his decision. I already did.

What were the dark forces plotting? If I were chasing someone like me, who became more powerful with each key, what would I do? I had escaped once. They wouldn't kill me for fear of releasing the power of the single key I carried within. Then again, they might decide the release of that single force wouldn't be enough to cause real damage to their takeover of humanity. Whatever was being planned would have to hurt me enough to distract me from completing the mission. And then I remembered the blood on the walls. The faces of those I loved flashed in my mind's eye. *There isn't much time. Was there ever?*

3

Flames licked toward the evening sky as several campfires burned. Around them sat more villagers than I expected, those who didn't fear my arrival as a sign of the start of terror. The smoke clung to my hair like blood-sucking insects drawn to skin. Dinner consisted of vegetables and some unknown meat roasted over a spit. I wasn't a camper. I longed for the pleasure of lounging at my desk with a plate of sushi, checking email, picking up my cell phone, and connecting to the world around me. What I wouldn't give to lose a couple of hours in a blink, documenting patient notes or internet shopping to avoid going out and doing the real thing. I was actually missing the technology, never guessing that I would.

"What do you think, Sara?" Matt asked.

"I'm sorry. I drifted a bit."

"Do you have any thoughts or feelings on the direction we should set out in for our hike tomorrow?"

I might've been guided at certain times pertaining to the keys, but the truth was I'd had too much to think about with Mary Ann's safety, the blood on the temple walls, and Kevin. I had given little thought to what direction the gateway was. Besides, as the guardian of the key, Topetine should know exactly how to get us to it.

"No. I'm relying on Topetine. What about you? See any future events we need to be prepared for?"

"Oddly enough, nothing. It's as though my ability is weakened or there isn't anything coming. And that's not likely." He smiled and sipped the dark liquid in his cup.

"Your energy in this part of the world is not quite as strong as in the US," Topetine said, stepping into our circle and sitting beside me. "Too many other forces are at work here." She flicked her fingers back and forth to emphasize an invisible energy among us. "That may change upon entering the gateway. Can't really tell till we get there."

"That explains why Matt and Juno didn't see the 'writing on the wall' at the temple ahead of actually finding it," Aria said.

"Don't worry about that," Topetine said. "Whoever's blood was used to draw Sara in to see that temple, assuming it was no powerful illusion, was already lost to the Dark Lord. Nothing can be done. Besides, two of the village guards went to check into the matter and said they found no evidence of a killing."

Aria and I looked at each other in disbelief. "We know what we saw, all of us," she said.

"I don't doubt you, my dear. This jungle is filled with all sorts of magic."

A commotion drew my attention away from the conversation toward a larger group that had gathered.

"They dance to the serpent god and the spirit gods for our safe return from the next realm," Topetine explained.

Any earlier doubt about the population of the village was put to rest as I scanned a full crowd that saw our visit as a sort of holy celebration. Children played the US version of soccer among several staked torches, while many of the adults sat around a fire smoking and drinking wine made from the fermented pulp of cacao seeds. I peered into my own cup, now empty. The wine tasted nothing like chocolate, but did the job of any strong liquor by making one light-headed in short order. After only a few sips, I had begun to feel the effects. I must have finished it while in deep thought and without a care for the dizzying effect. The sensation mingled with residual smoke that hung in a ghostly cloud around the village, lifting me to a lighter place.

Happy. They all seem so happy. And that reminded me of the weight of the world that hung in the balance. Faced with what might be a brutal hike in the morning and my head swimming in relaxation, I said good night and headed for the hut.

I sat on the step at the entrance and unfastened my boots, tapping the caked mud from the soles. The evening was quiet in this part of the village, just a short distance from the center of the festivities. I gazed up at the stars twinkling against the black sky and closed my eyes. A sense of complete peace joined with the lingering stillness in the air. One deep breath filled my lungs as a light breeze passed overhead, and the relaxation was nearly enough for me to doze against the post beside me. I opened my eyes and headed inside, setting my boots beside the pack resting near the door. As I reached to slip my shirt over my head and with an eye on the bed, a knock thudded, echoing across the small room.

Just ignore it. I cursed, knowing I couldn't. I ran a hand through my hair and turned toward the door.

"Sara, may I come in?" It was Kevin's voice that took me from my thoughts of diving under the covers. I hadn't seen him after dinner and thought he'd decided to turn in early, perhaps bunking with Mac.

"Sure. Come in." I smoothed my shirt down over my hips.

As he entered, I knew it was best to keep the distance he was establishing for his sake as much as for mine. I wasn't going to react to the sexual draw of him and make this situation between us any worse. I was well aware with my relaxed and inebriated state, resisting him might take a bit more effort. As he entered, something prickled in the air between us again.

Keep it together, Sara. Just send him on his way. "I'm sure Mac wouldn't mind if you shared a hut with him." *Good girl.*

"That isn't going to happen," he said, tossing his pack next to mine.

I glimpsed at it and back to him. "And why not?"

"He's staying with the guardian, Topetine."

"Not a problem. I'll find somewhere else to stay." I took a few steps toward my pack.

"Stop this."

"Stop what?" I asked. "I'm giving you what you want."

He closed the distance between us and glared at me.

I brushed past him, reaching for my pack, and opened the door. Before I could fully exit, his hands gripped my waist and pulled me back. In one quick maneuver from him, I'd dropped the pack and was staring down his backside from over his shoulder, struggling against his hold on my legs. The door shut with a slam as he kicked it. Everything that had been building raced to the surface and poured out of my fists and onto him.

"Put me down. I swear to God I won't tolerate being—" I was slammed onto the mattress. My breath left me in a single gasp. He was leaning over me. My legs dangled at the knees over the edge of the bed and my wrists were clasped in his hands at my sides.

"Let. Me. Go."

He never moved. Hardly blinked. "No."

"Fine." I brought my knee up between us and pushed hard into his chest, causing him to shift backward and release one of my hands to deflect my leg. My full intention wasn't an aim to hurt him, but merely to leave the hut, if I could break free of his grip. I turned into him and landed an elbow into his forearm, providing the desired effect of releasing his other hand, and bolted. Before I could make it to the door, he went for another hold and I blocked him. His hands moved quickly to find another hold, but with each attempt, he was met with my block. I swung again, but my fist was caught and released. Fury swept over me in a light sweat that broke out across my skin as a tremor ran through my arms. We fought for what felt like minutes, he trying to get the upper hand, and I to get enough distance.

"Damn it, Sara! Enough!"

He ducked behind me, reached down, and grabbed me at my knees, lifting me upside down. The quick motion sent my head spinning with no help from the earlier drink. Before I could get my bearings, he tossed me on the bed again and pinned me solidly beneath him. My breath came in and out fast. I had no ability to fight or I would have. I wasn't going to be held against my will. I lay beneath him, puffing in and out, trying to catch my breath.

"I'm done playing," he said, inches from my face.

"Oh, is that what you were doing? Because I wasn't."

"Good. When you calm down, maybe we can talk."

"After the way you—" I paused to take in another gulp of air. "I have nothing to say to you."

"Even better. Then you can listen." He had my arms pinned above my head. I turned my head to avoid the intensity of his stare. Those brown eyes flecked with gold had a way of putting me under a spell. "It's so easy for you, isn't it, to break a tie with someone? Or better still, to never let yourself feel for them."

Ouch. I looked back at him and saw the pain in his eyes. "Is that what you think? That I don't feel for you? That it's easy for me to keep the distance between us?" He stared at me. "Creating distance is what *you* decided to do, so you wouldn't fail in your mission, you said. I gave you what you wanted, trying to make it easier on you."

His brows pulled together in a fit of frustration. "It isn't easy," he said with an edge to his tone.

"I'm sorry you're having difficulty finding the best way to fulfill your duty to the Soltari. Really, I am. But maybe if it's this painful for you, you made the wrong decision." He pulled his head back slightly and I realized he thought I meant the wrong decision in agreeing to join me in this life as the warrior who would protect me on our mission. What I meant was that he'd made the wrong decision to distance himself from me. I closed my eyes, reminded of Eldor's words. *Be patient with him, Sara.* Kevin was reading my thoughts, as he often did. I could tell by the silence that would otherwise have been filled with words. I opened my eyes to see he'd cleared the pain that consumed his vision.

"You will not handle me. Let go of me," I said in a softer voice, pulling at my wrists.

"Not yet. Not before I help you understand that you cannot succeed in this mission on your own. I'm with you. Got it? I travel with you. I'll take whatever means necessary to protect you, and..."

I'm going to have you. No, love you. I don't know. It was a scramble of thought I heard as he finished the sentence in his head rather than aloud.

Kevin hadn't touched me in quite some time, and the weight of his body on mine with the grip on my wrists was turning me over inside, melting my emotional defense, and shifting my anger into hot-blooded attraction. I knew the gentleness contained behind that strength. The contrasting sides of him had always been my undoing. I felt his heart thumping against my chest. His eyes moved from mine to my lips, down farther still, and back. The prickling I felt between us when he entered the hut was now throbbing, alive with electricity as he covered me.

He planted his lips on mine, forcing them open to receive him. I struggled beneath his solid frame to get free of the grip and gain some control. And then my body relinquished its fight and my struggle slowed. My hips pressed into him, defying my intent further. His lips lifted from mine. I opened my eyes to see him staring through me. "You remember, don't you?" he whispered. And I saw the vision of the bond we created as spirits in his mind's eye, the dream I had awoken from as the ship reached landfall. He released my wrists and smoothed a hand over the top of my head.

"I remember."

"I was hoping they would give that memory back to you," he said, referring to the Soltari. He tilted his head and placed another kiss on my lips, softer this time. He shifted, allowing me to move beneath him. But I didn't. His eyes searched mine.

"What are you looking for?" I asked.

"If you remember how we came to be united souls, then I'm sorry to say your wall of defense is severely fractured, love. And maybe you were right, that I made the wrong decision to distance myself from you for the mission. I'm not certain yet."

I looked deeper into his eyes as a quick flash of color crossed them, like a flicker of colored lightning. I recognized it as the same as that belonging to the spirits that bonded in my dream of us.

"There you are," he whispered, staring past the jade green to something else behind them. *Does he see the same in me?* He bent his head and kissed me again deeper, trying to mingle our spirits as we had so long ago. I pressed a hand against his chest with an uneasiness that suddenly came over me.

"Wait. What do you mean you're not certain yet? You distance yourself or you don't." He moved beside me and I pushed myself up, leaning back against the pillows. "You know what it cost me to give all of my trust to you." I'd never allowed myself to trust a soul following the abandonment of both of my parents. Along with their departure from my life went any belief in the chance of being loved by people who should care the most. But Kevin had worn down my defenses. "Why would you dangle the emotions between us in front of me only to pull them away again?" I shook my head in disillusionment. My blood heated as the words rolled off my tongue. It was all I could do to maintain my patience while he formulated an answer.

"I was sent to protect you on this mission. And loving you has been a distraction that nearly got you killed. That mistake, being distracted, would have cost us all the lives on Earth and more."

"But it didn't."

"It's not over yet." His eyes were as intense now as when we were pressed against each other. "I find that distancing myself is an even greater distraction." I opened my mouth to protest, but closed it as he continued, realizing he was working out his decision as he spoke. "It seems that as I consider my duty to protect you, it may include guarding your feelings."

"I'm quite capable of watching out for—"

"Yourself," he interrupted. "Yes, I'm well aware of that." He moved closer. I wasn't sure it was the best idea, and still, I remained fixed against the pillows. "It took some work and patience to get you to trust me, as someone who says they love you and means it. But somewhere in that locked memory, hidden deep in your conscience, you do remember our connection beyond this world. Maybe all of the details aren't clear yet. But the knowledge is there." He paused. "And that makes it impossible to keep my distance from you."

Confusion disappeared like vapor into the air. I leaned closer.

"If we're in this together, you have to be certain we're in all the way." I pressed my lips to his. Enough holding back. I'd had my fill of it.

His kiss came rough. I was rocked through to my core with the intensity he'd been suppressing. His lips ground into mine, opening wider to take more, meeting the need in both of us. Our breaths were exchanged for quiet pants as we shifted angles and pulled from each other the desire we'd kept contained under a mask of dissolution. And then he broke away, leaving me gasping at the sudden halt and wanted affection.

"As much as I'm tempted right now, I will not make love to you with pent-up frustration."

"I'd call it passion."

"That's because you don't care about the difference. You're holding irritation toward me. I feel it from you."

"I thought you liked my aggressive side." I leaned back, considering his comment. "Do you really think I can't be tender?"

"I know you can but not right now."

Two ways to handle this. Both options, attempt distraction and return to passion or lash out for what felt like an insult, were considered in a fraction of a second.

"Your life didn't provide for tenderness, since you witnessed your mom's murder at age seven. Yet I've seen your ability to express it. Although it's been some time."

Something flashed in his eyes that I'd crossed a line.

"You wanted to talk," I added. The emptiness of rejection replaced the press of him upon me as he moved farther away. *I'm sorry.*

He turned, leveling a gaze at me as though he didn't know what to do.

"That was out of line," he said, pausing to gauge my reaction. I didn't move and cleared my mind of any thought. "Any mention of my mother and her death is off-limits."

"Fair enough." I shifted closer to the edge of the bed. "The only irritation I'm holding is if you can't decide if you're distancing yourself or not. Indecisiveness is irritating. But I meant I was sorry." I was sure he had heard the apology, because there wasn't a time I could recall when he wasn't listening to my thoughts, except when I made a dedicated effort to block him, and most often, I didn't.

"Are you?"

"Of course. If you keep hurting me with your words, there will be nothing to work out. And that's what you came here for, isn't it?"

"I'm not sure."

Yes, you are.

He raked a hand through his hair. "I needed some sleep. I need to protect you."

I felt the corner of my mouth lift. "It's more than that. And if you think you're sleeping without resolving this, you're more blind about the matter than I thought."

Kevin hardly slept, anyway. He was known in the realms as the Last Great Warrior. He was used to handling challenges, restructuring his plans to fit a situation. Having trouble on his mind meant no rest. During the time we'd spent in Cape Cod growing close, almost four months ago, he was awake and usually in his home office typing away on his laptop. Now, without any electronic devices or patients to attend to in the role he'd chosen as a doctor, he was both in and out of his element. *So strong and fierce.* And yet the soft spot beneath the exterior armor was what called to me now.

I stood from the bed, walked to where he was, and planted a single kiss on his cheek before peeling my clothes off and crawling under the covers. I was tired and I couldn't help him with his decision. The details made in the planning of this quest had been attended to long ago by the Soltari and the Alliance. Whether we could alter that plan or the consequences of going against it was still a question. It occurred to me now that where we went wrong was that, while I'd chosen to keep an emotional wall against loving anyone, Kevin had chosen to retain the tenderness of the connection. We were operating as polar opposites who loved each other with the same goal, for the sake of a successful mission. To save each other and what we held close, one of us would have to change our position.

"If you stay, and you're welcome to, turn out the light, will you?"

My decision to remember everything Kevin did about us, the

battles we'd fought, the connection we shared had been solid. The memories of our previous lives returning in pieces to me could pose a new problem—having to deal with the emotions I'd blocked for thirty-one years.

"I'm sorry if I hurt you," he said, sliding next to me a few moments later.

"Me, too." I was lost, stuck between the fear of letting the wall of safety fracture even more and the desire to pull him to me that would close out that fear forever. His fingers brushed a few strands of hair off my cheek.

As I lay with him pressed against my backside in the dark, I was comforted by the warmth and solidity of his body. I missed the closeness we'd shared at his home at the Cape, had craved it several times since. And yet a dissonance settled in the pit of my stomach. *Am I strong enough to hold on to us and still retain the focus required? What if my fear of losing him to the evil that hunts us is greater than my drive for the key?*

He kissed the top of my head and trailed a hand down my back. And I felt the answer to the latter question in the form of an ache, as it seeped through my skin and touched my heart. *Why couldn't he have chosen not to remember our connection?*

4

Kevin blinked up at the ceiling. He'd thought about bunking elsewhere, like outside the door of the hut she had chosen. He gave her space while she talked around the fire. And yet it didn't escape his attention how she'd watched intently while the boys played ball. How her eyes lit when one of them had stumbled and bounced back up to regain his pride. Would she remember how much she'd wanted a child with him, once, in a time long before this life? They had talked of what it would be like one day if they were lucky enough to be free of the Soltari's requests. As much as he disliked it, Sara was right about needing to keep some fraction of that wall of protection to see this quest through to the end. He'd work out the closeness he hoped to have with her in due time. With her memories of their lives together slowly being restored, the entire issue seemed weighted in his favor. One small concern stemmed from it, though—whether she could balance the mission with the return of emotion.

In a single fluid movement following her words inviting him to stay, he'd turned off the small gas light and stripped his clothes to slide beside her. The frightened tiger that Sara was at times had returned when he'd first entered the hut. He had expected it. He was so in tune with her emotions and thoughts, in part because she never tried to block him and, too, because he had been bonded to her thousands of years earlier, that any form she chose in any life was recognizable simply by the sensations from her. The energy she carried was so strong and connected to him that when he'd first glimpsed her in the emergency room of his hospital that night a few months ago, he hadn't needed a second look before racing to breathe life into the body that had nearly been destroyed in the accident.

It had taken a delicate touch to soothe her back to the gentle spirit he knew was contained within. He swept her hair from her cheek, leaving an ear open for the taking.

"Remind me what you remember," he whispered.

Her movement was almost undetectable, but Kevin had caught the angle of her head, as though she wanted to lean into him, and the hush of a breath that escaped her lips. It was his signal to press closer. He'd learned in this lifetime how to tame the tiger, his love, and how to crack the iron wall that blocked her emotions. It had taken awhile but her response was proof that, given enough time alone, he was capable of locating the point of affliction and handling it with all the precision of an expert fine-tuning an instrument. He felt her internal struggle to let go or show him her strength once more. Tonight, the weak point was fatigue.

He leaned over her again and whispered, "Show me, Arwyn."

Using the name she kept in the immortal world, he knew he could reach her at an even deeper level. His fingertips trailed the length of her back and extended as his hand slid over her hip. The gentle slopes of her body, especially where her neck curved into her shoulder, were smooth and elegant, the perfect graceful image covering a strong and willing fighter. The combination of power and beauty that she was made his heart beat faster, desire pulsing through every vein. He inhaled a breath at her hair and took in the physical sensations of silk and fire-smoke that joined with the heat of her backside against his body. It was pure necessity that he have her, but have her on her terms. She turned into him then and slipped a leg between his. He sucked in a breath at the touch of that long, silken limb to his most sensitive of areas. Her lips teased over his and a hand gently cupped his face, then lifted. Her fingertips trailed from his jaw, along his neck, and slowly across his chest. It sent a shiver through him with the need to take.

Maintain control. On her terms.

Her fingers stopped at the scar he'd received fighting the shadowed demons when he was first introduced to their power. Her palm pressed against him.

"Please," he whispered, sliding a hand along her side and feeling the swell of her breast. *Subtle curves. Softness. Strength.*

She drowned out his next few words, covering his mouth with hers, gently at first and then with all the want and need he'd felt from her earlier. She, too, had suppressed the same desire with so much difficulty before the argument. When her lips left his to trail across his chest and make their way down his abdomen and lower still, he heard her whisper, "Tender enough?"

"Sara," he groaned as his head lifted from the pillow to see her and fell back again. He wondered if it was her intention to make him suffer. He couldn't take the strain much longer. His body was alive and prickling like a live wire under her expert hands and mouth. "Need you."

"Not yet, my love."

Both palms slid down his chest and across the taut muscles of his abdomen as she took him into her mouth. *Too much. Need you now.* He sat forward, gripped her under her arms, and lifted her onto him. As she bent forward, her lips went to his ear whispering the language they had spoken in another realm, another time, far from this one. Dear God, she was remembering more.

"Yes, mine forever. Now," he urged.

She wrapped her fingers around him, but he was faster. With his hand pressed against her back, he flipped her on the narrow mattress and arched into her, finding silk once more. He called out her name, "Arwyn," as the quickening beat of his heart sounded in his head. Her heart was open to him once more. Had it ever closed?

She continued to speak in the language they'd known long ago, gasping at every other word for breath. The language, with its more fluid sounds and syllables, said more in meaning than the familiar

English of Earth would. And in between those sweet pauses for air, she was keenly aware of more memories than he had guessed.

Her heat was refueling the fire he'd built and carefully kept to simmer until she was ready for him. The softness that hid the strength within and her quiet moans of pleasure, stroke after stroke, were more than he could stand. When she gripped him, the sensation ripped through him in waves, causing him to quicken his pace and ride out the storm to its tantalizing end in a shudder.

"My sweet Cerys. How I've loved you...and missed you." He'd never heard the words *I love you* from her lips, these lips. But tonight she'd said them in the beautiful ancient speak in the heat of their passion. He held her, breathed in the sultry scent of her skin and smoke-filled hair, while the arm she draped over him slowly stroked up and down the length of his spine, until her hand fell gently away.

"You're my love, always. I'll never let anyone take that from us," he whispered over her hair and rolled onto his back. She curled into him, fast asleep. And time stood still. If only it would forever.

He wanted her like this, safe, with him, expressing their love without the threat of Tarsamon or the Soltari breaking their bond. Had she remembered that yet?

5

I've got to find a way to maintain some sense of detachment before...
Kevin caught my arm as I stumbled over a fallen tree trunk, interrupting my memory of last night and a concern that I might make a choice, if need be, to protect him over the mission. Deep in thought, I'd been glaring into the dense brush thick with foliage and somehow missed the protruding log that jutted into my path.

"I got it, thanks." It amazed me how I could move gracefully with a heavy sword one moment and trip the next. I glanced at Kevin. *How did I ever manage the stiletto heels on our dates, when I have trouble hiking through a jungle in boots?* My eyes scanned ahead. After being sure there were no more large protrusions in my path, I redirected my attention to the spot just beyond the sweeping branch of a copal tree. Something was there, maybe not in my immediate view, but it was lurking.

"We're close," I said. My head began throbbing, a signal that the gateway taking us to another place in time was near.

"That we are," Topetine said. "I'm to take you first to the J-man."

"The what?"

"The medicinal healer."

"I'm not ill. And we don't have time for delays. Tarsamon and his forces can't be far behind."

"Preparation for your entrance to this gateway is required, my dear. It's written in our scrolls."

What scrolls? Prepared? What could that entail?

I followed her with the others close behind, stepping out of the open space and into the thicker brush. When I placed my hand on the hilt of my sword, sensing an unfamiliar and strong presence, Topetine reached out to touch my arm, stopping me.

"All is well."

Do I trust her? I took a couple more heavy steps, staring at the back of Topetine's head while I decided. *Well, you'd damn well better. She's the only one who can lead us to the key.* The sensation nagging at my senses didn't feel dangerous per se, but uninvited. No need to approach in defense when there was no threat. Not yet, anyway. I relaxed as we continued to follow her past several dogwood trees and a collection of flowering shrubs into another open area.

The intensity in my head was beating inside my skull like a child throwing a tantrum. Topetine stopped and I took the opportunity to sit, tilting my head forward into my hands, hoping to reduce the pain. Once I passed through the gateway, very near judging by the immense throbbing in my head, everything would be better. What was the reason for needing to be "prepared" anyway? A hand on the crown of my head distracted me and I looked up through narrowed eyes into the wrinkled brown face of a man wearing a colorful feathered headdress and a robe with additional feathers down the back that peeked over the top of his shoulder. The child beat against the walls of my skull a little harder, protesting the sensory-filled outfit in front of me. Seeking refuge for my eyes, I lowered them past a necklace with a centerpiece carved of small bones to the man's bare chest.

"The pain is almost blinding, Light Carrier," he said in a cracked voice. He extended an open palm in front of me. I took it and began to rise with him. I was in no mood to argue even the simplest request. At five feet ten inches, I stood almost a foot taller than the man. *A powerful man.* Despite his actual size, his presence as a high priest was what seemed largest of all. In his other hand he held a pipe. My eyes drifted back to the man's face as he sucked in a breath from it and blew a small cloud of smoke into my face. I took it in and coughed.

Okay, that was just rude.

As I tried to justify the action, somewhere knowing the cloud wasn't meant to annoy, the throbbing in my head lessened instantly, and I found myself wishing for another breath of the wonderful spiced cloud.

My eyes began to relax and my gaze drifted past him to about six or seven tall stones similar to those Kevin and I had discovered in Randun. Did the little priest know of the power that drew me to the stones? Did these work the same way? The J-man turned and began walking away. As if led by instinct and the lighter effects of his cloud, I followed, until he stopped at a stone platform the size of a conference room. In the center were flowers that had been placed in the shape of a large wreath. He proceeded up three steps toward the circle with me in tow.

"Gather around," the J-man instructed. He took my hand and led me past the flowers into the center of the circle. Two things became very clear—a stone altar in front of the standing stones and the realization a ritual was to take place. Three other men of equal age, probably elders in the village, wearing similar feathered cloaks, stepped forward, placing offerings on the altar, and then joined us in the circle. "A sacrifice is required to the deities to be called to this order," the J-man said. *What?* I wanted to protest any such sacrifice where I was concerned. But instead I turned to Kevin, who stood next to Topetine. My eyes shifted past them to the faces of the members of the team. All were stoic, signaling everything must be okay. *But how? Did they hear the same thing?* "Show us the sign of the Light Carrier," he said. I held my open palm facing him. The ring that had been given to me by Cerys began to illuminate the inscription on the silver band as if it did so on command. It sought those pure of heart as though it were a key itself to unlocking the next passage on the quest. The lettering engraved on it would only glow when the ring had found its mark.

The J-man placed his open palm against mine. Another of the men stepped forward with a bowl containing what looked like a poultice, appeared to bless it by saying words over it I did not understand, and then dipped a thumb into the mixture, marking my forehead and temples. The J-man took my hand in his and brought out a knife. I resisted the urge to draw my hand away. *Dear God.* The small scar left from Magdalene's knife in Randun was still white. The thought of being cut again on the very finger that had recently healed was what caused my stomach to somersault. I closed my eyes, swallowed, and opened them again, gazing at the cracks of blue sky that shone beyond the leafy branches above us. The humidity somehow seemed heavier with the awareness of a sacrifice hanging over my head. I took in a slow, deep breath and shifted my attention to the eyes that studied mine.

Calmness surrounded the priest. He blew another large puff of smoke into my face to inhale, followed by one more for good measure, assurance that I was indeed as relaxed as he appeared. Tranquility filled my being, and my muscles defied the earlier desire for escape, slipping under the magic of the pipe. I was in tune with the J-man's energy, felt everything that he did, including his intent on fulfilling the ritual at hand. The third man moved beside me, dipped a brush in a bowl of clear liquid, and sprinkled it lightly inside the circle, then proceeded toward Kevin and repeated the same words before moving to each member of the group. *A blessing or prayer perhaps?*

"Do you, Light Carrier, give your gift to the gods willingly?"

A childlike voice called to me in the back of my conscience. *What gift would that be? My finger? My blood? My life? Can I say no?*

"Yes," I replied, under his spell. I blinked before looking at the other priest standing beside the J-man and felt the sharp point of the knife cut through my skin. The pain shot from my ring finger past my wrist as the nerve endings, so sensitive in the fingers, protested the intrusion of his blade. He quickly turned my finger into the bowl that the priest held. The blood fell and spread across the water, consuming it in a pool of bright crimson. The priest took the bowl and departed to the altar. I watched as he dipped his fingers into it and sprinkled it from the left to the right while he chanted. He was busying himself with other tasks of some sort concerning the *gift* while the

J-man applied an ointment and a small, clean cloth to my wound, still holding my hand in his. The smell of smoke redirected my attention to the priest at the altar and to a small fire he had created to the right of where he stood. He sprinkled a dust into it that caused the flame to spit and crackle as a colorful ring of red-orange lifted into the air.

I was drawn back to the J-man by the touch of his hand to my cheek. He held his pipe, sucked in deeply, and blew a cloud of white of smoke into my face, followed by another. As one not accustomed to smoking, I began to cough again, before the sensation in my lungs eased and gave up resistance and want for clean, humidified air. By the third intake, my head was as light as the smoke that floated above me. I would need to sit soon, either of my own accord or under the direction of anyone close by. The priests guided me to the center of the circle and the J-man approached the altar. Colorful circles rested like bubbles of light on the outside of my vision. It felt as though I was viewing the altar activities in a dream state.

I looked down to see I was in fact sitting, but didn't remember doing so. I couldn't see the other members of my team as orbs of orangey-red and blue-green light blocked everything except that which was directly in front of me. The feathered J-man approached and sat. Without a word, he took my hand and unwrapped the bandage. I could see he held the knife again. *What is this? I've already given...*

The blade pressed against the wound, stinging, cutting off my thoughts as it closed the wound.

Burning hot, so hot. My throat opened to scream, but instead I sucked in a quick, deep breath. A tear fell from my eye and the next breath caught in my throat.

"All is well," he whispered. The burning sensation was replaced by a cool, wet cloth, leaving the remnants of a dull throb, a welcome respite from the searing heat.

"Do not enter the circle," the J-man said, raising his hand and directing his attention toward where I had last seen Kevin. I was unable to sense Kevin's feelings or hear his thoughts following my meeting with the J-man. It was a powerful tobacco, laced with strong herbs that were causing my abilities to be blocked and a hallucination of colored light to fill my vision. A chant began and I closed my eyes, feeling only the spinning in my head and the throbbing of my finger that seemed to move in rhythm with the lilt of the J-man's voice. A whisper floated on the breeze into my ears. Without understanding how, I recognized it as the serpent god Topetine had spoken of yesterday, Kukulkan. I opened my eyes and saw something behind the shoulder of the J-man. I squinted, trying to press away the colorful circles to sharpen my vision.

Just an illusion, I reminded myself.

A white spirit shot through the foliage and glided toward me. I felt my back straighten and my eyes lock on to the form.

"Welcome, gods of the spirit world," said the J-man.

Could he see them, too?

"Ixchel, goddess of the moon, medicine, and the underworld."

I saw Topetine approach the circle and shift into her jaguar form. She crouched and dipped her head to the goddess, whose transparent form resembled a jaguar. "Itzamna, creator of all, may the portal to the spirit world be opened for the Light Carrier and her companions. Aluxes (a'lushes), guard the Light Carrier and those she holds close on the mission for the key."

The J-man placed his hands over mine, folded in my lap. Several ghostly white forms filtered through the trees and approached the open stone temple.

"Kukulkan, bring the light of the sun to Metnahl, the underworld, for the acquisition of the key."

Clarity of mind was returning to me in fragments, alleviating the lighter, dizzying sensation felt moments earlier. And as it did, the image of a snake with feathers extending from its head down its back shot forward from the depths of the forest, slowed its pace, and rested its ghostly image two inches from my face. The mouth of the snake dropped open as if to speak. This one bore the colors of the medicine man's feathers. I felt my eyes go as wide as dinner plates, but I didn't move. I couldn't.

The hands that covered mine left and brought forward a small gourd-like jug. The J-man drank from it, followed by the priests. The image of the feathered serpent retreated into the forest when it was my turn to drink. I took the jug handed to me and tilted it back against my lips. A smooth, sweet flavor of wine crossed my tongue and slipped down my throat. I handed the gourd back to the J-man. The air began to clear of the spiritual entities that I could see, and with it, my focus returned.

Powerful herbs, whatever they were.

I was invited to stand and cross the circle of flowers. I glanced at the other members of my team. Kevin studied my face before his eyes dropped to my hand. I had completely forgotten the sensation of being cut and burned. Even as my thumb stroked over the loose piece of damp cloth around my finger, I felt no more than a mild ache.

"Follow him," Topetine whispered from behind me, referring to our feathered leader. She was in her human form again, and I wondered if in fact she had ever changed or if her jaguar form was just another figment of my imagination. I followed the medicine man while the priests slipped into the forest without a word. We were led to a cave opening about a half mile from where the ritual took place. The J-man reached for my hand and put a bottle into it, no bigger than the size of my palm.

"A gift for you," he said. "One drop is all you'll need to cloak your energy from being visible to others." He closed my fingers around the bottle and patted them. "Keep all tools close at hand. They will serve you well on your journey." He turned to leave.

I tucked the small bottle into a pocket in my shorts.

"Is this our gateway?" Juno asked before I could.

"It is," replied Topetine.

"Are ye well enough to go through?" Mac asked, eyeing me as he stood beside Topetine. Kevin's hand was at my back. At our last encounter with the gateway in Scotland, a sensation of light-headedness would signal we were near. But I felt nothing of the sort, not even the pounding in my head as a sure sign of the gateway.

"Yes, quite. Perhaps the smoke I inhaled had some effect on my ability to sense the pull of the gateway's force."

"If that's so," Kevin said, "it means we could pass through at any moment." He turned to Aria, Juno, Matt, and Elise standing close behind us. "Be watchful. Stay close."

The entrance of the cave was black, with only the light from outside shining a couple of feet inside. I stepped forward, careful that I might fall through the passage. As I lifted my right foot once more, it made a sucking noise and stuck in something thick. *Mud?* I glanced down to see a pool of red, slicked-over mud, and my foot caught in the center of it. *Blood.*

An ugly hum sounded, as though a swarm of bees was approaching. "Something's coming," Matt said, pausing and lifting his head as though scenting the air. "Tarsamon." Kevin drew his sword with the others and closed in behind me. Topetine stepped to the edge of the red-brown puddle.

"The blood, it's a sign from the serpent god," Topetine said.

Are you sure? I wondered about the temple we'd crossed yesterday on our path to her that had looked as though there had been a recent slaughter. *Is this mess connected to the one in the temple?*

"That was different," she said, reading my thought. "No time to explain it further now. We're on the right path. We must hurry. Go!" She shifted from her stout, pudgy, middle-aged person into her jaguar form. She was a gorgeous creature, graceful and menacing, with golden eyes. She snarled and cocked her head toward the cave entrance.

"They'll follow us inside, through the gateway," Aria said, referring to the dark forces.

"We can't fight Tarsamon's army this close to the gateway. It's too risky. Go!" shouted Juno. With Kevin at my back, we rushed into the damp darkness of the cave, each step heavier than the last. I looked behind me to be sure we were all together and saw Topetine stalk inside behind everyone else. Mac was only a few steps ahead of her. There was no sensation to guide me and limited vision, as my eyes adjusted from the outside light filtering through the tree branches to nothing but black. I sheathed my sword and extended both hands for sight, placing them against the cave wall as my fingers began sliding along the crevices. *Aren't these caves known to be full of stalagmites?* A vision of tripping and impaling myself on one of them entered my mind and left as quickly as it had come.

"Focus," Kevin reminded me, listening again to my thoughts.

"I'm trying. Got any ideas, I'll take 'em."

"Your ability to sense the pull of the gateway is present. Bring it forward. Concentrate." His hand rested at my back and I did as he instructed, feeling for the sensation that usually directed me. I closed out the thought of what was coming and centered my concentration on the portal.

"To the right," I said, wondering how I was going to manage that in the dark. A flashlight clicked on, as if in answer, and I saw Juno beside me, Elise close behind him.

I heard Mac say something as the flashlight flicked in his direction. A howling sound like that of a fierce wind came from behind our group. I shot a look back over my shoulder to see the daylight had begun to gray.

"They're almost here!" I shouted. At the same time, I saw from the glow of Juno's flashlight there was no place to go but down. The cave echoed of the wind blowing outside and I swore I heard my name, as I had when I approached the gateway in Scotland. *Is it the gateway or Tarsamon calling? Damn! Does it even matter?*

And then I felt the urge to enter. The only problem was that there was no way to go but down.

"Give me your flashlight," I said to Juno. "I need a better look." He tapped my arm with it. I took it and aimed it in front of my feet. A small step, what looked like a slide, and more blackness. *Jesus.* I shined the light toward the others. "Sheathe your weapons. We're going down there," I said, pointing the flashlight back down. "It's a step, a slide," I said, pausing to be sure I couldn't see anything else. "And hold on."

"That's reassuring," Aria said.

Another howl came billowing through the cave, this time louder. A flash of light streaked brilliance across the dark cavern, temporarily blinding us again. It was the sign of the gateway recognizing my energy to allow us passage to the location of the key. This time it would be the underworld we would arrive in. My heart began to pound at the unknown, while adrenaline filled my body at the evil approaching behind, pressing us forward.

Does the underworld mean death? The thought raced through my head. One final attempt to try and understand what I couldn't know. *It can't mean death. But what's coming behind us does.* I had to remain alive and so did my team to recover the last key in Egypt. *It's why the J-man gave me the potion. I'm expected to live. No going back, only forward.* And with that thought, I took one drop of the liquid. Maybe it would buy us some time. If the shadows couldn't detect my energy, they might abandon the cave to look elsewhere.

I looked behind me to see the light at the entrance of the cave had been snuffed out by dark gray. The shadows were at the door. Kevin grasped my waist as I stepped down and slid forward to where no footing remained.

6

I blinked open my eyes to see a leafy green plant dangling overhead, as I grasped at any sensation from the environment. *More ferns.* Voices could be heard not too far away. My sword and the potion had made it through the portal. The blades Cerys had given me pressed uncomfortably into my back. I sat up to see Matt and Aria a few feet away. Kevin was lying unconscious a mere arm's length from me. As my team and I had learned from our last experience through the gateway in Scotland, it wasn't unusual for the force to have an effect on our consciousness while traveling through a passage in time. I assumed the effect was due to the G-forces that pulled us through the portal. In Scotland, I'd been the last one to wake and simply assumed the others were better at handling the trip. I bent over Kevin and put a hand to his cheek. He looked like he was sleeping. I put two fingers to his throat. His pulse was strong and steady and I breathed out a deep sigh.

"Hey," I said, running a hand across his forehead and over the top of his head. He didn't appear to have any bumps. A menacing growl redirected my attention to the jaguar that stood a foot from Kevin's feet. *Topetine?* Another growl.

"You're quite menacing in appearance. Do you have to snarl?"

It won't be long before the dark energy determines the entry point to this realm. Once the passage is opened, they will assume the Light Carrier has passed through, whether they detect her energy or not. It's not safe out in the open.

I heard her thought as she stared at me with those golden eyes. The risk of danger explained why she had not shifted back into her human form.

"Where do we go?"

Wake him and follow me.

I turned back toward Kevin, who began to stir. "Hey. Wake up." I brushed another hand along his cheek. With the team already gathering, I settled over him, bent down to kiss him, and nipped lightly at his lip. It caused the desired effect of rousing him quickly as his eyes flashed open. He frowned at me and his tongue prodded his lower lip. Topetine snarled loudly, causing him to jump.

"He's awake now," Juno said. "Let's go."

Kevin pushed himself to stand and joined the others already drawing their swords. We moved at a quick pace, pressing past soft, knee-high foliage.

Sorry, love. I sent the thought to him as I walked beside him.

"Couldn't you have just shaken me or something?" he asked.

"You weren't responding to my gentle attempts to rouse you." A tiny smile crept from the corner of my mouth. A distinct *humph* floated into my ear. Maybe I did enjoy it a bit. The recent fight that led to him pinning me to the bed had not completely departed from my memory.

"I'll remember this one," he said. "And you'd do well to hope that delivery through the next portals rouses you before I do."

I smiled bigger. A movement from the corner of my eye drew my attention from Kevin to where I'd seen the rustle of leaves.

The landscape consisted of a cover of tall ferns with scattered, towering trees, some with trunks as large as those I'd once seen on a trip through Yellowstone Park. Through the fingerlike branches was a gray-blue sky. I scanned the leafy green tops of the lower-level plants. Another shift of fern branches and a giggle this time came several feet from where we stood. Juno stopped, either seeing it or sensing its approach. A third movement farther ahead was followed by childlike laughter. *What is this?* As an empath, I sensed happiness in a place I should feel at the least cautious. *Got to find shelter, safety from the shadows.*

Stepping forward, I gasped, stopped from further movement by the immediate appearance of a troll-like man whose face grimaced back at me. His protruding tongue was touching his lip and I realized he was mimicking Kevin's expression after I'd woken him. I looked at Kevin and back to the man. He wiggled an index finger at me as if to signal *no, no* and bounded off, laughing.

What the hell?

"Aluxes," Topetine said. She had shifted to her human form, evidently feeling safe with the distance we'd put between ourselves and the gateway. I glanced behind us. There was no sign of invading dark forces. "They protect the forest and love to imitate humans. At least that's the legend of our people."

"They're supposed to protect us?" I asked.

"They will," Topetine answered.

"A forest of childlike men?" Elise asked, her tone dipped in disgust.

"Shake it off, huh?" Juno said. "At least they aren't angry childlike men." He nudged her shoulder and kept walking.

"How did you ever make it through Scotland with him?" she asked, lowering her voice to me while her eyes followed Juno.

"He likes you. So he's particularly annoying this time around," I replied.

"Just over that ridge," Topetine called. "Should be a village, underground."

"Who, in their right mind, lives below the soil?" Mac mumbled beside me.

"They've entered the gateway," Matt called. "Hurry." He grabbed Aria's hand and directed her in front of him. Juno, trying to seem discreet, paused, staring ahead until Elise caught up with him. Topetine shifted back to the precision and speed found in her jaguar form and we raced for the ridge.

The rustling among the ferns grew to look more like waves rolling over the blanket of green but was heading in the opposite direction, in the direction we'd just come from. No time to slow and get a look behind us. I sheathed my sword, trading it for the shorter blades on my back. I remembered my ability to utilize the energy around me to form a shield of light as I headed straight for the ridge. The familiar warm sensation in my center below my rib cage grew hotter, and a white glow began emanating from my clothing, preparing to surround me in a protective shield against the shadows. Since I'd obtained the first key, the power of its additional protection was hidden away in my core and the only evidence was a branding on my skin. The ability to create such a protective barrier had become easier with a mere thought.

Topetine stopped, cocked an ear left and back, then turned and went over the ridge. She ducked into what looked like a large animal den.

I glanced at Kevin as we approached. "Are you sure about this?" *It looks big enough but...*

He angled his head toward the hole in the dirt, lifting his chin. "Go," he said. "We're supposed to follow her." I shot a look over my shoulder, past Aria, and saw a huge movement in the distance where we were moments ago. Screams were coming with the rolling of the foliage. *Are they from the demons or the forest trolls?* "Sara!" Kevin shouted above the increasing noise. I crouched beside the den, allowing the others to enter first while holding the blades in front of me.

A piercing cry ripped above the screams of demons and Aluxes. I stood and turned in the direction of the sound to catch one of the faceless demons headed straight for us, its flesh-colored body far ahead of the others like him. My blood shot to boiling within seconds of seeing it, adrenaline pulsing through my veins. With the scent of near catastrophe still fresh from the last battle, I extended the image of the lighted shield I held, creating a bubble for the remaining team members as they followed Topetine underground.

"Go! Don't fight them now," Kevin shouted to me above the noise.

But he needed the space, the fraction of time to get below to safety and not risk being caught, so I remained with the light encircling me and the area around the den that might grant him that protection.

Kevin dove through the shield away from the security and, in the flash of speed he carried, severed the faceless demon's head. I flipped over the body as it tumbled to the ground. He sliced at the back of another that had come from behind him. I spun once and took off its head in one clean swipe of my blade. I felt a quick exchange of electricity between us and turned immediately to fight the rest of the evil close behind. But there was no need. The wave over the green foliage continued to rush in our direction but with no more demons. *The trolls?*

I stashed the blades and slid on my belly down the small, visible dirt path at the entrance of the hole and fell into a pit with the others. Kevin dove in behind me. With Kevin here and Topetine missing, we stared at each other, listening for any sounds above ground. Maybe the entire army of demons was delayed in getting to us. *Any moment.* All remained eerily silent. No rumbling of battle above ground. No shrieks could be heard. And still my heart pounded. The heavy throb in my ears began to subside and I had the strangest sensation of how a rabbit might feel stealing away from a predator.

As I scanned the room, I was surprised at the amount of space. It was as though we'd slid into a good-sized cavern about eight feet tall and several feet wide. The dirt floor matched the expectations of the rabbit hole it appeared to be from above ground.

"Maybe that drop of potion bought us a little time to get as far as we did," I said, huffing out a breath.

"Yeah, but close is close," Kevin said. "And I didn't like you out there with the team underground. I don't need to remind you—"

"No, you don't," I interrupted. "I made a quick judgment call based on what I saw and what I could handle. In that instant, I decided it was safer, better overall with the time we did have to get everyone in first."

"Are you guys going to argue about who's in charge on this mission?" Aria said, reminding me Kevin and I weren't alone. "Put it to bed already, will you? We'll do what's best in each given situation, agreed?"

My gaze shifted from Aria to Kevin and back. "Agreed."

"Well, good. I thought we'd have to go through it all again," Juno said, angling past me, closer to Elise.

Juno was right. There was no need to argue about who was in

charge. I'd given up my stubbornness after the last close call in Scotland and more or less agreed to either Kevin or Juno being in charge of security while I focused on obtaining the key. That was how this quest was supposed to work. But there were caveats to any plan. Nothing was ever as simple as it appeared on the surface. I was used to being a leader, not giving up the role to someone else. And changing thirty-one years of behavior didn't happen over a few weeks.

"If you'll follow me." A man with yellow eyes appeared from out of nowhere, startling me. He was holding a torch in one hand, slightly above his head. Strange, I didn't recall seeing him when I slid into the den. He pulled a second torch off the wall and handed it to Matt. He wasn't anything like the trolls and instead stood about as tall as our other jaguar friend when not transformed.

"Shifter?" I whispered to Kevin. He had a much stronger ability than I to detect the gifts of others.

"Something else. A priest or medicine man, perhaps."

I can live without seeing another one of those anytime soon. The man's energy seemed to shift under my awareness as his eyes darted to mine. *There will be no more cutting and burning, under any herbal influence.* Kevin smiled, hearing my thought, and touched a hand to my back as we fell in behind the others.

"The dark shadows cannot gain access here," the man said. "Above ground, you are open to the elements of evil." My thoughts went to the location of the key and the potential battle waiting for us if it was not underground. We followed him through the tunnel and farther yet down several steps.

"You're welcome to stay in any open room," the man continued, pointing the torch toward one cave opening and lighting the torch on the wall just outside. Matt raised a brow in our direction. Kevin shook his head once and reached for my hand, pulling me past the entrance. "In the morning, there will be a party that will join in helping you to locate the key."

What party?

"With all due respect," I said, "this team is more than qualified to search for the key." *Especially if Topetine is still our guide.*

"Indeed. But the magic that resides in this forest is unknown to you and your team. You will be safer with the additional protection and another guide that has been sent," the man replied. He continued forward, eyes set straight ahead.

Kevin's whispering lips were at my ear and his hand stroked my hair. "Trust. You have to trust those we are led to, love. There are many who are part of this mission."

"I trust nothing, no one, until all three keys are collected. And even then, trust is questionable."

Of course, darling. You wouldn't have it any other way. I heard his thought and caught the corner of his mouth turning upward.

"We'll take this one," Kevin said, referring to the last cave-like room at the end of the dim passage. He wrapped a meaty hand around my wrist and pulled me inside.

"What the hell do you mean yanking at me like that?"

"Sorry, but I didn't want any conversation about what was going to happen next. I'm tired."

"Fine. Do it again and you're taking an elbow for the trouble." I unloaded the pack off my shoulder and set it beside the bed.

"I haven't seen Topetine," I said. "We need to find her." I turned to see Kevin raking a hand through his hair. "I'll find her."

"She's here. No need to rush off. Remember, she entered first. She's probably communing with the other members of this world."

"I can't rest until I know everyone is safe and accounted for."

"Which means *I* won't rest until..." he mumbled.

"You're free to stay. I don't need you by my side at every waking moment. And like the man said, I'm quite sure I'm safe below ground."

Kevin moved to stand in front of me. "I like your strength. Strength I knew was hiding behind your profession of doctor and wealthy family image, and of course, the beautiful features of this face." His hand stroked my jawline.

"But you miss the weakness you first saw in me, right?"

"You were never weak, just unaware of what responsibility had been heaped upon you. Sometimes I wonder, though, what happened to the softness of this beautiful woman?" His hand reached to tuck the hair behind my ear. I couldn't remember a time when I'd seen his eyes half-closed and shadowed.

"She's remembering. Like you wanted," I answered. "I have a mission to accomplish, and I don't need you to help me track down Topetine. It also means I can't rest before I do." I placed a palm against his chest. "You rest. I'll be back soon." And with that, I kissed his forehead and turned to leave.

"All right. But if you aren't back in ten, I'm coming to find you."

I shook my head without giving him a second look. "Okay."

Faint voices could be heard ahead on the path that was more like a hallway with the torches burning on each side. *I could be sitting at home, curled up on my sofa, watching a comedy, rather than risking my life chasing the keys. God, what I'd give for a good laugh right now. What exactly was my turning point to agree to this quest? So much has happened since that first visit to Ardan. Oh, yes, the shadows infiltrating the humans. I couldn't ignore that as proof.*

The voices grew louder, confirming I was on the right path to finding Topetine. The shadows weren't the only reason I'd chosen this path versus ignoring it. Each member of the team was threatened by the same evil that hunted us, sure. But were they, too, held hostage by the Soltari's decision to punish if I failed? In the end, in the case of failure, both outcomes were the same—an end to our immortality. The truth of the matter was that I was on this quest to protect our eternity and save humanity. The keys were the promise of fulfillment of this difficult task. Once my eyes had been opened to what existed and the path Tarsamon had taken into Earth, the blissful ignorance of believing shadows and demons were figments of a troubled mind and continuing as a psychiatrist and humanitarian were off the table.

I finally understood why Kevin wanted to remain so close. Neither of us wanted to lose all that we had gained over thousands of years and numerous missions together. One goal with two individual ways of getting to the same end result. Had it always been that way in each mission? Was our motivation not only the good end result from saving a realm but to avoid the separation? If so, I was about to have a real problem with it. C-05 had mentioned something about losing his partner and said if I only knew the truth behind what I fought for, I would question who I gave my loyalty to. I couldn't recall the rest of what he'd said at the time. His sword had been angled in my direction with the full intent of interrupting my quest, permanently. While killing me wasn't going to bring someone he loved back, it would have been payback to the Soltari for what he'd lost.

As I turned down another hall, a faint light glowed at the end and the sounds of voices and laughter grew louder. *A party? Some sort of celebration, perhaps?* It was inconceivable given what waited for us above ground. The sounds reminded me of Mary Ann's laughter and mingling with the donors at one of the Forrester Foundation galas. I stopped at the end of the hall, remembering the gown I'd last worn and how beautiful I'd felt with the two most important people in my world beside me, Kevin and Mary Ann. I'd give anything to wash the sticky humidity and J-man's smoke from my hair and skin to feel beautiful for a night.

So many people. How is that possible in what appears as a compact underground enclosure?

I stepped farther into an enormous dining hall, torches blazing on every wall and people drunk on wine or spirits. My eyes scanned the faces of the individuals who looked so much like Topetine, matching height and Mayan characteristics. Stone gods were attached to the rafters as though keeping watch over their children. My eyes flicked back to the group. *Happiness.* It was a sensation I would've liked to get lost in just once on this quest. I stopped to gaze at the scene and commit it to memory for a particular dark day when I might need a reminder of joy.

And then the noise began to die down into whispers and heads turned in my direction. My eyes found their mark toward the front of the room. Topetine left the table where she had been sitting. My eyes traced her path along the wall, where she moved with haste. The other faces were frozen in a stare, having forgotten their previous bliss. She looped an arm through mine and turned me away.

"My dear, I'm sorry but you cannot be part of the underground world."

"I don't understand. They must know who I am. Their faces say so. Why are they so"—I paused, trying to define the feeling I sensed at their stern looks—"fearful?"

"Well…" She let out a breath and shook her head. "You are a truth that was foretold to them. You are a reality of the evil that has entered their world."

"They hate me then? For what I must do?"

"No. They fear the end of all things is near. Before, it was a story, a folktale. Your presence is a distraction and a reminder that what lurks above is truth. They've seen you with their own eyes and there is no longer a choice to deny what was foretold."

We'd stopped in the hallway a few steps from the room where I hoped Kevin was now sleeping.

Topetine spread her hands wide. "For now, the people may be drunk enough to get back to their conversations and more drink."

"Maybe, but they looked damn well sober enough when they saw me. Have I just put them at risk?"

"No, no. We, the members of the underworld, have been preparing for your arrival." She smiled up at me through closed lips, realizing I didn't understand what she meant. "I will instruct them. And if you need me again, I can hear any call from you, verbal or otherwise." And she winked, signaling her ability to read thoughts, too.

"I didn't mean to make things difficult for you."

"Never mind that. Now, you get some sleep," she said. "You are safe here. Your energy is not detected by the evil above us. And there is a man there"—she pointed to the door where Kevin was—"who desperately needs his rest so he can fulfill his task tomorrow. I'm sure he sleeps better with you beside him. The morning brings a new day and a new opportunity for the key. Now go. I have work to do yet, back there." She angled her head in the direction of the room of people.

I nodded. "Okay. Good night." She patted my cheek like a grandmother might before sending a child to bed and turned toward her "work."

As I stepped closer to the room where I'd hoped Kevin was already sleeping, the sound of several hushed whispers nearby distracted me from joining him. I stepped past the entrance that was ours to the next.

Seems I'm not the only one with a plan to sleep later.

I knocked gently and pushed open the door, which had been cracked open, to find a few candles burning and the entire team, including Kevin, hovered over a small table. As more light from the hall filled the small space, heads turned.

"What's going on? What are you looking at?" I moved to peer between them.

"It's a map of the underground village," Matt replied.

"Ah. It wouldn't happen to indicate any clues for where we will be going in the morning?"

"None that we can see."

I squeezed between Aria and Elise to see an architectural drawing of a village that was quite extensive, not the compact enclosure I thought it was. Rather, it was a like a small city with tiny, square inked images, replicas of glyphs or the Mayan language. The meaning of which was obscure to me.

"Where did you get this?" I asked.

"It was rolled up and crammed between the wall and the bed," Elise said. Juno, a former military member of the US special operations force, would never cozy up in a strange location without first searching it thoroughly.

"We believe the direction we'll head is this way." Juno pointed to an area of map that showed an opening from the village ceiling to the exterior. I speculated that the size was about as large as the room and the meeting I'd interrupted moments ago.

"We don't have to worry about what direction to go because Topetine is leading us there." But a closer look at the map had me curious. "Now that you mention it, though, how is it possible that there is an opening in this village and we are not yet overrun by dark shadows?"

"We were just discussing the possible answer to that before you walked in," Aria said. "We think there is some protection here and here," she added, pointing to opposite sides of the entrance. "But what, we can't possibly imagine."

"Unless this map is out of date and the villagers have since closed those openings, maybe in anticipation of our arrival," Elise added. Aria lifted a brow in consideration.

"Topetine should be able to explain," I said. I sensed something was being withheld. "What? There's something else you're not saying." Glances darted around the table to Kevin, then Matt. "What is it?"

"Sara, we have a job to protect you," Matt answered. "We're trying to figure out the best way to do that by anticipating the level of evil that could be waiting." He paused. "We don't want to trouble you with the plan."

Trouble me? I sensed the white lie as if they'd called it out as such. They didn't want to tell me because I might disagree, the way I had last time, creating a larger problem. As if fighting a bunch of faceless demons and shadows wasn't problem enough.

"Oh, for Christ's sake already. After Scotland, I learned not to disregard such plans. I realize you've got your job and you know how to do it. I've also got mine. I won't interfere with your direction, as long as you don't redirect me from the guidance I receive toward obtaining the key."

"Fair enough," Matt said.

"I'm getting some rest. You should do the same."

I left without the plan being shared. *What is it that's so important I can't know? Something they can't risk telling me.*

Had Juno and Matt been honest about their abilities not being as strong in the Yucatan? What if they were as strong as ever? And if so, had they seen a coming event, one that concerned them enough not to share?

You're tired. You're overthinking the whole thing, Sara.

But that thought felt wrong. Kevin. We'd made a pact with the Soltari that emotion that could distract us from the mission would not be allowed. Kevin agreed to it to join me on the mission. What if the others had to agree in a similar fashion, used as another form of protection aimed at ensuring the key was collected without interference? My resentment toward the entity I served was growing and without hard evidence to support it.

I flopped on the bed, the room dark as soot, with no windows to capture any semblance of moonlight that might have streamed in from a crevice in a man-made window. And in the quiet and peace, I lost myself in the blackness and drifted to another night of restless sleep.

7

Slow tapping on my stomach woke me. I peeked under my eyelids. A candle glowed in a corner of the room.

Strange. I don't remember bringing that with me.

Stirring from a short figure standing beside me had me wide-awake and slamming into Kevin on the opposite side of the bed.

"Who the hell are you?"

Kevin lifted himself up, less concerned about an intruder in the room than I. *Some protection.* Of course, with eyes fully open, what appeared to be a male figure, somewhat troll-like but in a pudgy, cute sort of way, was really no taller than a child. The Aluxes didn't live down here, did they? I hadn't seen any of them.

"Hell are you," he repeated.

"Aluxes," Kevin said at my ear.

"Yes, Alux," he said, nodding. "Belly of light." He pointed to my stomach and then patted his own.

"He knows?" I asked.

"Knows it, the light you carry. Come. We go."

"What? Go where?"

I turned to Kevin. "If this is what it's like to have children, it'll be a cold day..."

"We go," the little person pressed.

"Fine. I'm awake. Couldn't be more than a couple hours of sleep,

I'm sure, but let's go somewhere." My body was moving, but now that the alarm of an intruder had passed, I wasn't so sure my mind had caught up yet, with its sour mood spilling over into my words.

"Wonder what the chances of getting coffee or tea are," I added, stumbling out of the bed.

"I would say pretty good," Kevin answered. "We may have passed through to another realm, but I believe you're still in what would be considered a modern-day Yucatan, or close to it, darling."

"Am I? 'Cause I don't recall Aluxes in my history books."

"Come, come, come."

"Yes. Don't pull me."

Kevin laughed softly and got out of bed. I narrowed an eye at him and followed the little creature out of the room in the direction of the great hall.

Topetine and the other members of the team sat at a table, talking and eating. *Wasn't I just here witnessing a similar event? Did Topetine ever go to bed?* The faint aroma of cooked meat and baked bread lifted to my nostrils and, with it, the scent I'd been looking for, coffee. It seemed too early for food and my stomach gave me a quick warning not to try it.

"Sara, good morning. Ah, and Kevin." I turned, not having realized he was behind me. "Did you sleep well?" Topetine asked.

"A few more hours would be nice," I mumbled.

"Just fine," Kevin answered in a cheery tone that often cracked through one's skull before the first sips of coffee.

"Sorry I had Grim wake you. But we must get an early start."

Grim. Now there's an appropriate, relatable description for how I feel.

"Please," I said, holding up an open palm. "I'll be ready to discuss travel, er, hiking in a few minutes."

"I've not seen ye so cranky, lass," Mac said, scooping up what looked like a pile of mashed potatoes from his plate.

"Yes, well, a couple of hours of sleep will do that to most people."

"There's a warm pool down the hall and to the right. May help ye wake and lift your spirits."

"Yeah, it's like a spa, without the massage," Aria said.

"But I'm sure the massage could be arranged," Juno added, nodding once at Kevin.

I slanted a look at Juno. "Thank you, yes. I think I'll find it." I snaked a piece of bread to go with my coffee and headed in the direction instructed, passing little Grim, who was gobbling down something that looked like oatmeal.

Grim, huh? He must have woken someone else up early to earn the name. Wonder how he ended up here, anyway?

He's our messenger, our connection to the outside world. I heard the thought come to me and angled my head to see Topetine raise her cup in my direction. I forced a smile. All would be set right again after I soaked in the spa-like bath Mac had mentioned.

After tracing a path down the hall, I entered a room with a wide pool of water set into the ground. Steam lifted off its surface and disappeared into the air like a ghostly mist. The ceiling was open to the sky. Tree roots trailed like long, hanging vines from the ceiling into a pool that could have welcomed a hundred people or more. The roots provided additional privacy to the numerous rock formations surrounding the edge. I sipped from my cup, noting the solitude. No voices. No one. Not even Kevin. I'd walked straight into the tropics, underground. Was this one of the protected areas on the map? It had to be safe enough if my team recommended it.

I set my cup on the edge of the pool. Without a soul in sight, I peeled off my clothes and stepped into the tepid water. My skin prickled at the warming and my muscles relaxed into softness. I closed my eyes and took one more step so that the water teased at my shoulders. Within seconds, the sensation of gentle movement eased me further into relaxation. I let go of a long breath and inhaled another cleansing intake of steam-filled air. Mac was right. This was working to ease my tension. I peered under my lashes to see the water was swirling in soft currents around me, and not like the massive jet tub in my workout room back home.

How is this working? I tilted my head to see below the water's surface.

The small ripples pulled back and dipped into another separate smaller pool. I wanted to step back, but the sensation of being under a relaxed hypnotic trance was too enticing. I stared into the area a foot or two in front of me. Within the swirls of water, a picture began to form in the smaller pool, that of several people communing. *The Alliance?* One of the men began shouting. The picture clouded with black and reemerged as Tarsamon. *Are these waters trying to show me something? A message, perhaps?* Then the pristine forest of Ardan came through. And as though I were sailing across it high above the trees, I could see the realm Tarsamon called his. An area in Ardan he'd been exiled to. Never to have further contact with the rest of Ardan, he'd created a place of evil in one world that was believed incapable of holding such a force. To make it more his own, every bit of life in the trees had been sucked dry, and the thorny, clustered stems of bushes where soft leaves once clung and thrived were all that remained. Surprising to me was that the image showed Tarsamon had been a member of the Alliance. Could that be true? If so, how could anyone have been so close to the Soltari and yet have turned so evil?

"They're mystical waters."

I awoke from the trance-like state in an instant and turned to see Kevin leaning against the doorway, cup in hand.

"They can only show you the truth."

"Reading my thoughts again."

"Darling, I've told you if you don't want to be an open book, impart a block."

"I didn't expect that I would have to in a bath. Alone."

He smiled and glanced to the ground as he approached. "May I join you?"

"As long as you stay on your side. I can't afford to get caught."

"Caught," he repeated. "Caught taking a bath?"

"You know very well what I mean."

He set two cups next to mine and proceeded to pull his shirt off, followed by his pants.

"There's no one who's going to *catch* you," Kevin said, stepping into the pool. "This part of the dwelling is occupied only by Topetine and a few others." He sunk a little deeper. "They're ready to leave when we are, by the way."

"We shouldn't keep them waiting then." I moved to exit but he circled an arm around my waist and guided me to him instead.

"I don't think they'll mind if we take a few minutes. Besides, weren't you desperate to get the scent of smoke out of your hair?" He reached for one of the cups and brought it closer.

"You listen to everything I think."

"When you allow it, love. Which is almost always. Does it really bother you?" He tipped me backward until all of my hair was wet and cradled me against him. His closeness never ceased to send warm tingles racing down my neck and arms, a feeling I found irresistible.

"For the record, yes. But does it matter?" I sat up to see him staring into my eyes.

He smiled bigger. "No. Because if it bothered you enough, you'd block me."

True. And I had done so only a couple of times in the past, when making a decision that usually involved him. The fact was there was little I cared to keep secret from him, even if I was able.

With arms wrapped around me, he poured some of the shampoo into his hand and proceeded to rub the fragrant scent of rosemary and mint onto the top of my head, working it through the strands.

The water began to lap against the sides, soothing me back into the trance again, as the pool began creating another image. This time the vision was Kevin administering CPR, the urgency in his face and pain in his eyes so clear. The water changed to center on the image of the person he was working so hard to save. Me. I felt my brows close together.

Of course. The accident. What a mess it left of me. That's how we had met in this world. Before the memories had been restored, Kevin's mannerisms had been very familiar. The way he slid his hand through his hair when faced with a difficult decision. The way he had stared through me as though he knew me, and the way his touch alone was the only one I trusted, ever. He was the one person I felt most comfortable with, with no reason as to why. And all the excitement of him had remained in this life as with the others in each kiss and every expert stroke of his hand.

The vision swirled in the pool while Kevin's fingers worked at the ends of my hair. I felt him guide my head backward once more into the water, as he pressed his lips firmly against mine, holding them for a moment. Fingertips trailed over my breast and a palm flattened against my abdomen.

"Not here," I whispered.

"Why not?" he asked at my lips and lifted his eyes to scan the area. "There's no one coming to disturb us."

"Let's just say I'd like to be sure there isn't."

The water skimmed over my face once but not by Kevin's doing. He held me tight against him. But as my eyes darted from the water to his face, his gaze was no longer on me. He helped me as I'd lifted myself up, sensing a disturbance. The circumference of the motion of water had grown larger, enclosing both of us in the circle's center.

"What's happening?" I asked.

The visions flashed quickly—the scenes of our first bonding at his home in the Cape, the weapons used for our fight against the dark forces, swords, energy that I could manipulate into spheres of light, the neglect I'd suffered as a small child and the wealthy adoptive family that had rescued and provided so well for me, and lastly, the ring I wore. It functioned like a key, unlocking our passage through the realms. We stared as the water came to life, our history for the last thirty years. A woman appeared that I didn't recognize, gagged and tied to a chair in a dark, swirling current. The scene belonged to Kevin's memory. The picture of his mother continued twisting through the current. Her anger and fear could be felt by both of us.

Jesus. She knew he was going to kill her.

"No," Kevin said in a distant voice, trying to fight back the memory of the stranger standing beside his mother as he watched. *Did he recognize the man?* The back of the head of a seven-year-old Kevin could be seen, but not the tears that assuredly streamed from his eyes.

The flash of a knife blade turned in a man's closed hand. A muffled scream from a child and the vision cleared.

"My God," I said under my breath and grasped Kevin tighter. The waters grew more violent, sloshing against the sides. Kevin and

I moved to leave the once comforting bath but were held back by the force of the water in the center, tugging at our legs.

"Matt, Juno," I called. Matt and Juno appeared within seconds, with the others close behind them. "Get us out of here!"

Kevin held an arm tight around me as the water began to rise but never spilled over the edge. Juno planted himself flat on his belly and extended an arm out for us to grab. Reaching back was unproductive with the resistance, like quicksand, that held us in place. *At least we aren't being pulled down.*

"It's not harmful," Topetine shouted from behind Juno, referring to the water now at our necks.

"The hell it's not," I yelled back.

"Relax into it."

Juno continued his reach with Matt and Mac joining in. Kevin's fingertips reached Mac's extended hand and he held on. No matter how hard Mac tried to pull, the force of the water was stronger. We didn't seem to be getting closer to the edge.

Aria's ability to calm the effect of nature wasn't working, either. Probably because this had nothing to do with Mother Nature and more to do with some mystical elements of what felt like a natural environment. She stood beside Elise, tiny sparks fading as soon as they were created, a distinct look of anger plastered across her face.

"No matter what happens, hold on," Kevin shouted over the rush of water that had now encased us in a funnel. His arm was still stuck outside, holding Mac's grasp. "Don't let go of me, do you hear?"

"Yeah," I shouted back, nodding to him. "Strength, not fear," I told myself and wrapped both arms around him tight. He let go of Mac's hand and wrapped himself around me. With us cocooned in a naked embrace, my earlier fear came to fruition as the bottom of where we stood fell away and we were pulled downward in the funnel. Several splashes interrupted the funnel's shape, but the water held tight its form as we descended to what felt like a place still farther beneath the surface.

8

C-05 moaned in agony as his arms were pulled farther from his body. Beads of sweat trailed along the sides of his temples toward the tendons standing out from his neck. The shackles that held his wrists bit deeper into his skin and the muscles that joined each shoulder were frying. He'd been pinned to a rocky cell wall by his wrists and ankles for two hours that felt like ten.

"You've done nothing to get me closer to her!" Tarsamon's voice slammed against the gray stone walls into C-05's ears. "If anything, you've delayed me, allowing her to get closer to finding the second key. You had opportunity in Scotland. I granted you that much and you failed. Miserable creature." Tarsamon leaned into C-05. "For your sake, you'd better hope the demons can find her and the same forces protecting her don't deny us entry into the realm as they did in Scotland."

"She was here, my Lord. I brought her to you as you asked." He cried out again in pain. "You saw her."

"And you let her slip right out from under you, while you were in the same room with her. Stupid man." Tarsamon paced the cell, his black shroud hiding an invisible face. Sara had been rescued by the only power known to break the space-time barrier and allow her human form to return safely to Scotland. C-05 had heard of such power but had never seen it used. The elf, Seria, referred to in the realms as the white witch, had provided Kevin a brief lapse in time to get Sara out of Ardan and back to the safety of the elves protecting her. How could he have anticipated that level of intervention on Sara's behalf?

It wasn't until Tarsamon stopped and glared at C-05, the red points of his eyes piercing straight through him, that C-05 realized the life he'd given up meant he was forever going to be at the mercy of a higher power. He wasn't sure if there was a better side to be on, that of the Soltari or Tarsamon. Punishment of other members, like him, who had failed a mission had been fierce by the Order. This, however, was the first time he'd ever been shackled to a wall or beaten.

With a power as strong as the space-time fracture of the white witch, he never guessed it could penetrate the strength of the dark energy Tarsamon had accumulated in the relatively short time of almost fifty years. That said, he'd only ever known of the trolls, faceless demons, and shadows that resided here, not the level of accumulated power. The location had been converted into nothing more than a wasteland with thorny remnants of bushes and dead trees, standing like skeletons, row upon row. Nothing grew and nothing lived. And anything that did find its way into this side of Ardan wasn't allowed to remain living for long. Usually as long as it took for Tarsamon's army to locate and kill. When he had been found, C-05 had to race to find a chip to bargain with after he'd demanded to see the beasts' leader. He'd given up any connection to the Alliance to save his own life in exchange for his connection to the Light Carrier. Now that she'd slipped from his grasp, C-05 needed to find a way to stay alive, even if it meant begging for the pathetic life he would have under Tarsamon's rule.

C-05 moaned louder as the restraints yanked ever tighter.

"You don't seem to be paying attention to the severity of the issue. I wonder if you realize what's at risk."

He knew all too well. At risk was the end of Tarsamon. For C-05, the risk he'd taken was about something else. During the last quest, C-05 had lost the love of his life, his eternal partner, to the powers that governed the balance between good and evil. He gritted the name *Soltari* between clenched teeth. The entity was despised by Tarsamon and himself for the act of punishment. In the end, the Order was responsible for him hanging in these shackles. Separating him from his partner had made him increasingly bitter, and the memory of it was its own demon that devoured him from the inside out. Still, he'd managed to proceed on the quest for the keys as a lead contact for Sara's team, until he ventured too far on the search for his love and was forced to bargain for his life.

"Anything," C-05 gasped. "Anything you need from me I'll do."

"Of course you will. What choice have you left yourself? Question is, do I need you?" Tarsamon stopped in front of the tiny window that looked out into the perpetual dark gray sky. The sound of howling dogs, possessed with the same evil that drove the rest of his force, echoed in the distance as he began formulating a plan. "I'm going to need to be sure my agenda doesn't get muddled going forward. I can't trust you to handle the task alone. But I believe there's a way you could assist."

"Yes," C-05 panted. The links to the shackles clicked open, dropping him to the floor like a sack of rocks.

"I'm very disturbed that your failure to stop the Light Carrier has interrupted my consumption of the energy on Earth and distribution of it to the growth of my army." He paused and glared at the crumpled form of C-05. "For that you'll pay." A maroon orb danced beside Tarsamon. C-05 cast his gaze upward just as the sphere zoomed straight for him. He lifted his arms to block it, but it was no use. The orb slammed into him, filling him with dark and painful thoughts, including those of torture experienced by the woman he still loved. He knew the visions might not be true, probably weren't. But he also wasn't going to be able to stop the flood of negativity flowing through his veins until the power of the orb wore off and his energy was restored, outside of Ardan.

"Now, tell me what you've learned of those who protect the Light Carrier in the Yucatan."

"The guardian," C-05 gasped, exhausted. "The guardian will have her blessed by the holy priest." He grabbed more air. "The J-man."

"What power does he possess?"

"He has a connection to the god Sara will try to reach to obtain the key." C-05 turned his face up to see Tarsamon. "He will have instilled a marker on her that the god will recognize once the key is found."

"What does this marker look like? What power does it hold?"

"I don't know. I hadn't gotten that far in my research. But it was foretold that it is unmistakable when found."

"Get yourself together. You leave for the Yucatan within the hour to trace her energy through the gateway. And this time you'll be under careful observation."

Were the demon shadows he'd already sent ahead to the Yucatan going be Tarsamon's eyes? The Dark Lord could shift into almost any form, could move between worlds, and carried strength greater than all C-05 had encountered. Still, with those abilities, Tarsamon had been banned from entering Randun to stop Sara from obtaining the first key. Evidently, the collective magic of the Druid priests, a group of educated individuals, philosophers and magicians, was more powerful than the energy even the Dark Lord held. He had not uncovered any information to suggest all three locations had the same type of protection the sacred Druid priests offered. And yet he was being sent on another task to retrieve the Light Carrier. How would Tarsamon place him under observation? He did have the ability to see into other worlds even if, for some reason, he couldn't bring his energy into it. That had to be it. He'd watch him from the dark side of Ardan.

C-05 was transferred out of the small cell and into the room he'd been given upon his first arrival, containing a few more human comforts including a full bath, large bed, and a desk, should he require it. Despite the appearance of comfort in such a space, it was no less a cell. All that awaited him beyond the boundaries were more orders and tasks. And that meant he was nothing more than another one of Tarsamon's trolls. How had he sunk this far beneath his prior respected seat on the Alliance, where his job was to carry out orders for the Soltari? Either way, he was and had always been someone else's servant. His circumstances now were as good as a death sentence. There couldn't be any more he could lose. What was becoming all too clear, however, was how much he didn't want the pitiful existence that awaited him in Tarsamon's prison. But that would only be a reality if he returned.

9

The rush of water severed our hold on each other. I sucked in a quick gulp of air as we were sent plummeting into the center of a cenote, a cave filled with jewel-colored water in shades of turquoise and brilliant blue. Rays of sunlight pierced the water's depth, leading the way toward the surface and another sweet breath.

"Over here," Kevin said as I broke through and grabbed for air. With an angling of his head, he directed me toward an edge leading out of the water. I followed him to the embankment, noticing the outside streaming light into the cave. It was as if we'd fallen down several floors of a building through a water channel instead of an elevator, with the cave opening facing the sky and jungle. As I climbed out of the water, clothing began to drape across my form.

"It never ceases to amaze me how the magic in these realms knows what to dress us in and when," I said, recalling the change in clothing when we arrived in the first realm of Randun. I lifted my arms at shoulder height as the unknown power finalized the last curves of black fabric. "Not bad," I added, eyeing the finished garment of a lightweight black cotton gauze top over durable fitted pants of the same color and the ever useful boots. "Thank God it isn't another dress."

"But you look so good in them." He chucked me under the chin as he finished fastening the button on his pants. My lips curved into a smirk.

"The jungle is no place for any sort of dress, no matter what the ancient Aztecs wore, not when a good pair of jeans or leggings has been available for some time." I pressed a flat palm against the black cotton material that had been twisted in just the right places to conceal. The gauze would be cooler, too. And where was I to store my blades? *My blades. Where the hell are they?*

Several splashes hit the water and plummeted beneath the surface. Within seconds, the faces of the rest of the team popped up.

"You dove in after us?" I asked Juno. He was the closest to where Kevin and I stood.

"We can't let you go without us," he called. "You at least need Topetine to guide you." I couldn't argue with that.

"Out of the way!" Juno shouted. We all glanced up to see nothing, until a few seconds later, several blades dumped out of the same orifice as we had. "Our gear." Matt, Juno, and Mac dove for it, with Aria and Elise following. I placed my belly flat against the rock and reached for a pack floating close by that looked like the one Juno had when he loaned me his satellite phone. Beads of water rolled off the top. *It wouldn't surprise me if it's waterproof.* The man was always prepared. My dagger shone at the water's edge. I climbed over the rocky surface to retrieve it. But there was no sign of the blades I'd worn at my back upon entering this world. Kevin waded into the water fully clothed to retrieve the glowing white-blue light just beneath the surface. *My sword.* The signature light called to me. With the tail of his shirt, Kevin lifted the hilt and set it on the nearest rock. The blade had been blessed by the elves at its creation, providing a protective energy that did not allow anyone else to touch it.

"How long of a hike do we have to get back?" I asked as Topetine stepped closer.

"We're not hiking back. The stories of my people tell of the magic of the waters and that as time approaches for light to reign over darkness, the gifts of this world will come together to lead the Light Carrier to the key. That's the force of the water that delivered you here."

"I thought you were leading us."

"I'll direct you on the path. From here, we need to access the scrolls."

"Do you know if this is the only path to where we are?" I cast a gaze to where we'd fallen into the center of the cenote. C-05 and the demons that chased us last night would no doubt be close behind.

"There are miles between us and where we entered. This is the shortest path but not the only one. The energy is programmed to tune in to yours. But because your team was able to fall in the same manner through the channel, it's possible even the same path remains an open door, if they aren't stopped by the Aluxes first."

"That means they'd have to find an access point around the safety of your fort," Matt said.

"Yes."

Did the map we were looking at last night have any access points? I suddenly regretted leaving too quickly for rest.

I turned to see if anything else was left behind as Mac and Topetine started off out of the cave. We followed until they abruptly turned and disappeared into what looked like the wall. As I drew closer, their disappearance turned out to be an illusion. A narrow passage existed behind the immediate rock formation facing us. Inside, the walls were cemented in shells of all sizes and colors in a mosaic pattern. The path in reminded me of an underground drug tunnel between Arizona and Mexico that I'd once seen in a news clip. I only recalled it because I'd wondered why a drug cartel would take the time to create such an elaborate corridor. The passage grew darker as we delved farther beyond the entrance of the cave.

"Juno, you still have that light?" I asked.

"I wouldn't expect it to work after the bath we took," Elise said. But the light flickered on.

"Lucky for you I come prepared with waterproof gear, sweetheart," Juno replied.

"I'd expect it," Aria said as another light from Matt streamed past us, "from our former Special Forces men."

Matt and Juno had met during their recruitment in the military.

Not long after, they discovered they were on the same mission for the keys.

"It's like the descriptions I've seen and read about Shell Grotto in Kent," Elise said, switching gears, as we all gazed at more of the patterns covering the cave walls and ceiling.

"Who built the one in Kent?" Juno asked.

"It's not known for sure but there's speculation about the Knights of Templar, or that it had something to do with a Phoenician goddess. It's been open to the public since the 1800s and has damage to it. This one is pristine."

"Well, we don't really know what time we've stepped into. Do we?" I asked.

"This passage was created by the J-men, medicine men, like the one you met with to prepare you for coming here," Topetine replied. "They wanted to conceal the great library of the Aztecs. It was never meant to be found, not by accident, anyway."

"That library was destroyed by the Spaniards if my recollection of history is correct," Kevin added.

"True. With the exception of one."

I lifted a brow at that. *Before the Spaniards in, what, the early 1500s? Geez. I doubt anyone would have thought to write about Aluxes in the history books when so much was at risk of being lost during the time.*

"That's why it's a legend, love," Kevin whispered at my ear, again listening to my thoughts.

"Here we are," Topetine said, turning left. As we entered, Juno and Matt shined their flashlights up and across the room. As if instructed by an unseen force, torches came to life at different points on the wall to reflect more of the same covering of shells on every inch of wall space. Books were stacked on numerous shelves in all directions. I peered around a hidden corner to see they did indeed wrap around us. When I turned back, a man was standing in front of us, his eyes set on me.

"I present to you the Light Carrier," Topetine said. "Passage is sought for the location of Kukulkan and the second key."

Instinctively, I stepped forward, wanting to shake the man's hand in front of me to be sure he was real. He had to be a ghost. There was no other entrance or exit that could be seen. The air alone was as stale as the pages of text contained upon these shelves.

"Your hand," the figure said. I obliged and extended my right hand with the silver ring.

"Yes. You may proceed." But he held my hand firmly in his.

Feels very real. How did he get in behind us without one of us seeing him?

"Remain still." His other hand extended past my wrist to my forearm and flattened against it, pressing harder. My skin grew hotter beneath his grip until it was burning like a branding iron, reminding me of a time when Kevin had removed a mark the demons had made in the same area of my arm when I'd stumbled into the darker side of Ardan. While I stood locked in place, I felt my brows close together and my breath quicken as I accepted what this man, J-man, ghost, whoever he might be was delivering. The heat extended from the area on my forearm and up, encompassing my torso, chest, and head, until it exhausted itself and came out as beads of sweat that ran from my temples down my neck. The room started to float, or perhaps I was, as I could not feel my feet any longer. The light grew brighter and a subtle fog settled across my vision. For a brief moment, it felt as though I was falling, and yet there was no sensation of pain. I was indeed staring at the ceiling but in a trance. I tried to speak but the sounds were trapped from escape.

"How long will she be out?" Kevin's voice floated into my ears.

Hey, can't you see my eyes are open? What do you mean "out"?

His hand swiped across my cheek. *You okay?*

I heard his thought, just as I'd heard his voice. *Yes. Some sort of trance. Can't speak.*

Can you stand?

"She'll be fine in a few minutes," Topetine said. "Go ahead and lift her up."

Kevin's firm hands behind me pressed against my back. At the same time, my body shifted either on its own or with help, likely both, into a standing position.

"The passage has been opened. Proceed with caution," the man said. I blinked and saw the last remnants of a figure disappearing through the rows of books in front of us as though he'd never been there.

On the lowest shelf, books were replaced with rolls of paper tied with string I was sure I'd not seen earlier. A strange urge propelled me forward without assistance. I pulled at the string and carefully unrolled the papyrus, scanning the first and second pages before stopping at the third.

"Sara?" a voice called from behind.

"Let her be for a moment," Topetine answered. "The spell cast over her allows her to read the text. It's her destiny to seek out the Scrolls of Life for her meeting with Kukulkan."

I continued scanning the document, unfamiliar with the language it was written in and yet fully aware of its meaning. There were drawings. One was similar to the map of the underground world. Another was of a mountain, containing a fire within its depths. The picture was roughed out as though someone had wanted to show the inside of the rocky terrain in a sliced or sectioned version. A few more instructions were listed following the drawings, along with key codes, but to what, I didn't know. When I was finished, I turned to face the team.

"We need to go to the place known as the Bloody Basin and free the serpent god. Only then will the key be released."

"Did that document tell ye where we'd find such a lovely place as that?" Mac asked.

"I know of it," replied Topetine. "From here, we'll need to be very cautious. The same protection we were afforded last night is not a guarantee once we leave this cave and the cenote."

I grabbed a torch on my exit from the library. All was rather quiet as we made our way back through the hallway to exit the cave.

"Do you feel any different?" Kevin asked in a low voice.

"A little, but I can't put my finger on it."

He nodded but remained silent, his thoughts consuming him. I could feel the energy that changed around him, the same heaviness as I had when he'd come into the little hut yesterday. *Must be his worry that has that familiar vibe to it.*

"I'm sensing some danger," Matt said. "Juno, are you getting anything? My vision is clouded." A swish of swords being removed from their sheaths sounded.

"Same sensation. No detail," he answered.

Juno, Matt, Aria, and Elise moved ahead to the front, while Mac, Topetine, and Kevin flanked my sides, as much as the narrow hall would allow.

I placed the torch against the stone as we stepped into the bright light of the afternoon that greeted us with the heat and humidity of the day. I was blinded by the sun, my eyes battling to adjust to the contrast from dark to bright light.

"Continue straight ahead," called Topetine from behind.

Yeah, as long as we can see straight ahead. I gazed down in search of a path as we stepped from the rocky surface of the cave floor to grassy terrain. The sound of a sword against stone rang out, causing me to shift my focus up. I reached for the bottle the J-man had given me and realized it, too, had been lost with the blades.

"Here," Kevin said, tossing something in my direction. It was the potion. "I found it floating near the sword."

How? Someone must have thrown our belongings in after the team followed us.

"Topetine's comrades," Juno said, answering my thought. "They were behind us when you called out. We asked them to send the gear if we disappeared like you had."

Kevin stepped in front of me. At the same time, I heard a loud growl from Topetine, who had shifted into her jaguar form. My eyes adjusted to the light in time to see shadows peeling from their hiding places in the shade of a nearby cliff. Aria and Elise took down the first two. Juno and Matt were at their back to take down three more. I fumbled with the top of the little bottle, trying to open it with my thumb, my blade in the other hand. I swallowed two drops and stuffed the bottle into the only safe place available, at my chest where the material knotted the tightest. *How long until this stuff works, if it works?*

High-pitched screams could be heard a short distance away and moving closer. Until this potion took effect, my safest bet was to stow the blade and use the energy found in the extra protection the Druids had given me in Scotland. With each key, the gift of another level of protection was provided. It was an additional measure, layered into the planning of the quest to help us brace for the increased risks we were expected to face. The only caveat was that I had no idea what gift was offered in each key until I needed it. The Druids had granted me a boost to my defenses in the form of a stronger and longer-lasting barrier against the more forceful beasts of Tarsamon's malicious band.

I imagined the white-blue light of the shield and lifted one open palm to the side and one directly in front of me. As though my mind only needed the outlet through my hands to make it real, the barrier sparked to its full illumination in seconds and expanded from my hand into a square encompassing those within its reach, a span of about twenty-five feet. I had almost everyone embraced within the safety of the shield, except Kevin and Mac. I shifted my attention to the two men.

The call of the evil was louder and higher-pitched with each passing minute.

"The shadows we kill are signaling the others' approach," Matt shouted.

A dark wave rolled across the landscape, covering everything that was green in shades of gray and black. Mac and Kevin were deeply involved in a fight with unrelenting forces. I ran toward them, extending the shield farther so that it would encompass them in its protection. The barrier had a lifespan that, from my last experience in Doune, wouldn't hold for very long.

I continued toward the men, calling to them, only to have my voice drowned out by the sound of the screams and a new sound, like static. The shield I held began to fade and so, too, did the hand that held my blade. All of my energy was being cloaked, even that of the sword that carried the same connection to me. The wave continued rolling toward us.

"Sara's hidden under the protection of the potion," called Aria.

She stomped past me, the determination in her eyes promising destruction. "With any luck, that stuff really will keep them from sensing your energy."

From the vantage point atop the rocky formation and path running alongside it, we could see the Aluxes in formation below ready to intercept the wave of dark shadow moving toward us. *They must reside in all areas of the Yucatan.* As they headed straight for the dark wave moving closer, their skin color changed from flesh to yellow. I glanced back to where the Aluxes had set their battle line in time to see the black shadows hit them and fall to ground level, their misty dark forms absorbed into the soil at the feet of the trolls.

Topetine was still in her jaguar form and turned to me as though she could see me and snarled.

Follow me. She bolted with the team chasing behind her.

We can't outrun them and the shield will expire. I sent the thought to the rest of my team with the ability to receive messages telepathically.

We remained high above the Aluxes as we rounded a corner that sloped downward under the cover of trees, losing sight of the battle below. A vicious snarl from Topetine rang out before we met up with her seconds later, standing over a now deceased demon dog. Its neck was turned at an uncomfortable angle.

The protective shield faded around us, exhausting its energy, while the drops still kept me hidden. The break to catch our breath reminded me how much more difficult it was to recover with the blanket of humidity weighing upon us.

Mac leaned against the wall. "How did the wee creatures do that?"

When an Alux's skin turns yellow at the sign of danger, it produces a toxin to the shadows. Topetine shared her thought. *The Aluxes only need to pass through a shadow to disable it permanently. We have to keep moving. The danger hasn't passed.*

I turned my attention to the sky, thankful the J-men had thought to grant us the additional protection this far from the safety of the underground dwelling. All was clear in the late afternoon, for now. No evidence of additional shadows descending from above or around us.

"Are we close?" I asked.

It's not too much farther.

"I can't get a read on anything around us," Juno said.

"Nor can I," said Matt. "Our abilities to see what may be coming are blocked."

"That might be expected," said a voice that came from out of nowhere and likely the other side of the rock face. "It can't be helped right now." We whirled around to put the voice to a face.

Topetine lunged toward an object that had come too far into her personal space. In one swift motion, the team drew their swords.

C-05 stepped over the carcass of the demon dog Topetine had taken down. Feet behind him stood a pack of gray seething hounds with yellow eyes. Their back legs were human in appearance, very muscular as they crouched, ready at the command.

Never thank your lucky stars too early.

"Let's see. You all wouldn't be here without your precious cargo in tow," he said, pointing his sword at no one in particular. "Where are you, Sara?"

My eyes roamed across the terrain, assessing. More of the dogs were being held by the faceless flesh-colored demons that I'd learned from previous experience tracked the energy of their prey for a kill, and as such, the demons had no use for eyes or a nose to scent. They were created for tracking energy by sensing it, usually with a call to destroy it. But the dogs were another story. And that sense to hunt was keener than a cheetah hungry for her prey. The dogs began to lunge with impatience, as if they'd caught the scent of a meal. I placed both hands together to create the white sphere of light that would attack several of them at once if thrown. That's when I saw what tempted them. *Not now.*

The potion had begun to expend its energy and I was slowly becoming visible once more. *Was I supposed to take the entire bottle? No.* One drop was all the J-man said was needed to cloak my energy. But I had taken two for good measure. There was obviously some work that needed to be done to iron out the kinks, specifically the longevity of the protection I'd been given.

"There you are," he said as my body came into full view. Swords drawn, the team stepped closer to me, but there was still some distance to close. C-05 smiled. "I knew I wouldn't have to wait too long."

"You've looked better," I said, glaring at him. "I thought for sure your new master would have taken your soul after you failed him." C-05 had made a valiant attempt to stop me from obtaining the first key, but still had been unsuccessful in keeping me under house arrest in the dark world.

"How did you find us?" Elise asked.

"Elise, darling, glad to see you're feeling better."

She growled under her breath, and it was as if Topetine had made the sound.

C-05 had almost killed Elise in an attempt to take her energy so he could shift into an exact mirror image and try to fool me, lure me to trust him. His attempt had failed when my senses detected his energy to be off, or rather, not the usual sensation I would have felt had it really been Elise.

Kevin's, Juno's, and Matt's thoughts were colliding in my head as they tried to figure out the best way to escape. Topetine killing the demon dog had likely led C-05 to us. Unless there was another option, battling would call even more evil to us, reducing our chance of escape.

"I was going to lead this mission. Once. I knew where you were going. Tracking your energy was easy once I arrived in the Yucatan," C-05 said, answering Elise. "Really, one piece of information led to another and then the rush of the little fellows. Dark shadows don't chase evil, after all. But enough about me."

He shifted his gaze back to me. "You're outnumbered."

"That may be but it's never stopped us before," I said.

C-05 glanced to the orb of light I held. "You bear the mark of the J-man. Do you know the power you carry?"

I shifted my gaze to see a mark on the underside of my forearm, where the ghost figure had gripped my arm.

"As if I'd share that knowledge with you." And no, I didn't know what the burn mark on my forearm meant, or more accurately, if it meant anything at all. I didn't even recall receiving it. Had the figure who'd given me access to the scrolls been a J-man?

"I've never enjoyed our conversations much," I said. "And you can't have anything of value for us. What do you say you get out of our way?"

Step back, Sara. Kevin's voice trailed through my head with his warning.

"You always have a direct way about you that I so admire," C-05 said.

"You'd better be sure you're successful this time, or you're a dead man." I lifted my other hand to create a shield. "But then again, you already are." He took my reference to him selling his soul to Tarsamon and narrowed his eyes at me.

C-05's sword jutted out before my shield could fully compose, snagging my pants and piercing my skin as the blade cut into my left upper thigh. I kept my eye on him, feeling the sting and warm trickle of blood inching down. C-05's other hand reached toward the sky and dropped as he signaled the demon dogs to be released.

With Kevin's lightning-quick speed, his blade was at C-05's throat in half a second. "Call them off."

"I've got nothing to lose anymore." And before Kevin could react, C-05 was gone.

"He's shifted," Kevin called out. "He's still here." But the dogs had already been released and were making their way straight for us.

"You okay?" Kevin asked.

"Of course. Let's get out of here. We don't know how many more are behind them." I lifted a chin in the direction of the heat already coming for us.

I threw the sphere into a group of demons that had arrived too close to Kevin and sent another hurling into a group of dogs aimed at Topetine. I whirled, sensing the need to look behind me. *No time to run.*

Two dogs leaped at my back, smacking against the shield, and were thrown off, howling. The force was enough to send me stumbling forward, landing on my knees. From previous experience, when the demons hit my shield, it struck them like an electrical current. But after a few tries, they appeared to develop resistance, so that it didn't take long for them to hit the shield without so much as a whimper.

An unfamiliar cry rang out above the confusion. I scanned the immediate area and spotted Kevin fighting a group of the demons with Mac and Matt at his back. Juno, Aria, and Elise were doing a fair job of keeping several dogs off me. *Where's Topetine?* I ran to where I'd last seen her, throwing another ball of fire in front of me to clear the path. As I did, a massive black paw shot out in front of me.

I leaned over Topetine, expanding the shield to encompass us both in its protection. "Where are you hurt?" Before she could answer, I saw drops of blood mingled in the black fur, wetting it. *Her back leg.* The injury didn't look bad. But I couldn't tell if it was a surface wound or something deeper like a torn muscle. "We have to get out of here. It's our only chance for them to stop the fight against the others." If I left, the demons would have no reason to fight. At least, that's what had happened when Kevin and I escaped the shadows in New York. "Can you walk?" A sharp growl, followed by another, rang out, warning me to stay away. "I'm not leaving you. We need to hide you until we can get a better look at your injury. Can you shift into other forms?"

Never... tried. Topetine pulled herself to stand and with a limp started to follow me.

One more of these ought to do it. I reached for the small bottle of potion.

Shit. It must have fallen when I... I lifted my gaze to the area I had thrown the first ball of fire, now crawling with dogs. There was no way I'd be able to recover the precious liquid. I threw another sphere before ducking with Topetine into a crevice at the edge of a rock formation.

"Lean into the wall. Feel its coolness in the shade, its roughness, and close your eyes," I told myself. I pressed my back against the uneven surface and said a prayer. I'd only shifted once before, when I was first getting reacquainted with my supernatural abilities in

Ardan. Back then I'd joined with the energy that was the tree, feeling the strength in its root structure, strong and secure, and the bend and sway of the branches. I hadn't made an attempt to shift since. Topetine and I had to try to distract the evil that was scenting our energy before more of the beasts found our hideout. Topetine leaned into the wall, more out of necessity than desire.

"You have to focus on every detail of the rock, the way you understand the energy of the jaguar that resides with you," I said, holding still against the surface. With any luck, our energy would blend enough into the formation to confuse the beasts. To my knowledge, they had no direct order to attack my team, but rather had set their attention on finding me and possibly the guardian. The real threat was our ability to get to the key. There was a chance, if I was captured, that it would be unlikely I'd be killed. Supposedly, my death would release the power of the keys I held. I was betting Tarsamon wouldn't take that risk, if the belief was true.

As I pressed into the crevice and started to concentrate, I glimpsed Topetine. She slipped into the rock formation more easily than I. The only evidence was a small trail of blood streaking the gray surface of the rock. With a bit more concentration, I slid into the same concealment and saw that the dogs backed off the team, noses scenting the air. They'd lost the trail, hidden within the substance of the rock. Kevin turned to see what was happening. He was connected to my energy and knew at the very least if I was present or away. A strange call sounded in the distance, possibly from C-05. The dogs turned in response and headed down the embankment in a dark rush. The faceless demons held firm. Though there were not as many of them as the dogs, they could still pose a threat. As I waited to see what call might come next, I felt something tighten around my throat, constricting my airway.

"I seek not to kill you, just to prevent you from completing your mission."

What? Impossible! How could he have? He must have seen me running toward Topetine.

Unable to breathe or fight, I could no longer hold my concentration against the rock. I fell from concealment to the ground, gasping for breath. I turned my head toward the wall in time to see C-05 unveiling his hidden form beside the place I'd fallen from. He had the ability to shift into any form, inanimate or living. His arms braced around me in an instant, locking my arms behind me to prevent creating a shield or weapon for defense. Matt and Kevin, with their supernatural speed, were beside C-05 with a double threat, but he still held his razor-sharp blade to my throat, undeterred. I doubted if Kevin and Matt were fast enough to stop the swish of a blade across my pulmonary artery. From the looks in their eyes, they knew it, too. They were gauging their options.

"She leaves with me," C-05 said. "I'll not kill her, but I can't promise what the Dark Lord intends." C-05 lifted his chin toward the demons that waited and they came rushing in answer. Juno, Aria, Mac, and Elise took on the first of several that headed toward them. Matt's gaze flicked to my side.

Topetine.

"Blasted bloody coward," Kevin said. "I'll see you dead. Mark my words." He dropped the arm that was raised to strike and slashed low, aiming for C-05's leg. I saw the blade come down at the same time the fierce growl behind me rang out. Topetine lunged from the wall and, with her head lowered, slowly started for C-05. A hair quicker and the jaguar would have been on top of him. Instead, C-05 had angled us away from the wall, our backs toward the overhang of a cliff where he could see my team. I felt my eyes widen at the demon behind Kevin. Matt turned and, in one quick motion of his sword, had the head rolling away, while Kevin stalked toward us, unmoved by the action and with the look of death in his eyes. Topetine crouched, eyes intense, as she judged the best angle of attack. I felt the pain of her earlier injury radiate through me and gasped.

Another movement from behind the men redirected my attention. "Look out!" I shouted. I took the risk of the blade still at my throat to send the warning. Aria and Elise continued battling the evil at a steady rate, but that wouldn't last long. The demons were approaching faster with each kill. Kevin was steps from us when another jumped on his back. C-05, with his blade still angled at my neck, stepped away from the scuffle. Kevin threw himself and the beast to the ground, attempting to wrestle him free as Matt rushed toward him. A blur of flesh and color rolled past us and off the edge.

"No—" My cry was cut off as C-05 took a step backward and had me tumbling with him over the embankment.

10

Kevin warned me not to underestimate C-05's abilities. And while I didn't know all of what they were, one of them was indeed speed. He'd whisked me out of site before any one of the members of my team could find me. My hands had come free in the fall and I'd put up a relentless fight. I was pleased that I'd opened his lip and caused blood to gush. Kevin hadn't missed when he'd struck C-05's leg, either. Blood oozed from the gash and there was a slight limp to his walk. Too bad Kevin had missed the main tibial artery in the lower leg. He would have bled out in minutes. Despite the damage, C-05 had managed during the battle to keep a hand on me as though his life depended on it. It probably did. I was surprised he was alive as it was and wondered what he'd bargained with this time to stay alive.

The last image of Matt and Kevin played over in my mind. *Are they okay?* Matt's speed at the very least matched Kevin's, and I hoped that, with his help, they had made it safely over the edge of the hill. *Maybe it isn't as far a drop as it seems.* That was the only thought I would let myself believe. *Is there a ledge that would brace their fall?* There was no room for distraction or to allow my thoughts to wander to the darker corners of what might be. Kevin was known in Ardan as the Last Great Warrior for a reason. I'd seen him battle more than two demons at once and make it out alive. He had fought dark, energy-absorbing shadows and survived a battle alone in Tarsamon's world when he was training to develop his skills. I didn't know if he had ever gone over a cliff before, but I wouldn't let myself believe that he wouldn't survive this mission. He had to. *I'll get back to him. I'll see that he's okay.*

C-05 and I had been walking for what seemed like a couple of hours, without water or food. My fingers had stopped tingling and were growing numb. I stretched against the binding he'd wrapped around my wrists and behind my back as fast as someone tying a hog in a contest. My sword and dagger were gone. Probably left behind, where we'd tumbled off the cliff edge. And the potion I'd tucked safely at the tightest part of the knotted dress was lost in a chaos of seething dogs. That meant I'd better find a way to get free of the bastard who was my keeper if I intended to hold on to any chance of survival, not just for me but for Earth and a future I longed for with Kevin.

"Where are we going?"

No answer.

It must hurt to talk. Good. God, how you deserve so much more.

He grabbed my arm, causing the binds to dig deeper into my skin, and pulled me with him down a slope under the canopy of hanging tree roots.

"Sit," he directed, releasing my arm.

I stood immobile, debating whether to listen or make a break for it. Deciding I wouldn't get far, I sat in the dirt and leaned against a wall covered in moss. Getting off my feet did feel good. But the momentary rest reminded me I'd only snaked a piece of bread in the early hours of the morning. My stomach cried out for nourishment. Resting also brought pain. I needed a distraction.

"I'm not going to lead you to any location," I said.

"If I wanted that, I would have taken your jaguar friend with us."

He must have guessed Topetine was our guide. Then again, his abilities at sensing people and their energy were keen. He would have detected her abilities. If he'd been hiding, he had likely read her thoughts. Did he know of the Bloody Basin?

I huffed. "I'd have liked to see you handle a jaguar, even an injured one."

He shot me a wicked glare. My stomach grumbled loudly again and I shifted my gaze to my feet.

"Can you at least loosen the binding at my wrists so blood may flow again?"

He cut a few pieces of low-hanging roots, looping softer grasses around them, before maneuvering behind me. For some reason, the action should have warmed the cold-as-steel feeling I had for him, but it didn't. I was being held against my will and without any protection. I leaned forward as he quickly replaced the binding, tying the knot as a sailor might while giving me the tiniest amount of movement. He then tied a longer binding around my waist and attached it to a piece of dead tree trunk, forcing me to give up my position beside the soft moss.

"I'll be back. We need water."

"What if something happens to you? You can't leave me unable to fend for myself."

"I'm sure as hell not letting you free from that trunk. Deal with it." And with that, he limped beyond the entrance and out of sight.

I struggled with the binds for several minutes before giving up. I was exhausted from the day's activity and no food. I'd forgotten about thirst until C-05 had mentioned water. That was dangerous because dehydration often snuck up on its victim. I closed my eyes instead and drifted, awakening each time my head lolled to the side. After several attempts at sleep, I finally gazed up at the sky to see dusk had settled. I knew very little of the Yucatan. I didn't even know what year I had landed in after sliding down into darkness, following the J-man's ritual. Was I still in the Yucatan? It looked like any other picture of the jungle of Central America. We hadn't seen any ruins on the hike. If the Spaniards had not yet arrived, and I guessed they hadn't with the library still intact, it would mean the time was at least before the early 1500s. But what if that library was hidden from the invasion by the Spaniards, and it had survived? There was no telling what year I was in. Maybe it didn't matter. The focus was the key and the guide that would lead me to it. *Topetine. Is she okay?*

New York. Mary Ann's homemade pasta sauce. I'd give anything for that hot meal. Hell, I'd give anything to lick the inside of a street-car hot dog wrap-per right now, so long as it eased the hunger pangs.

Further fantasy was disrupted at the sound of footsteps from be-hind. C-05 stepped beside me. The ankle of his pants where he had met Kevin's sword was torn and wet up to the calf. He placed some-thing that looked like fruit beside me. But there was little I could do with my hands tied. He crouched beside me and picked up one of the red, bulbous objects that looked similar to a Roma tomato.

"I'm not untying you. If you want to eat, and I know you do, you'll take it the way it's offered." He held the fruit up a bit higher and I bit into it. He set what looked like an expandable bottle filled with water in front of me.

"Why are we still here? Shouldn't you have delivered me to Tarsamon by now?"

"Not yet." He cut into one of the other objects, handed me a piece before taking the rest. "You're quite valuable. And I have something to acquire."

I didn't respond right away. Instead, I mulled over his meaning. He once said he had lost a love of his after failing a mission for the Soltari. But he couldn't possibly be stupid enough to think to use me as a bargaining chip. Could he?

"You'll get both of us killed if you try to use me to bargain for what you seek. You know that, don't you?"

He didn't answer but instead put the water to my lips. I took in several swallows before turning my head away.

"What is it you want?" I asked.

"Nothing you can get me. Not directly, anyway."

A moment passed between us in silence.

"The forces on each side are greater than you and me together," I said. "I hope you have your plan worked out."

"There is no other choice. I'm not giving myself to the darkness."

"I thought you already had. And you'll risk the lives on Earth, all of them including yours and mine, to get this *thing* you want to ac-quire?" I shifted back against the log. "So what's so valuable?"

"You should understand better than anyone."

I waited before answering. "You want to be reunited with the woman you love. Is that it?"

"Your connection to Kevin can be severed forever and that doesn't anger you toward the Alliance or the Soltari in any way?"

"I admit the thought of it has unnerved me," I confessed. "But I'm not going to take on the Soltari, an entity I'm allied with." *Will I?* "Maybe if you were to help me and the team, there might be a way we can appeal to the Soltari."

"Impossible."

Probably. "It's the Soltari you aim to do business with, bypassing the Alliance altogether, isn't it?" I released a breath. "I don't take you for a stupid man."

"Humph." He shook his head.

"Because only a stupid man would think he stood a chance of surviving after trying to negotiate terms with a demon lord." I shifted uncomfortably against the stump. "Oh, that's right. You already bargained with him for your life once. I forgot. That doesn't seem to be working for you, does it? 'Cause I gotta tell you, you look like shit."

He finished biting into one of the items he'd brought back with him and tossed the remaining flesh on the ground. "You talk too damn much. You know that?"

"Yeah, we can't all be perfect. Besides, as a psychiatrist, it's my profession to talk and listen. And I haven't heard anything that suggests you've got this plan of yours worked out."

"I've got a better chance with the Soltari. But I'm willing to see who is more interested in you."

"Then you're willing to die to find out. Where is Tarsamon, anyway? Shouldn't he be with you? Not that I don't have plenty of his forces after me."

No reply.

Did Tarsamon hit a barrier against entering the realm, similar to the barrier that prevented him from entering Scotland?

"If such a barrier was in place, the demon dogs and shadows never would have made it through," he replied to my thought.

"So, where is he?"

No reply.

"You'd better not get us both killed taking me from my team to ..."

"Stop talking, will you? I'll think of something."

Tarsamon would never bargain again. He might have gained valuable information from C-05, but he'd also lost me once. I'd obtained one key and was well on my way to the other before being captured. At least C-05 understood the odds. But what other choice was there for him? If Tarsamon caught him, he'd kill him for not handing me over. The killing would assuredly involve torture since C-05 used Tarsamon's forces to take something and not deliver on the goods, not right away, anyway. And the demon lord might risk killing me being that I only had one of the keys. They knew I'd only grow stronger as I obtained each of the remaining two. From what I had learned from Mac, to release the keys, I would need to exchange my life for them. I hoped he was mistaken. If not, Tarsamon might risk release of one into the world, perhaps believing he could control the eminent power of a single key. I would lose my eternal bond with Kevin and end up lost like C-05. That wasn't in my plan. With this half-baked scheme C-05 had created, I was left with one option; I'd have to escape him.

"Would you consider retying my hands in front of me so I have some basic use of them?"

He stared at me. I cleared my thoughts in order for them not to be read by him. Even though he didn't appear to have a well-thought-out plan, he had been clear that the small, scattered development of one didn't include killing me, not immediately.

"Don't try anything," he said.

"I won't try anything if you're not stupid. Deal?"

He shook his head, annoyance washing over his face, as he grabbed the joined wrists and cut through the binding. "Clasp your hands together in front of you. I don't need you creating any fireballs."

I did as he instructed, satisfied I'd bothered him. With any luck, I got him to think a little more about who he would approach first with me as his bargaining chip. Not that I had any intention of being that chip. Problem was, I had no plan of escape yet. I'd have to wait until he was asleep to be sure my thoughts were safe enough to construct a strategy for getting away and back on course for the key.

C-05 had more energy than I thought. It must have been three hours before he finally fell asleep. I had even dozed for several minutes at a time, waiting him out and hoping he wouldn't remember to tie me to anything immobile. He hadn't. Either he'd forgotten or decided not to. As I stared at his sleeping form slumped against the wall along the only path out of the cave, thoughts of sneaking past him played through my head. If he slept as lightly as Kevin did, I wouldn't have a chance. *Should I wait longer or test the depth of his sleep? And risk more waiting or, worse, being stuck with him? No way.*

All C-05 wanted was his love to be returned to him. I didn't know who she was or if she was worth his life. But I couldn't blame him for taking such extreme measures if what he said was true. But could I trust love or hope as his only motivation? Probably, because it didn't look like he had anything left. The Soltari had betrayed him. He'd given his soul away to Tarsamon. He'd lost all that he'd once cared for. That's the price for selling out to the other side. I had my own concerns. Those that involved saving Earth. I had to get back to Topetine and get the key or I'd find myself in a similar situation as C-05. I'd choose death before I'd join with Tarsamon. And while the threat of losing the only person I'd ever loved loomed over me, there was still a chance for Kevin and me, as long as I could slip past C-05.

I leaned forward and pushed myself to stand, all the while watching for a flicker of an eyelid or twitch of a muscle. Quietly I stepped, trying to place each foot on the softest ground available and avoid the loud, gritty cover beneath my feet. I slipped across C-05's outstretched legs, holding my breath, and sidestepped to the entrance of the cave, never taking my eyes off him. As I turned to leave into the open jungle, I crashed into the solid form of a man measuring a few inches taller than my five foot ten. He wrapped one meaty arm around me and covered my mouth with his other hand, silencing my gasp.

11

"Sara?" the man whispered.

I nodded, unable to speak. Contrary to how he was dressed, his energy didn't feel ominous. I glanced at C-05, who began to stir. A flash burst across my vision, blinding me. When it cleared, I was no longer in the cave or any immediate area surrounding it. Faint moonlight scattered across the evening sky to reveal the lush vegetation had disappeared. Tents were strewn across a desert landscape, with a smattering of stubby bushes and a few trees between them.

"Who the hell are you? And where are we?" I asked, shifting my gaze to the man. Behind him, torches highlighted a group of men dressed in the same rugged leather attire. *A uniform? Are they military?* The man I addressed was hooded and wore a red cloth around his middle. Numerous straps were belted across his chest and waist, holding swords and daggers of different types.

Il partember de katesh. The man began unstrapping two swords from his waist, leaving the daggers in place. "Never again."

"Come again?"

"The one parted by the four famines," he translated.

What famine? Parted from whom? My usual analytical mind was at work trying to find answers to questions that didn't matter.

"I lead this army from another time, another realm. We are here to aid you. I pulled you from that cave you were in by tracing." He paused, taking in the questionable look that must have been plastered upon my face. "The ability to move energy from one location to another. In this case, yours and mine. Not to worry, you are still in the Yucatan."

"Thank you. But I must get back to my team. I was in the process of doing this before you interrupted me."

"Your team will catch up with you. The detour for us to intervene is a necessary one." He squatted on the ground beside a fire. "How far did you think you were going to get bound and stumbling through the dark, anyhow? Don't you know of the predators that hunt in the depths of the jungle?"

"I would have made it farther than staying with C-05." *Maybe.* I reconsidered as thoughts of large cats and anacondas floated across my vision.

I didn't understand what was happening. And something told me I wouldn't be provided an explanation. "Can you at least free me of these binds?" I held my wrists out to him.

"Not just yet." He extended an open palm in invitation to join him by the fire.

I stood looking at the flames and the open space beside him. I couldn't run. Well, I could, but because he was a tracer, I wouldn't get far before he found me again, and the effort would be fruitless in the dark, not knowing how to get back to my team. I acquiesced and sat near him.

"How did you know I was in need of aid?"

"A signal came from the one you are joined with."

"Kevin? You know Kevin?" *So he's alive. Thank God.* "Is he okay?"

"Aye. We've known each other a long time. Cerys is the name I know." He turned his gaze from the fire to me and slicked back the hood. "And yes, he is well."

I breathed a sigh of relief. The light gray eyes of my new captor blazed into mine, reminding me of Kevin's intensity when we had first met. This man's facial features were similar, too—angular jaw and high cheekbones but with a nose a bit shorter and wider. Despite the dim light, the eyes were clear and intent on fulfilling a goal, whatever it might be.

"If you know of Cerys, who are you? Are you human or an entity?" His grip on me in the cave should have been convincing enough.

"An ally. I'm a little more human than what you understand human to be on Earth. I have the same ability as you or your team to speak with the entities as well as mingle with humans when I choose."

"Why won't you free me if you're an ally?"

He leaned closer. "I have something for you." He reached a hand behind him into the air, keeping his eyes fixed upon me. One of the men came over and placed an object in his open palm and turned away.

"Why would that keep you from untying..."

In one swift motion, the man held tight my arm and stabbed me with a syringe, injecting a solution that began to burn as though he'd held my flesh to the very flames in front of me. I screamed, unable to control myself as the heat raced in every direction from the point of delivery. I fell onto my back in agony. Despite both wrists being secured, I reached to rub the immediate area and disperse the pain. But because the intensity was spreading rapidly, nothing eased the burning sensation.

"What did you shoot me with?" *Is it like a venom that I have to cut, suck, and spit out?*

"The pain will subside soon."

"I didn't ask you that! What is it?"

"DNA enhancement. A cell restructuring is taking place. It's not harmful to you, though it may feel like it."

Harmful? Deadly is more accurate. Every cell feels like it's splitting and on fire in the process.

I was lying on my side, holding my arm with one hand while trying to process what I'd just heard. I'd hardly said more than a few words to this man who said he knew Kevin, and before I had decided whether to believe him or not, he was restructuring my DNA? Was that right? My eyes began to twitch, while my body twisted against the effect. DNA restructuring wasn't even possible on Earth yet.

"Free my hands," I shouted.

"Not until the transformation is complete."

"Holy hell. You're dead, if this doesn't kill me first." I screamed once more. I'd never felt this much pain, ever. If I could be seared alive, this had to be what it would feel like. My body writhed in uncontrollable agony. Sweat broke out across my skin in response.

All the while, the man sat next to me, staring into the fire. Minutes passed like hours in torture until the pain gradually eased, finally releasing my body from the wave after brutal wave that left me shivering in a cold sweat. The man angled his head toward me and picked up a heavy, dark-colored blanket, placed it over me, and gently scooped me into his arms. Only then did I become aware of my gasping breath. Exhaustion from the effort I'd just been put through. But why? Why had he injected me with a chemical to restructure my DNA? Rage began to combine with the shivering. Once my quivering jaw stopped impeding my attempt to shout at him, I'd demand answers.

He set me down, still shaking violently, under the canopy of a tent. "You're recovering. It won't be long now."

It won't be long before I kill you. I don't care how scary you look under that hood.

He smirked. "He warned me you'd fight, and fight hard, your Kevin, that is."

"Ee...x...pp...lain," I stuttered.

"My name is Jade. I travel the realms with my men, soldiers. As I mentioned, Cerys and I have been friends for quite a long time."

"No."

He lifted an eyebrow at me.

I wasn't sure if all of the individuals I would encounter with supernatural abilities would be able to read thoughts, but I decided taking a chance was the fastest way to get to the heart of what I really wanted to know. How he knew Kevin, or rather Cerys, could be understood later.

What is the effect of what you injected me with and why did you do it?

He tucked the blanket tighter around me. "Your body was in need of enhancements to help you avoid the danger that hunts you," Jade said, confirming to me he could read thoughts. He turned toward a stuffed pack and unzipped a compartment. I watched every movement, while the larger muscles in my body began to slow their contractions. "The effect will take some getting used to but I imagine you'll fall into it with some ease."

I sat up, pulling the blanket around my shoulders, as I continued to shiver.

He turned back to me with a knife in one hand and a canteen and cloth in the other. "Do I have your word you'll not use light energy upon me and my men?"

"I don't like being held against my will."

"I need your word before I untie you. Then, I'll explain."

"Yes," I answered reluctantly, holding out my bound hands to him. "No fireballs."

"That's a fine knot job," Jade said, slipping the knife between my wrists. He stashed the knife and drenched the cloth in water before lifting it to my forehead.

"I'll do it," I said, stopping him. He handed me the cloth and I pressed it against my cheeks first, then my eyes. The dampened material felt so very good against my previously burning skin that I didn't want to pull it away.

"What effect?" I pressed.

"Drink first. You need it."

"Not until I'm certain you haven't laced it."

"Ever the untrusting soul. He warned me about that as well." Jade took a deep drink from the canteen and handed it to me. I swallowed as though I had thirsted for a week.

"You'll need food, too, but that can wait," he said. "The DNA restructure you've undergone allows you to shift."

"I could shift before that injection by joining energy with any inanimate object," I said.

"That won't do you a damn bit of good when fighting evil that can scent your energy like a hungry dog. Tarsamon has a weapon that is stronger than the shadows or dogs."

I stared at him in silence, contemplating the analogy as one I often used, which meant he was quite familiar with Tarsamon's dark forces.

"You now have the ability to shift into a hawk."

A hawk? My gaze floated to the remaining light of the fire outside the tent. The ability to fly, I considered, could be useful in escape. But would I know how? And how very awkward, to say the least, to have this body mutate into a bird, with feathers covering skin and claws for hands. I closed one of mine into a fist in wonder. *Would I still be me, Sara?*

"Of course you will," Jade said, answering my thought.

"A bird of prey," I said more to myself. "And to think I had almost become a vegetarian." Before I'd set out on this quest, the only meat I had been eating was fish. The kind found in sushi. I had all but lost the desire for the texture of the other selections at the local grocery. The thought of meat made my stomach turn, even though I'd not eaten much in the last several hours. "Is this a temporary effect on my DNA?"

"Until you release all three keys."

End of life, if Mac is correct about the release of the keys. Can't think about that now. "How will my team catch up with us? The scrolls said I'd need to get to the Bloody Basin."

"Then we go there, after you eat and sleep."

In all that had happened, I'd forgotten about the need for more substantial food than a piece of fruit. But as Jade began unrolling what looked like bread and cheese from another cloth inside the pack, my stomach grumbled.

"Here," he said, handing me a hunk of each item he held. "Settle your stomach and you'll sleep."

"I doubt it," I mumbled. "Thank you." As I took a bite and then another, my nerves did settle. "How long have you been on this mission to aid me and my team?" I asked, trying to learn a few facts about my new captor.

"Long enough. We were called to action by the Alliance. And judging by the situation I found you in, it was a good call."

"Excuse me, but I was doing fine making my way out of that cave before you appeared."

"Again, how far did you think you'd get?"

I hadn't considered it beyond getting past C-05 and cutting the binds on a sharp rock. Maybe I would have followed the trail back the way we'd hiked and met up with the team. I could've have tried to reach Kevin via telepathy. But I didn't know if that would work.

"You'd have run into Tarsamon before you found your team. Face it. You need help and you need to trust someone."

"And you're supposed to be that someone?"

He shrugged a shoulder. "I've got a small army. You've got, well"—his eyes skimmed over me and he continued eating—"yourself."

He sounded like Kevin, too, when he was upset.

"Trace me to my team." It was meant as a request but came out a little harsher than I'd wanted, sounding more like an order. "Please," I added.

"Not gonna happen. The dark forces are expecting you to be with them. It's too risky." He stood, ducked under the tent entrance. "Get some sleep."

He called a couple of names, and from my limited view, I saw three men approach. "No one in or out. Got it?"

"Yes, sir."

"Wait." Hunched over, I walked to where the two flaps of the tent met. "At least provide some proof Kevin is okay."

"I'll see what I can do."

Minutes passed slowly into an hour, then two. When I grew tired of listening to the men and their card games, I spread the blanket out, lumped one end into a makeshift pillow, and placed my head on it to sleep. *I've got to get to the Bloody Basin area. But without Topetine, how?* Jade had said we'd go there. But how did he know the way? I'd discovered that small piece of information in a scroll, deep in what was a hidden library. There had been no map or instruction to get to Bloody Basin.

With time to kill, I reflected on my new captor. He was sent to "intervene" by the Alliance. Was that a result of an order from the

Soltari? Where else would he have obtained a solution to restructure DNA? He also knew of Cerys, my Kevin, but Kevin had never mentioned anyone like him to me.

My eyes began to close in longer increments at the mere consideration of being safe. I could spare a few minutes of rest, couldn't I? *My team. I have to find my team. They'll catch up, remember?* With the faint sounds of laughter and lighthearted swearing in the distance, I drifted into a warm, comfortable sleep and into the world of Ardan.

My visits to the mystical realm were often a calling for someone to provide direction or to share information. The familiar dirt path appeared beneath my feet. The sky was black as soot with the smallest shred of steel-blue on the outer edge of a would-be horizon if the sun ever rose here. I'd never seen it, not in this lifetime. I felt as though I were alone in the early hours of morning, but that was a false sensation. My experience in Ardan had proven the person responsible for summoning me was watching for my arrival. And as Kevin had once said, the presence of my energy was felt before it was seen.

As I stepped past the trees that lined either side, a sensation crawled up my spine that someone was behind me. I couldn't see anything more than what was within a two- to three-foot span of a circle by glow of a faint blue light, its source unknown.

I'd been told by the elves during my first visit to Ardan that I couldn't be hurt here. But I'd also been told Tarsamon's forces were not allowed passage on this side of Ardan. That had proven to be false when they'd crossed the guarded boundary that divided him from the rest of the realm, causing a battle to ensue as Tarsamon tested his strength, or rather that of the guardians of Ardan—the wolves and the elves. I stopped on the path at recalling the memory and turned to look behind me. Nothing. A hand on my shoulder jolted me back around to face front. Standing before me was either Kevin or Cerys, but I couldn't see his face clearly. The eyes had been the main identifier for me. Kevin's were warm pools of brown with gold flecks and Cerys's were a vivid cerulean blue. Both had similar angular features, high jaw, and long bridge of a nose. Why couldn't I see his eyes? They were shadowed.

"Who are you?" I asked. The energy felt like Cerys's, as warmth spread over that same shoulder he had touched, calming and full of love.

"My darling." He sounded like Cerys.

"Why can't I see you clearly?"

"It's part of your transformation." He lifted a palm to the direction in front of us as if inviting me to see. As I looked on, the darkness lifted and in its place were twinkling lights. The sky was lit like Van Gogh's *Masaustu Resimleri*. The shades of black and gray swirled in clouded hues of blue and white. Where cloudless dark could be seen, shiny, diamond-like stars were sprinkled in varying sizes across the heavens. The beauty had been topped with a crescent moon.

"A moon," I said under my breath. I'd never seen one in Ardan to explain the glow coming from above. *Why now?* The colors that lit the sky had often been a mystery without the prior existence of a moon or stars. I centered my attention on each detail, too much to absorb, before lowering my gaze to a field of colorful blooms illuminated by the brightness of the sky.

A hand gently swept back the hair from my neck and a kiss was put in its place, followed by another. The sensation sent the familiar tingling across my shoulder and down my arm. He turned me to face him and set his mouth upon mine, soft, wet, as sensual a kiss as I ever remembered.

Wait. A tiny voice in my head said the spell was meant to seduce and I felt myself falling deeper into him with every second his lips were on mine. *And why not? Why not allow myself this pleasure?* Two fingers slipped beneath the strap at my shoulder, while an arm slipped behind me and a hand held firmly at my back, easing me to the soft Earth below. All the while, his lips never left mine. I slid my hand through his hair and cupped his neck, urging him against me. I felt his hardness press into my center and knew this was no memory being shared from a past life, but reality. It was a closeness I longed for in the joining of spirit and flesh. To feel that complete was nothing more than heaven, one as beautiful as that sparkling above me.

There had been too much struggle and focus on the quest. *Let go,*

I told myself as he eased my shirt to the waist, exposing me further to his expert touch. I opened my eyes, ready for him to be studying my reaction, as he always did when he held me close. But his eyes were not on me. There remained a shadow across them, making them blurry, almost visible through a cloud of smoke. He bit into my neck gently and sent another wave of passion racing through my body. I lifted my chin, giving him more access. He pressed into me once more, just before his hand slid up along my thigh, closer to the center of what burned for more of him. I heard him gasp as he reached the area of the mark that had been branded into my lower abdomen by the Druid priests upon obtaining the first key. I opened my eyes, head still angled back, to see Cerys walking toward me. My heart stopped its rapid beat of lustful want and froze as though it had been struck by an ice pick.

My attention shot to the weight of the person pressed against me as the entire image began to disappear. My eyes were fixed open to see the stars had faded, as had the moon and soft bed of flowers. Replacing the lit sky was an odd green glow that surrounded me and the lump beside me. The man who had been covering my form was now hooded and lying with one leg covering mine in the tent where I'd dozed. The flap was closed to conceal us, but my shirt was indeed at my waist.

Jade.

"Get off me!" I shouted.

He covered my mouth with a meaty, rough hand. "You were so close. You were almost there."

"Not for you, I wasn't." I struggled against his pressing weight and protruding firmness.

"Listen. You were shivering again. I tried to comfort you, and one thing led to another. I shouldn't have..." His voice trailed off. *Damn straight you shouldn't have.* His cheek was rough against mine as he spoke into my ear. "I fulfilled my mission to the Alliance, an order from the Soltari, to transform you to help you survive this mission. All you need to do is allow me to hold the key for you. I won't keep you from getting the other two."

"Screw that. Get off me," I mumbled under his hand as I continued my struggle against him.

"Sara, stop." His hand remained pressed against my mouth and he lifted his head to look at me. "I need to ensure that the Soltari do not put my men through another torturous famine."

What?

"I only need one of the keys to press the Soltari to change their methods." He paused. "Please. It would be a merciful act."

What the...? So many thoughts raced through my head at once. Mac told me the only way for anyone to take the key was for me to willingly give myself up to that person, but that any genuine protector of the Light Carrier would never request this of me. For one, they couldn't hold the power of the keys, and two, true protectors understood it to be my responsibility alone to fulfill the mission. This man, who claimed to know Kevin or Cerys, wanted me to give him the key. It didn't matter why, because it couldn't matter. Even if he had some ability to hold the power of one key, without all three, I was unable to complete the mission. The result would be a tremendous loss of life on Earth, not to mention my eternal bond with Cerys. And what of the façade to seduce me in Ardan? If Jade had been successful, there was so much more to have lost than the fear of another famine.

My mind jumped to another page of the quest, wondering what kind of entity punished so severely? What had caused the Soltari to issue a famine, much less four of them? Was C-05 right that if I knew the true nature of what I fought for, I'd think otherwise? He'd said that to me on the last quest. Maybe he was right. But there wasn't time to contemplate that now.

My blood was boiling at what he'd tried to take from me, the lie of pretending to be a man I cherished, and having no intention of protecting the key I'd already worked so hard to get. This wasn't the place I needed to be. I had to get back to my team as fast as I could. And I sure as hell couldn't trust anyone to help me do that. I felt the heat on my skin as it flooded my veins and broke out in another sweat. My vision sharpened. I saw every pore on Jade's face, even in the shadow that cascaded across from the hood he still wore. With all the strength I had left, I shoved against him. And to my surprise, he moved off of me. *What? No fight?*

Free of his weight, I stood to face him. "How could you try to take the key when you must know what's at stake? No one can hold the power of it but me." My voice lifted higher and cracked. Sweat rolled down my temples.

"Calm down, Sara. You'll want to get a grip on that anger."

He might have been a few inches taller and built with taut muscle, but that was no match for the wicked temper that had been brewing for hours. I lunged with the intent of throwing a right hook to catch his jaw good and hard and missed as my legs gave out and a loud screech pierced the tent. *My God!* I'd shifted into the hawk. *Why? Did my rage cause the transformation? Is that why he warned me to get a grip on my anger?* Jade made an attempt to grab for me but missed. The tent flap opened as one of the guards peered inside to see if assistance was required. *An opportunity for escape.* On instinct, I flew through the small opening, blinding the guard with the brush of a wing as he grasped at nothing but air.

I soared above the camp, in awe that I was indeed flying, before resting on the branch of a tree at what felt like a safe distance away. I doubted Jade would trace to a limb for the off chance he'd catch me. I just needed a few moments to think.

Where to now? Kevin. The team. Back the way I hiked with C-05. Which direction is it?

My keen senses honed in to the former location. And as I set myself to take flight, the little voice that guided me whispered, "Ever the untrusting soul, for good reason."

12

A figure paced the edge of a village set in the heart of the Yucatan jungle. *A jaguar. Topetine?* In the torchlight that lined the building, the head of the animal turned and angled up at me. With surprising grace, I landed on the branch of a tree within a safe distance to what I hoped was the Mayan woman and, within seconds of landing, fell to the ground, naked and human again.

"For Christ's sake," I said under my breath. "This is going to take some getting used to."

"You'd be better off remaining as a hawk in this place, my dear." It was Topetine. She'd shifted, but unlike me, she was clothed. "Wait here. I'll be right back."

I hid in the concealment of large leafy plants, watching as she moved to a nearby dwelling constructed of rock and straw. Her movements were slow and casual, as if she'd lived there her whole life. A man stopped to ask her a question, they shared a few words, and she continued strolling until she was out of sight.

Several long minutes passed. My focus remained fixed on the rock wall she had disappeared behind. The sensation that the rest of my team was near filled my body, but there was no other indication of their presence. As I wondered if Topetine was indeed coming back, she appeared with something rolled up in both hands.

"Here. They should fit well enough." She handed me the bulky object while looking over her shoulder to see if anyone had seen her cross into the jungle.

"How is it you transform with clothing?" I asked, unrolling the garments to find a shirt and pants, a hooded cloak, and shoes.

"Practice. You get used to shifting enough and the Powers That Be begin to understand your needs and provide for them."

The clothes were styled for men, and I slipped into the slim pants, rolled up the sleeves of the shirt to my elbows, and slid my arms through the dark army-green cloak.

"Cover your head. Your hair, with all of the red highlights, will give you away as an outsider."

She tucked my hair behind my ears, as though she were my mother about to send me off to school.

"What is this place?" I asked.

"A village your team and I were passing through on our way to find you." She paused. "We've been delayed by some of the villagers."

I detected a warning in her tone. "Why?"

"How long have you been able to shift?" she asked, switching subjects.

"This is my first time."

"I suppose I could've guessed." Her eyes narrowed as they skimmed down and up again, taking in my dressed form. "Well then, to shift, you have to become angry or remember a painful event. When it wears off, you'll return to your human form. If you want to remain as a hawk, you'll need to hold the painful thought or anger at the forefront of your mind." She pressed her lips together. "Why is this your first time?"

"A man, a soldier I think, rescued me from C-05. He said he was directed to administer a DNA-restructuring agent."

"Directed by whom?"

"The Alliance. He said it was the Soltari who had ordered it."

"This man, how was he dressed? Leather? Guns or knives?

"Knives, mostly," I said, recalling the arsenal he carried on his jacket. "His name was Jade. You know of him?"

"I don't know him, but the story *of* him and his army has existed in Ardan for as long as I can remember. He's known a great deal of suffering. He's never been known to intentionally hurt someone tied to the Alliance, but you can't trust anyone except the team that walks with you on this quest. Do you understand?"

I understand a lot better.

I nodded. "Where are the others?"

"They're in there," she said, angling her head in the direction she had come from with the clothing in hand. "But we aren't going."

"Why not?"

"You have a task to complete and time is of the essence. There is little of it to spare."

"My team . . ."

"Your team needs you elsewhere."

"What are you keeping from me? Why won't we be getting the key together?" She stared at me, not offering a response. "Something's wrong. Something you don't want me to see." I turned my attention toward the dwelling, what little was viewable from our hidden place behind a few trees, and recalled she had been in her jaguar form when I arrived. A sure sign something was indeed wrong.

Topetine gripped my arm. I glanced at her hand and met her stare. "I need you focused. You want to help your team? Get the key. Simple as that."

"What's in there?"

Her hand dropped from my arm. "So stubborn." She huffed out a breath. "If I take you in, you have to promise me two things—one, you will not reveal yourself or your abilities, and two, you will leave with me immediately no matter what you see. Understand?"

"Is Kevin okay?"

"Yes." She paused without moving. "For now."

Alarm filled me, but my feet remained rooted as I contemplated her request. "You believe it best I shouldn't intervene here."

"You'll kill him if you do."

Goddamn it to hell.

"I need to see for myself."

"Your word first that you'll follow me."

"Seems to be a popular request," I said, remembering Jade asking for my word before untying me. "Of course you have my word. I'll follow you."

"We'll pass through the gathering of people as though we belong and head to the Bloody Basin. No stopping. Understand? It's important that you not show any interest."

"No interest." Rigid with tension, I hoped I could hold myself together and act like the one thing that mattered most meant nothing. I would do what I must to protect Kevin. And God help me, if that meant ignoring the situation to get a good look, a full assessment, then so be it.

I walked close behind Topetine, head fully concealed in the cloak. My hands were balled into the sleeves to hide the ring that identified me as the Light Carrier, but only to those pure of heart. I wasn't taking any chances that anyone would spot me.

We passed beneath an arch and proceeded down a corridor toward the growing sound of chanting. *What are they saying?*

Not now. No thoughts, no words, and no actions. Nothing.

I lowered my eyes as we entered the huge chamber, where a large crowd of villagers had gathered. The chanting was almost deafening, as I followed Topetine through the multitude of people bumping and chiming for a better view, of what, I couldn't know. Sliding between them, I scanned the floor-to-ceiling height, several feet high. Torches lined the walls of the dingy hall that looked like a mix between an old barn and a prison. Straw was scattered about the floor. My eyes froze on a row of chains dangling midway to the floor, one after another, from the center of the ceiling. My breath caught and my eyes held. At the end of each chain was the upper half of a torso. No sign where the lower half of each body was. I didn't see Kevin and breathed a sigh of relief. And yet I wouldn't be content until I could see him, alive.

"Ye'll not want to be here, lass," said a familiar voice. I angled my head to see Mac. "May I help ye out?"

In my surprise, I hadn't noticed that I'd stopped following Topetine to gawk at the gory sight. "Yes," I answered.

Mac knew what I was doing there and so did the rest of the team.

From what I could sense from them, they were terrified I'd react. But to what? The sight of the bodies was gripping, but not enough to make me react to nameless, deceased men. Then, I saw Kevin. As I followed Mac to the opposite end of the hall, pushing past a man holding a pitchfork, our eyes met. Tears welled as I fought not to let them spill over. My heart jolted to a stop in my chest. Inside a metal cage, stripped to his waist, Kevin was chained to the bars. Some of the villagers were poking him with jagged sticks, calling out ugly sounds, words I didn't understand, *waay* (wi-ay). He was bleeding from too many areas to count and looked as if he'd already been beaten. I wanted to shout at everyone holding a sharp object, rip them from their hands, and stick them the same way they were inflicting pain on Kevin.

Go! Get the key. Hurry.

Kevin's thought broke through my shocked state and my eyes dipped toward the ground. Mac pressed a hand against my back, urging me forward.

He's next. He's next. I can't leave him to that! Sweat broke out across my skin and my breath came into my lungs in short, halted inhales.

"He'll no' be next, lass," Mac said, reading my thought.

How can he be sure?

"But we canna hold them off long. Go!" Mac pushed me out of the hall into the corridor on the opposite side from which I had entered. Topetine stepped in behind me as though she'd been watching the entire time.

Kevin. My God! There's no time. My eyesight narrowed in focus to being pinpoint sharp and my legs gave out as I shifted again into the hawk form, unable to control my emotions at the images that were on an automatic rewind of Kevin in the cage and the angry intent on the faces outside of it. I looked behind me before flying off to see that Topetine had scooped up the clothing. I flapped once, then twice, with every intent of taking off. Instead, I hit something firm but soft and struggled. There were no more torches or forest or even ground, for that matter. Darkness surrounded me.

Topetine!

I called to her in thought but it came out as a screech. I continued to fight inside the object that contained me from flying.

"Hush now. We don't want any attention over here." The whispering voice that filtered into my super-sensitive ears was Jade's. "You want to save him, then you'd better calm yourself. I'll let you out once you do."

I immediately went silent and ceased to move, following his instructions. There was nothing that could be done to help Kevin if I was dead or held captive.

The air came in fresh and clean under the remaining dark sky above. And yet there wasn't enough of an opening in the bag I was contained in to make an escape.

"We need to be friends, Sara. Understand that right now and there's a chance we can save Kevin and you can finish your quest to save Earth." Jade held out an arm.

This mission wasn't under any control of mine. I couldn't fly away without Topetine to direct me to the Bloody Basin or with Jade's ability to track my energy and hold me captive. Caving to the realization, I eased out of the sack and onto his arm, wishing I could gouge his eyes. Maybe I could after I got the key. I'd show him what his precious potion could do.

"First of all, I'm sorry for the earlier incident in Ardan," Jade said. "Each of us has a mission and mine is protection of the armies that aid the Alliance. The key you hold would have been useful."

It's not being offered as a bargaining chip. I sent the thought to him, hoping he was listening. *Where's Topetine? She was right here only a second ago.*

I might have understood desperation that called for a powerful tool, but I wasn't ready to forgive his manner of obtaining it. I didn't have time for his apology, and it did little to ease my nerves after seeing Kevin and feeling an entirely new sense of urgency. I needed to find Topetine and get the damned key.

Topetine, the jaguar, needs to lead us to the basin.

"She's right here."

Topetine stepped closer, flanked by two of Jade's men. The sight of her washed instant calm over the alarm bells going off in my head. And yet the image of Kevin remained fixed in my thoughts, holding me in a feathered state. Topetine tossed the clothing she'd picked up to Jade and shifted into her jaguar form. She started off in a trot with Jade and two of his men keeping up with ease, as we made our way through the jungle.

After several minutes and upon entering a clearing, Jade lifted his arm and I took flight above Topetine, wondering if we could lose the men but deciding they might be useful for protection should we come upon another group of angry villagers. The beginning of a sunrise was lifting just over the eastern sky, providing enough light to see the jaguar's dark figure as dawn chased away the night.

What were the people shouting at Kevin? I asked in thought to her.

Warlock. They must have seen his abilities, either his speed or skill at protection with the light energy. It doesn't matter. The curse they were chanting is only said under the influence of demonic powers and will draw more darkness to him and anyone else caged. Your team needs our help fast, before they are revealed.

Demonic powers. Like . . .

Tarsamon. I'm sure he didn't think you'd leave Kevin. And that puts you in additional danger.

"You have the aid of my team at the village if necessary," Jade said, listening to the thoughts exchanged. "They are already in position."

Let's hope it will be enough. The evil is expanding faster than expected, Topetine replied in thought.

A plume of smoke followed by another lifted in the distance ahead of us. "Let me guess. The basin is in that direction," Jade said.

Topetine took off in a full run toward the black puffs, while I held pace with her above for a short distance.

"Stay with them," Jade directed, as the two men continued following us, but at the faster pace of a jog.

I angled my head to see Jade had disappeared, likely tracing to the location ahead of us.

Don't shift into your human form. Not yet, Topetine said.

I wouldn't if I could help it. The image of Kevin being jabbed with several sharpened sticks remained pasted in my memory, with the wind under my wings gliding me faster to the site of the smoke. I saw Jade standing a few feet from three objects. Only two were burning. As I drew closer, I could see a man pinned to the third shorter object, still clinging to life.

Jade held up his arm and I took the offering to land. I despised being what felt so much like his pet. But there was little choice, as he stood at the heels of the man, watching him twitch, inches from death.

Who is he? Can we save him?

"Not this one," Jade said, reading my thought. The man was pinned by his wrists and ankles to the wall of a temple. His blood-soaked hair dripped over his eyes and ran several paths over his bare chest. Burned into the center was a marking I didn't recognize. The colorful splotches of skin in red and purple were a testament to him being beaten before being tied until dead. His two accomplices were staked to posts, still burning. Jade angled his head toward me. "This is the work of the Dark Lord. You'd need the elves for him to have any chance at life. And I doubt they'd save him."

Sensing the change taking place in my body, I left Jade's arm and shifted again into my human form. The change was exhausting, leaving me breathless. If I ever recovered to the point where it didn't bother me anymore, I'd need to deck this man for adding another complication to my quest.

Jade reached into the pack he carried, crouched beside me, and handed me my clothing. "The shifting will get easier to manage as you learn to control your thoughts." He paused before covering me with the cloak. "We don't have time to mourn. You'd better get dressed quickly. Topetine will be here in a moment."

It wasn't Topetine I was suddenly feeling shy about but the two men who were with her. I snagged the clothing, my back facing him. "Turn around for a minute, will you?"

"I don't know what there is to hide," he mumbled but turned. "I've seen most of you already."

"Don't remind me," I said, letting the cloak fall while quickly pulling up the pants. "I don't trust you. And that's enough reason to hide anything."

The energy from the man fighting to live or die was suddenly familiar, as though his energy called down to me. Fully dressed, I moved closer to him for a better look.

"Why didn't they burn him with the other two?"

"They left him as a message."

I heard Jade's footsteps behind me. "That marking on his chest. What is it?" I asked.

"It's a Baphomet symbol. A satanic symbol. His soul cannot reincarnate again once brandished with this marking while alive."

I continued to stare at the two *t* markings with a figure eight lying on its side below. "Maybe we can help him. He's not dead yet."

"He's as good as dead, Sara. Leave him be."

I moved closer and saw something lift from the wall and move toward the twitching man. A shadow of some sort. But it didn't have the same ominous feeling as Tarsamon's demon shadows. I reached a hand toward the object but was stopped at Jade's abrupt grip on my arm.

"Don't touch him."

"Why?"

"That shadow is a necromancer. He has the ability to move between worlds, Earth, Ardan, anywhere."

"A what?"

"He conjures the dead, delivers their souls to another realm."

"That's ridiculous. This man isn't dead yet." I waved a hand in the direction of the pinned man. "Besides, I don't believe in such things."

"Whether you do or don't is no matter. I assure you that you don't want to come in contact with him. You will feel death upon you. Come. We have a key to obtain."

Why do I feel as though I know this man?

"You," I said to the man. "Can you speak? Who are you?"

Sara. C-05.

I felt my mouth drop open at hearing the thought. He might have kidnapped me, tried to hurt me a few times, even kill me. And yes,

I hated him. But he had shown me a kindness by offering me food and water as he considered his options. He had been desperate. And for a reason that resonated somewhere in my childhood, I had understanding for his plight. Perhaps it was compassion for desperate people. But C-05 hadn't worked that angle of my softer side. Instead, he had chosen to bind me with the intent to turn me over to Tarsamon.

"There's a message." Jade's voice startled me from my trance. At the same time, I heard the footsteps of Jade's men and the padding of Topetine's paws behind us.

Written in blood on the wall beside one of the men was a language I didn't understand. Jade read the message aloud.

"It sounds like the language you spoke when you told me who you are," I said when he finished.

"It is."

"Well? What does it say?"

"He is a gift from the Soltari."

"What?" I had suggested C-05 go to the Soltari to ask for mercy for betraying them and joining with Tarsamon. And this was what they did to him? They handed him over to the cruelest punishment known in the higher realms? "I thought you said this was the work of the Dark Lord."

"It is. He was given to Tarsamon, then marked and strung up."

"He must have returned to the Soltari, after you found me. Probably begged for his life."

"No doubt. The message says, '*The gift of mercy cannot be bestowed upon one who has left the light, for it will not be valued in life. It is only in death that one will understand the true nature of betrayal.*'"

"What does that mean, 'understand the true nature of betrayal'?"

"It means in death he will see clearly what he created in his life. This man's soul will be left to wander endlessly between realms, never to find peace or a place to call home." He continued to stare at the limp figure. "The symbol is fitting. Of the many who could have been chosen, the one associated with the Knights of Templar is the marking."

"Why is that fitting?"

Jade turned to look at me. "That symbol is believed to represent a deity the Knights worshipped." He paused. "Don't you remember?"

I shook my head.

"C-05 was a member of the specialized order in another lifetime, probably this one, too, or at least a Freemason. Who knows, he was so secretive about who he was as a human." Thoughts of my first meeting with C-05 rattled through my head. The locked-down facility in the basement of a towering office building with its numerous rooms and security, the driver who wouldn't provide details of where I was going, and secret messages delivered to me under code. "During his lifetime, where the Knights of Templar had their largest following, he was part of a network known as Christendom of the Fifth Order, C-05."

As the message began to sink in, I could feel tension building at the thought that any powerful entity that cared enough to protect the light would put in harm's way one who used to be tied to their own energy. The decision to punish was absolute. Was there no room for forgiveness when fear consumed rational thought? C-05 had come to Earth to be human. That meant he would not only think as an immortal but also as a human when faced with the fear for his life upon being captured by Tarsamon's forces months earlier. My fists clenched at my sides. I took in a deep breath to try and cool the anger simmering at the edge of human and hawk.

I'd learned from Cerys that C-05 and I had once been members of the Alliance, until he'd failed a mission and lost his eternal partner. It was his last wish to be reunited with her. He sought the Soltari's mercy because he'd lost me to Jade as his bargaining chip. Despite all that C-05 had done to sabotage this mission, this level of inability to forgive was unacceptable. If the entity would hand over a former key member of the Alliance, granted he'd sided with the enemy for a short time, would the Soltari banish me from Ardan, perhaps leave my soul forever lost in abandonment if I failed the mission? Not if I had anything to do with it. And I knew damn well I had only one chance to renegotiate my contract to fulfill this mission.

I grabbed the dagger resting in a pocket on Jade's chest and cut loose the binds, avoiding the necromancer that lurked toward one of the other staked men. Maybe what Jade said about the conjurer was true. Maybe not. I didn't care. A few months ago, I wouldn't have believed any of what I had experienced thus far.

"I'm sorry for you," I said to C-05. "You're a pathetic soul who made some bad choices, in my opinion. While you may deserve to die in this life, I don't think your mistake calls for you to die like this or pay eternally."

Why did I have sympathy for the man? I should have been pleased he was suffering, but that was never my MO, whether he deserved to bleed or not. And oh, how he deserved to bleed. I stared in consideration, watching his suffering and trying to block the feelings I could sense coming from him. He was trying to numb them but was unable, probably due to the markings on his body that condemned his soul to its personal version of Hell. Sorrow, pain, a sense of loss, and what was that last one that balanced on the very edge of sanity? I sharpened my senses in an effort to understand what he felt. Hopelessness. The man really had nothing left.

13

"You shouldn't have released the binds, Sara," Jade said.

"As if Tarsamon would give him another thought." I handed Jade's blade back to him. "Or even the Soltari," I added. "They were done with him when they gave him up. There's no more time to give to this. We need to hurry. Topetine?"

Just a little farther, she answered in thought.

Jade pulled at my arm as I started off. "You take risks interfering with powers greater than those you carry."

"I'll do as I'm guided, and generally as I please."

Dangerous woman. Going to get us all killed.

His thought echoed through my mind. Trust was a two-way street. The team sure as hell wanted mine, but a little trust was needed from them, too.

We hiked another mile before stopping in front of a large, moss-covered rock formation. Topetine shifted back to her human self, while I observed the object that looked nothing like a Bloody Basin. Instead, it could have passed for any number of the multiple rocks or cliffs we'd encountered since arriving in the Yucatan.

"You're certain this is it?" I asked.

"I've spent my entire life preparing for the possibility that I would need to lead you here. Only you could read the scrolls to confirm one of three locations. I couldn't be more certain, my dear."

"Well then, would you know...?" My voice trailed off and my fingers stopped picking through the vegetation at the sight of the Mayan symbol for a bat etched into the stone. It matched exactly one of three medallions I'd had before Cerys had confiscated them on the last quest in Scotland. Each was a sign indicating the particular location of the key. *This is it.*

The sound of rustling from behind had all of us turning to see Juno with palms up in the air.

"Jesus, you could've been killed," I said.

He angled his head to the side and flashed a grin. "That's why I wanted to show you I wasn't carrying a weapon. Not one you could see, anyway."

"Jade, this is Juno," I said.

"We know each other well," Juno said. They clasped hands and bumped shoulders together.

Both military. I should've guessed they already know each other. I continued my hunt for where I might find an entrance to the actual key.

"What news do you bring? What changes?" Jade asked.

"The Dark Lord. Both Matt and I saw him in the area as Kevin was captured."

"How exactly did that happen, anyway?" I interrupted. "With his strength and speed to fight demons, how did the villagers take him?" I stopped rummaging through the greenery and turned to Juno. "You and Matt are the strongest next to him. Now he's caged and in line to be cut in half and strung from the damn ceiling," I shouted. "Some goddamn protection! And I can't seem to find what is needed to move forward here." I splayed my hands in desperation. "You'd better hope we aren't too late to save him or so help me—"

"Sara," Jade's calm voice pulled me from my rant. "Get a hold of yourself. It's the solution from the injection. Causes a rage of emotion as it balances in your system. You need to steady yourself. Get control of the change."

I huffed out a breath and slanted a look at him. He was responsible, after all, for giving me the potent drug and the rage that went with it. The heat of my temper and the potential to shift had so quickly shot to the surface, threatened to boil over into a full-blown fight with a member of my team. "This is your fault," I said to Jade. "My apologies, Juno. I'm sure you did what you could." Though I wasn't fully convinced that he had done all he could. My team was one of the fastest, most skilled in the realm of Ardan. I didn't understand how villagers without the abilities the team carried had overcome them. "We have little time and I can't see any way closer to the key." The sound of fear in my voice surprised me.

"Topetine wouldn't have led you anywhere other than the proper location," Jade said. "The key is here." He turned back to Juno. "What about the Dark Lord?"

"He captured Kevin using the villagers. Seems a curse was cast over them as demonic spirit holders. They tricked Kevin into needing his assistance, feigning pain because he had the ability to heal."

Spells? Witchery? How absurd. Is that even possible? Tarsamon had a goal, and he was powerful, but I'd never believed in spells and black magic. Obviously. I'd set C-05 free from the necromancer without a second thought, despite Jade's warning. *Lady Mara is real.* The old woman I'd met in England, on the quest for the first key in the realm of Randun, had brewed a potion that allowed me to see Aria and Elise, to be certain they were safe. I'd seen that with my own eyes and the proof of it when Aria showed up later to confirm the vision. And the berries she'd given me that had conjured the white witch. I could now transform into a hawk from a substance. How much more proof did I need?

"*Had* the ability to heal?" I said, referring to Juno's last comment. I remembered seeing Kevin's healing ability once, when I'd awoken to find a burn from a demon on my forearm, a marking that began taking the shape of a cross. At the time, I'd dismissed it as nothing but a bad dream and a blister that would resolve on its own. I'd tried to hide the mark from Kevin to avoid his concern over entering the dark world alone. But when he spotted it, he'd covered it with his palm and the image began to fade after a few minutes, following a severe stinging sensation. The muscle of my arm twitched at the memory.

"He was stripped of his abilities. He's as vulnerable as any mortal right now." Juno shook his head.

"How did that happen?" I wasn't aware anyone backed by the Soltari could have his or her abilities removed. The fact was, I'd never considered it.

"Enough time in the presence of a negative energy, a toxic substance can infect anyone. It happened to you when you had the additional protection of the first key in Scotland. The fever only the elves could clear, remember?" I did. And I hadn't even realized that I'd been infected. "Kevin came in direct contact with the curse or illness Tarsamon gave to the villagers when he tried to heal them. The rest of us held back, stayed behind to help guard against a further attack, until we could figure out a way to get him out of there without getting all of us killed."

"Further attack? He's in line to be killed. It took everything I had not to blow my cover and get him out of there. Why are you here and not with Kevin?" I asked.

"Tarsamon. He…well…Matt and I saw him. We knew—" Juno stumbled.

"For God's sake, what are you trying to say?" I was losing patience fast. I needed information that Juno had felt important enough to bring, or else I needed to get back to finding the key. For all the things I didn't know, one thing was certain, I was short on time.

Juno took a deep breath. "We were looking for you. Kevin said he had given you a bracelet to help track your location should you become separated from him."

He had. And put like that, it sounded like I was a pet. In fact, the device was another level of protection. Should I get into trouble and Kevin and I were separated, it would send a signal to him, allowing him to locate me faster, similar to a GPS tracker. I had been wearing the device disguised as a piece of pretty jewelry when I'd been in Jade's tent. The silver ring identifying me as the one who would carry the power of all three keys was locked in place on the fourth finger of my right hand. It had somehow not slipped off. But the bracelet was gone. It was intended to fit as comfortable as a second skin and perhaps why I hadn't noticed it had been lost.

"You were safer not being with us when we came upon the village or you would have been taken. Matt and I received a vision of Tarsamon in a rage just before a black mist raced through the streets we were passing through. That mist filtered through every window, door, and crevice. The fog ended up being a possession that carried with it unbelievable strength. Kevin had already gone to the aid of someone crying out when he was overcome. We believe Tarsamon suspected that, by having Kevin captured, it would slow your path to the key. I don't think Tarsamon believed you'd leave him. Instead, you were supposed to fall into the same trap, to stay behind with the rest of us. Leaving, as you should have, was the best decision."

"You can thank Topetine and Mac for that," I said. "Without them at my back, I probably would have stayed behind."

"We continued the fight when he went over the cliff, Sara, when you were separated. Three of us went after C-05, but we couldn't see either of you, despite being able to sense your energy."

"What? Why? I was there, fighting him."

"I don't know why," Juno answered. "It may be that as you become stronger, so, too, do the forces that hunt you, and now us. You have to believe me when I tell you that for Kevin to have the small chance he does, we needed to conceal ourselves instead of fight once we realized what had happened, or we might all be caged."

"I do believe you."

"Never has a member of our team lost their abilities to the dark energy," Juno said. "Tarsamon has done more than grow his army. I don't know what resource he has tapped into to become stronger."

"We can't be concerned about that right now. Tarsamon took out his impatience and rage on C-05," I added. "I appreciate you filling in the blanks, but I've got to get back to this key for any chance to help Kevin."

"There's more," Juno said. "The vision also showed Tarsamon meeting up with you again, but not at the village."

"Dear God." And with that, I glanced to the sky. "Cut me some slack? Throw me a bone here?"

"Where? How much time? How much forward notice does your ability to see into the future provide?" Jade asked.

"We aren't sure where and it's hard to be accurate. Matt's and my abilities have been unreliable since crossing the entrance into the Yucatan. We were surprised to get the vision we did. But"—he paused, eyes searching left and right—"before this adventure, I'd have to say a day, maybe two."

I had one ear to the conversation but had already turned to continue my search around the wall of stone for another clue, beyond the bat symbol, that I was in the right area of this basin.

Why is it called Bloody Basin? The history of the Mayan culture was one filled with gruesome sacrifice, anything from decapitation, reaching into the chest to pull out and hold a still-beating heart, to disemboweling. Perhaps this was one of the primary sites of such ritual performances. *On second thought, I don't want to know.*

"Here," I said to myself.

The writing etched into the wall matched that of my ring, the words I'd been told by Cerys were only visible to the pure of heart. I looked up and around the rough surface as I fingered the crevices. "Damn," I said, placing two flat palms against the wall, fixing my gaze just above my hands.

"The key is highly protected," Topetine said. "It will open with the right combination."

"What combination?"

"Listen and feel how it guides you, my dear. It's trying to speak to you."

I was never one for meditation, at least not in this life. My responsibilities kept me much too busy. And right now, I'd give anything to be sorting out a behavioral or relationship issue with a patient instead of standing here trying to tune everything out to hear spirits guide me. While I had accepted that finding the keys was my task, every so often I'd have doubts that I was the right person to complete the mission. This moment was no exception.

I took in a deep breath, pressed my palms against the wall, and closed my eyes. The discussion behind me fell quiet. In my mind's eye, a picture formed of where I stood now, a vision of the massive rock, covered in moss. The upper corner above the writing lit in a soft white. Keeping my eyes closed, I reached my right hand closer to that light. I felt Topetine behind me as I stepped to the side. My hand shifted up and slightly right, following the same path as the mental image. The ring I wore on the same hand locked into a crevice in the wall. I opened my eyes. The ground trembled and the sound of grinding rock followed. My hand was still fixed to the space on the wall. With the ring locked to the stone, a small vertical crevice opened, freeing my hand and revealing yet another wall.

Damn! What is it that's needed? I had to find the proper combination, when all I wanted was a bulldozer to knock it down. *Think, Sara, think.* I stared at the wall facing me, now covered in squares of hieroglyphs, symbols of which I had no prior knowledge of their meaning. When Mac and I had been admitted to the location of the first key, there had been a riddle that needed to be solved. Could this be similar? The sensation of time pressing upon me and what might happen if I didn't complete this task before they…*Stop. Just stop. If there's a way in, there's a way out.*

I felt Topetine's hand on my arm. "Listen and you will hear. Only the Light Carrier can receive the message that guides her to the key."

"Explain this to me," I said, pointing above the squares to a set of fat lines and dots.

"That is of the old language, believed to represent time," Topetine said.

"And the hieroglyphs of the faces?"

"Believed by some to represent the secrets of the heavens"—she paused—"believed by others to be the record of history and the reign of kings."

Why, if I was going to be called to this task, did I not have more of an interest in history?

"Being that these glyphs represent the history of your culture, which do you believe?" I asked.

"It matters not what I believe. Only that you allow yourself to be guided."

"How in holy hell am I to allow myself to be guided when I have no idea about the message here? Tell me that." And yet, in my disbelief, I had been reminded that the ring I wore had been drawn to the stone, unlocking one passage. Could there be another?

The Mayans were believed to be intellectuals, who very likely studied astronomy. That's about all I could recall from my education, with a few snippets of fact that involved the Spaniards. As intellectuals, they might have had a healthy dose of curiosity regarding the heavens, even enough to document the study of them. But they most definitely would have documented a reign of cultural royalty for a more permanent record. My fingers traced over the glyphs, one by one.

"This is telling a story," I whispered to myself. "Can you translate these pictures?" I asked Topetine.

She moved closer beside me. "It tells of a battle between gods." Her fingers followed the glyphs. "I can't make out the rest. But here"—she tapped the stone—"there is reference to the Light Carrier."

"What gods?"

"It does not identify a specific god here."

"The key of understanding is what I seek. Does it make reference to that?"

She was silent. "The key is in the underworld, accessible only by the Light Carrier."

"Underworld. That's what these skeletons refer to, the dead?" I asked, pointing to another set of glyphs.

"The culture of our people runs deep into the spirit world. One must provide an offering for a gift to be bestowed by those who reside in the spirit realm. In this case, the writing and myths suggest it's the only way the key will be granted to you. Because the door has begun to open for you, it's a sign your energy is welcome in the underworld, Sara."

I didn't care to bring forward or meet any spirits. And I sure as hell didn't have anything to offer. But I needed the key. I turned my attention to the rock that had ground open. *Underworld.*

For some unknown reason, a flash of Kevin's unresponsive form blinked into my thoughts. "What offering?"

"Offerings are most often in the sacrifice of blood."

"You said it already recognizes me."

"It's a gift to the spirits that reside in the underworld."

I knew there's a reason I question religion and its so-called "practice."

"Jade," Topetine called. He and Juno had retreated steps from us, perhaps to figure out a plan, but hiked down to where we stood at Topetine's call. "Your sharpest blade."

He obliged. "Your wrist," she said to me.

I almost protested. My wrists were still sore from being bound. If Topetine hadn't been the guardian of the key, I would've told a seeker of such a sacrifice where to put an offering. Instead, I placed my wrist in her firm grasp.

She held tight with her small, strong hand and quickly swiped a thin, shallow line across, avoiding larger veins. She turned my wrist over and guided it over the glyphs of the skeletons, spilling several drops of blood. She then tore a line of fabric from her lower skirt and tied it at my wrist. At the same time, I could have sworn I heard my name being called in the distance, then Juno's. I turned in the direction of the voices and saw Matt leading the group, his arms extended slightly behind him, carrying something. Mac was behind him, followed by Aria and Elise.

"Stay here," Juno directed. "I'll find out what's going on."

Another sound redirected my attention back to the wall, as it began to grind once more, this time opening to reveal a dark cave-like room. The light that filtered in from the outside showed something lining the inside wall. Thinking the light outside was playing tricks on my perception, I slammed my eyelids shut and held them closed. But when I reopened them, the previous dark cave had been replaced by more jungle. The stone that had ground open was still open in an arch, as if the entrance was a doorway instead of solid rock.

I must be hallucinating. There's no other explanation.

"Sara, we must go," Topetine said. "Unlike the passages leading here, this entrance will not remain open."

I glanced back to my team to see Matt and Mac were indeed carrying something. But as they drew closer, I could tell it wasn't something, but someone.

Kevin.

Juno stepped out ahead of them, waving his palms in a *move forward* direction. "Go. Go get the key, now."

"Tell me he's okay first."

"Yes. There's no time for argument."

But I didn't feel any sensations from Kevin. I didn't hear his thoughts. And from what I could see, his body was limp. "You're lying to me. He's not okay, is he?"

"Listen!" Reaching me in a couple of strides, Juno grabbed my arm and leaned into my face. "Do you want to save him? Do you? Do you want to have a chance here?"

"Of course." I pulled from his grasp. Every instinct in my body wanted to run to Kevin and defy my responsibility to the quest. I needed to know, needed to see him for myself.

"Then take me at my word and do what I'm telling you without your stubborn nature getting in the way. For once, damn it. There's no time to argue. Matt and I have seen what could happen. And there are others coming behind Aria and Elise."

"What others?"

"Never mind that. We'll deal with it. But this ends here, everything, if you don't go forward. Understand?"

Not liking the lack of options and, worse, knowing he was right, I nodded to him. "Don't let him die."

I turned to Topetine, who, with a hand at my back, urged me beyond the arch, into the passage. The bright daylight faded into black, and several burning torches, concealed behind long branches, lighted the jungle. My attention shifted to my feet as they grew heavier the farther I stepped inside. Human skulls formed a boundary around us in the shape of a rectangle. I was reminded of the temple the team and I had passed through with its so-called sacrifice. The metallic scent of which pierced my nostrils as I cast a gaze downward and saw the reason for the heaviness at my feet. Topetine and I were standing in a pool of crimson about an inch thick. The metallic scent confirmed my worst suspicion, leading me to understand why it was called the Bloody Basin.

"We should expect a challenge, a test of some sort before the key will be released," she said.

"Of course." I stepped to where I hoped a pool of blood did not exist. It was never easy to obtain the key. I'd been challenged with Mac, the first guardian at my side, upon entering the abbey in search of the first key. Why would this be any different?

"Here," she said, directing me to a large rock. There was a small pool of standing water. "Drink, but don't swallow. Spit it out instead. Okay?"

I did as she asked, happy not to ingest the water. She followed with the same action. "Why did we do that?"

"It's a ritual purification. Anytime you enter a place where a god resides, you purify yourself."

I'm pretty sure that was anything but purifying.

"You have nothing to worry about."

"Time will tell. I sure hope you're right."

From out of nowhere, a ball rolled forward, tapping me on the toe of my boot. I searched beyond the trees for a sign of who sent the object, but all remained still.

"They want you to play a game."

"Who? What game?" I asked in disbelief.

"This is a game of souls. It's an ancient game of my people in which the loser must relinquish their life."

"I hope to God I'm not a player."

"You are intended to be the key player."

"Fabulous. Did the Soltari give any thought while hiding the keys that by asking someone completely unfamiliar with Mayan tradition to play a Mayan game, they may lose the entire quest?" *Why would they do that anyway? No. I have to look at this differently. There's something more to this than a game. There has to be.*

One of the tree trunks lit brighter, showing a circular form tied to the tree.

"How is this game played?"

"You must get the ball into the hole."

Basketball. I can do that. I'm five ten. Easy.

"Without using your hands."

I huffed out a breath. "Let me guess, if I use my hands I forfeit and die."

"You lose the game, yes, and a life is surrendered." She paused and picked up the ball. "This challenge is about your beliefs."

And I didn't think there could be a weaker trait I carry than trust. I'd never given much thought to my beliefs. Granted, they'd been tested plenty when I first entered Ardan and spoke to elves that looked like porcelain figures of the most beautiful humans I'd ever seen. Or when I'd learned of my ability to use light as a weapon in my defense against Tarsamon's shadows. My beliefs had been challenged and rearranged following the experience, and even earlier at the credence I'd given my parents that they cared for me at least as much as themselves. It hadn't worked out that way, of course. But I had landed in a good home, eventually.

"How deep is your faith, your belief in what is and what will be?" Topetine asked, pulling me from further reflection.

"I don't know."

"You'll know by the end of this quest."

She dropped the ball and a group of ten people appeared from the forest, two women and eight men. All were clothed in minimal garb resembling loincloths. Five of the individuals moved closer while the others remained on one end of the rectangular court.

"You are playing with the spirits of these sacrificed souls," Topetine said, leaning into my ear. "But make no mistake, they aim to win. They want to be released by the serpent god and freed from the underworld."

"Dare I ask if there's any other way I can lose this, aside from using my hands?"

"Whoever scores first wins."

Oh, yeah, no pressure. I might not have been confident about my beliefs, of what was or would come, or even my faith. But one thing was certain, Kevin and I, along with the rest of humanity, were knee deep in a pit at Hell's corner.

14

"You've got to call the elves to save him." Aria gazed at an open wound on Kevin's chest. "We can't wait for Sara."

"They won't come this far from Ardan, not for anyone other than the Light Carrier," Juno said. "We either wait for Sara or figure out how to get him to Ardan." Kevin's pulse was weak and his breathing growing more shallow by the minute. "Besides, he wouldn't want to leave Sara."

By the time Matt fought his way through the growing crowd of villagers, Kevin had been pulled from the cage and beaten with sharpened sticks and rocks. He'd been cut, for what Matt assumed was bloodletting, in honor of the gods. The priest overseeing the execution or sacrifice had been in the process of chaining him to the ceiling just as Matt reached him through the crowd.

"He's going to be leaving her whether he wants to or not if we don't get him some help," Elise said.

"Why did he lose his powers and we didn't?" Aria asked. "It doesn't make sense."

"He's the strongest fighter among us," Matt answered. "If the villagers were inflicted with a curse from Tarsamon, they would seek out the strongest individuals among us as prisoners, and we couldn't risk all of us being captured. As it is, we narrowly escaped the villagers. They've grown more powerful."

Elise shook her head. "I still say we should've pulled him out when they first caged him. It might've been harder to get him, but he wouldn't be on the brink of death."

"Matt's right, we couldn't risk all of us being locked up. At least he has a chance," Aria added.

"For how long, we dinna know," Mac said. "The villagers are no' far behind us. And I assure ye, they'll be comin' for their prisoner." He shifted closer to Kevin and put an ear to his face to listen. "Is he safer in there, out of view?" He lifted a chin in the direction of the arch that Topetine and Sara had disappeared through.

"I've got to believe it's unlikely the villagers would enter where a god is believed to reside," Juno replied. "But we don't know what's on the other side of that arch. And I damn sure don't know what the villagers are capable of under Tarsamon's control."

"I hate this," Aria mumbled.

"Well, he's dead out here for sure. Help me, Mac," Matt said, standing. It wasn't that Matt couldn't carry him alone. But to reduce any further injury, it was best to keep Kevin in a prone position. They'd managed to duck under the canopy of low-hanging tree branches and remain concealed until the villagers had run past them before turning and heading in the direction leading to the basin. The mystical location where Sara had entered would have been the last place they would look for Kevin. But if the town people knew about Sara's quest, it wouldn't take them long to circle back to this location.

"My forces are holding the villagers at bay for the time being," Jade said. One of his men stood beside him, the other having gone to fight with the rest of his unit. "But Matt is right, if this is a curse put upon the villagers, that hold is temporary. I can still trace. Is there another location he would be safer?"

"I'd say the village where we met Topetine," Matt answered.

"Tarsamon could reach him there," Elise said. "The underground caverns we first entered and where the Aluxes met the shadows is safer."

"I'll need someone who's been there to come with us to share the location."

"I'll go," Elise volunteered.

"Someone strong enough to also carry Kevin's weight. Juno?"

Juno was nearly as big as Kevin himself. He turned to Matt and Mac. "Keep a close eye on that doorway where Sara and Topetine went. They'll be coming through and we won't want them to be met by an angry mob, or for the mob to try to take Sara as a replacement for this one." He angled his head toward Kevin and bent to grasp Kevin's arms. "Hang on. We'll find a J-man for you as good as any doctor." And as he blew out a breath, he and Jade lifted Kevin.

"Stay and back them up if anyone approaches. I'll be back soon," Jade called to his right-hand man.

"And if they come back before ye return?" Mac asked.

"Follow wherever Topetine leads," Juno replied. "We'll find you." And with the image of the underground location fixed in his mind, he and Jade disappeared with Kevin.

Jade and Juno arrived in the dirt cavern. Torches were still lit along the walls as they had been before the team had left. With a great deal of care, Juno placed Kevin down on a bed in one of the empty rooms and rushed to the main corridor, nearly stumbling over one of the people Topetine had been having coffee with the morning they were swept away into the depths of the cenote.

"What's happened?" the little woman asked, flattening her palms against her long skirt. "Where is the guardian?"

"Follow me. We need your help or that of a J-man," Juno answered. He wasn't going to tell her that his cargo wasn't Topetine for fear she wouldn't follow him. Before the woman could answer, Juno had turned and rushed in the direction he'd left Kevin and Jade, leaving her no choice but to follow.

As she entered, the woman's gaze crossed over Jade and narrowed before resting on Kevin's lifeless form sprawled on his back. "What's happened to him?"

"The villagers were going to sacrifice him. He's been beaten badly and—"

"No, no, no." The woman waved her hands. "I can't help you. Not in this." She began to back out of the room but stopped as Juno stepped closer.

"What do you mean? He's part of the quest. He not only protects the Light Carrier but the guardian."

"She means she can't intervene because he was already decided for the sacrifice," Jade said.

"He bears the mark in honor of the gods." The woman pointed to a branding above Kevin's heart in the shape of a cross with an *X* through it. In the center was a swirled pattern. "He's untouchable."

"That's ridiculous." Juno leaned closer to her. "The mark was put there by cursed villagers."

The woman only shook her head.

"You'll help see that he lives or more will die, understand?"

Jade stepped between them and began speaking another language Juno was not familiar with. When the woman nodded, he said a few more words before she rushed off.

"What? Is she getting help?"

"Yes. The J-man you wanted."

"Just tell me you didn't promise her something undeliverable."

"I didn't have to. For one, her people believe the J-man is the only person who can intervene with health when the mark of the gods is placed upon the skin. And two, I told her that her gods would not be happy if the life of the guardian was put at greater risk with his death." He jerked a thumb in Kevin's direction.

"Good." Juno turned and bent over Kevin. "He's still breathing, but I don't know for how long. I hope you didn't scare her into taking off."

"Nah. She probably thinks the gods would be angry with her if she could've done something and didn't. That's what scared her to get the J-man. Trust me. She wouldn't risk the hell that she believes would come to her."

Both turned their gaze to the sound of footsteps and the appearance of a painted man in the doorway.

"She was quick," Juno said in surprise.

"Fear has a way of doing that." Jade shifted his weight against the wall and crossed his arms. "She wants our man out of here."

The J-man waved Juno away and sat beside Kevin. He held at chest level a bowl, the contents of which were smoking with the scent of burning leaves, as he began to chant. He shifted the smoke to the left above Kevin's head and then in the opposite direction, until he had finished. He set the bowl down and reached into a leather pouch crossed over his body. In the palm of his hand, he spat once and rubbed a red powdery substance together, then gestured to the woman, who brought a candle to him. The J-man then lit the red mixture. It sparked and sputtered as it came to life. As quickly as the sparks flew, they died at the single breath the man blew across his palm. The J-man dipped into the creation with an index finger, rubbed the red concoction between two fingers, and leaned over Kevin's chest, pressing his fingers into the mark of the gods on his chest while chanting.

Kevin's chest lifted off the mattress as though pulled by an invisible string and slammed back down. A black mist rolled upward and curled in the air above him before dissipating as though it had never been there.

Juno shifted his attention from the J-man to Kevin's form. There wasn't so much as a single twitch from the body. He wondered if Kevin had given up the fight for life, and held firm his position, resisting the urge to push the J-man away to check for a heartbeat. He and Jade watched as the man drew images with the remaining paste on Kevin's chest and reached for the bowl to repeat the same smoke ritual over him.

"He needs a medical doctor," Juno whispered to Jade. "And probably a cast. Look at his body, all bruised and skin torn."

"Don't underestimate him. J-Men are powerful healers, tightly connected to the spirit world."

The man continued his ministrations, first the red paste, then yellow, and finally a black paste. Each careful application was followed by another chant along with the smoke. When he had finished, Kevin was hardly recognizable. All Juno wanted to know was if he was still alive.

His conscience started to tug at him. *Maybe I should have taken him to Topetine's town, radioed for help, and had him flown out.* With the risk of Tarsamon or his demons and shadows coupled with the time it would have taken to do that, he didn't think Kevin would have made it. This was the safest place for him and the J-man was the best medicine they had to offer. *God help them if Sara was overcome by the same fate. Would the elves find a way then?* He put that thought aside with no room to give it attention. Had the team left Kevin, there would have been no help until they could have fought back the villagers.

Shit. The villagers.

"Don't touch him," the J-man said, interrupting Juno's thoughts. "Not for any reason."

"Is he alive?" Juno asked.

"His heart beats but his spirit will determine where it wants to land." The man packed the sachets of powder into his leather pouch and turned to Juno. "He has been cleansed of the Dark Lord's curse. Should the soul of this warrior decide to return, his powers should be his again." The man held a wrinkled index finger in front of Juno's face. "Touch him and the energy you carry will undo the work created to cleanse him."

Juno nodded. *Decide to return? Why wouldn't he?*

"I've got to get back," Juno said to Jade. He turned to the little woman who had held a position against the entry. "You'll watch over him but not touch him?"

"Yes, I'll keep an eye on him."

"Take us back to the team," he said to Jade.

"I need to get my soldiers out of the village. Do a count of my men. If a few villagers are capable of taking down a man as strong as Kevin, there is no telling what they or a dark curse will do to a small force."

"Take me to Sara's location first, then you can get to your men."

"You can't help Sara right now. That's why Topetine is with her."

"I need to protect the team." But it was Elise he knew he needed to fight beside. She was fast, but not as strong as the others. After the last encounter she'd had with C-05 on her way to Scotland, there was no way she was going to fight without him beside her. "This mission is crucial to the survival of Earth."

"I know all about your mission and the importance of it. If you want to protect your team, I need to be assured mine is safe first."

"We're wasting time here. Drop me at the last location and go check on your men."

Jade might be a friend of Kevin's from long ago and a damn good warrior, but the man had an edge about him. It probably came from being used to getting his way. Their military connection wasn't going to help them meet eye to eye on this issue. There was something at work beneath the surface of this commander.

"No can do," Jade replied. "It takes too much effort to trace both of us that quickly. It'll leave me weak, unable to fight."

"We'd better not lose a member of my team, catering to your more important needs, or you'll be answering to the Soltari."

"I'm looking forward to it," Jade said as he followed the path that would lead him to the village.

15

It was a game of life or death I wasn't skilled enough to play. Being required to participate somehow seemed a disservice to the other poor souls needing to win freedom from the underworld. My gaze fell to the pool of blood, then to the skulls. Everyone who had come through this point had to have been sacrificed. We hadn't met a single living person yet. And if every person that entered had to play this Mayan game, where were the winners? Where was the proof that anyone *could* win?

"Are you aware of anyone coming out of here alive?" I asked Topetine. "On second thought, better not answer that."

"I don't know that anyone has been here before."

"What are you telling me? The blood and skulls are a hallucination, like these spirits?"

"No. It's all very real. Anyone who has died is trapped in the underworld. Only certain spirits seek a way out. This point of entry was reserved for you, according to the glyphs. The blood and skulls represent sacrifice and a clear message that you have entered the realm of the dead."

"This isn't right and I can't explain why." The scrolls flitted through my mind's eye as if to confirm the sensory input racing through my head. "There was an image of fire in the scrolls. Nothing about a game. This is only an illusion, a form of distraction. Maybe it's for someone who got lost, God forbid. But it's not for me. Not when someone's life out there hangs in the balance." *Or the millions of lives on Earth.*

I started past the ghostly figures of players, uncertain if Topetine was behind me. I was looking for a clue, an inscription perhaps, and to get out of this jungle. Then, I saw it. A light emerging ahead that caught my eye, drawing me in like a ship in the night in search of a lighthouse. I stepped up my pace with a sensation that this was the way. It was a feeling I'd not had since arriving. I had to get to the center of that glow ahead. Call it trust or faith, I needed to get closer.

"Sara."

I heard Topetine call from behind me but I couldn't stop to turn around. The race to get to the light source was consuming, pulling me forward. *That's it. There. Just a little farther.* As the light came into focus, I stopped abruptly, as if my feet were under a control all their own, and stumbled backward, falling onto my backside. I'd reached the edge of a cliff. Gone was the jungle, answering my earlier wish, replaced by brimstone and fire. I'd stepped straight into Hell.

Clouds of smoke filled the sky in large, thick shades of gray. The light of the fire reflected off the puffs of smoke closer to the ground. The source of the fire was an enormous burning tree that reminded me of a banyan with its multiple layers of twisting, reaching roots. I shifted my gaze to the cliff across from where I'd almost fallen over and saw an orange glow coming from the center of the barren rock. On the side of the cliff, something moved within that rocky illumination that was very much in the shape of a snake. There were dark shadows that pulled from the many shaded rock and tree formations. Demons lost without a soul to consume glided over the landscape either waiting or watching. Probably both. There were also several faceless flesh-colored demons that had gathered around the burning tree, lifting arms to it as if celebrating another death.

How did they find this place?

I jolted at a touch of my shoulder. *Topetine.* She crouched beside me.

"What is this place?" I asked.

"It's supposed to be where the serpent god resides. But this"—she paused—"this is not where a god would live. Something has penetrated this sanctuary."

"But how?"

"I don't know how they found another way in."

"Maybe they had access to the scrolls?"

"Not possible. They were only open to the Light Carrier."

"Maybe they accessed them after I did, while we were delayed by the villagers and C-05." *But still, how did they find another way in? Was there information I neglected to read?*

If so, that meant if the dark forces had gained access to certain information I had unlocked, our quest for the key would be more challenging than I could guess.

"Tarsamon has been busy," I said, returning my attention to the shape within the granite cliff wall. "Is that your serpent god?"

"I'd say yes, but even I can't be sure from here. Legend says the serpent god has resided here for centuries, awaiting his freedom. This"—she lifted her eyes to the sky—"wasn't supposed to be waiting for us."

"Regardless, we're in it, and we need to figure a way out without getting killed. I need weapons. I don't have enough energy to fight all of them."

"The mark on your forearm given to you by the J-man is added protection, but I don't know how strong it is."

"Now isn't the time to test it," I said, spotting an area over her shoulder that might be a way in. "I've got to get to the other side."

"Do you see that figure perched upon the hill closer to the fire?" she asked.

On top of the granite hilltop was a long, thin creature with skin the same color as the smoke. She sat boldly erect on the lookout point, high atop an extension of a cliff. Jet-black hair flowed to the middle of her back and she had a wingspan the length of her body, as she stretched one feathered arm out and pulled it back. A long tail whipped casually from side to side. She looked like an angel. A graceful dark angel of Hell. She was keeping watch. As if she sensed me taking in her appearance, her head angled in our direction. I pulled

Topetine closer to the ground with me. The eyes were glowing, widened, and bright blue.

"She senses us," Topetine said.

"No, she doesn't. She's just watching." I knew because I could feel what another felt and when I looked at her, she might have appeared as alert as an eagle spotting its prey but she continued to look on and over. There was no sensation of alarm coming from her.

There's got to be a way in. Off to the left of where we stood was a bridge to the other side of the cliff edge. I didn't think either of us could make it across without being spotted.

"That bridge can't be the only way."

"Over here," Topetine said. Staying hidden behind the hillside, she shifted into her jaguar form and slunk close to the ground toward a rock that jutted out from the side of the cliff. I followed her, making myself prone with the rocky terrain and careful to remain out of sight of the demon perched on the ledge several hundred feet away. Topetine slipped into a crevice that couldn't have been more than three feet wide and shifted back to her human form. A dim light shone from deep within, growing brighter as we wound our way through the twists and turns of the tunnel.

"This is it," she said, stopping. "The sign for the guardian. We're in the tomb of the serpent god." Her fingers traced the edge of the square. The glyph was of a cat sitting in front of a crescent moon. Unlike the others, this one had been placed into the wall versus being carved from the existing stone. "There should be one more."

"The other is a piece to this one," I said. "Together the passage engages like a key to a lock."

"Yes."

I didn't know how I knew the pieces would fit together, just that they did. The information in the scrolls must be coming through as needed.

Though my eyes were on the lookout for the other glyph, they were more focused on the serpent as the attraction to this area drew me deeper inside and closer to the flame that burned within it.

Strangely, I couldn't feel any heat despite getting closer to where I'd seen the flame.

I was fully aware of time pressing at my back as I scanned the walls. How much time before Kevin gave up? How much time before the evil that guarded outside became aware of our presence? And had the rest of the team already encountered the villagers? Were they engaged in battle?

Just find the key, hurry, Kevin had said. His words repeated over again in my head, urging me to move faster.

Stay alive for me. If you can hear me, my love, stay alive. I'll make this right. So help me, I will.

My gaze rested on an object that looked familiar. The all-seeing eye. I hadn't expected to see it until I arrived in Egypt, the location of the last key. Topetine dropped to the ground and leaned forward, her head touching her knees and her arms extended in front of her in an apparent show of respect. The center of the eye was set in a beautiful blue lapis stone, the remaining part of which was outlined in copper and embraced with silver. On either side of the eye were two glyphs. One of them was a picture of a figure holding an orb up to a snake-like figure. The other was a jaguar staring out at us.

"This is what we want," I said.

Topetine stood from her position and stared up at the image.

I lifted my hand with the silver ring to the eye. I had a suspicion I'd need to provide evidence of who I was, the one able to hold the key, in the same manner I'd had to show it at the abbey in Randun.

The center of the eye sparked and snapped as several pieces of lapis fell to the ground. The sound of grinding stone from the wall in front of us revealed a blank area beneath the eye. I looked at Topetine just as we heard the sound of something hitting the ground behind us. I went back to where we'd found the first glyph to see it lying on the floor in three pieces.

Holding each of them in both hands, I studied them. "Will it work?"

"Only you have the power to see it so. The eye would not have lit if it didn't recognize you as the person who has reached full enlightenment through many incarnations and is chosen to receive the truth found in the keys."

I recalled one incarnation with Cerys, and not even with full clarity. So many pieces of the past were still missing. And I sure as hell didn't feel enlightened. Yet her words sounded much like Mac's when we had been tasked with solving the riddle of the first key. I had to trust in her words, whether my current belief disagreed with them or not. I carefully picked up the three pieces and carried them to the location of the eye and placed the left corner into the space that had been created, followed by the top and lower right corner. There were shavings of stone missing. I wondered if the eye would consider the glyph incomplete in some way. But there was no choice and even less time to doubt. This had to be it. With one hand holding it in place so that all three glyphs came together in the open space below the blue flame, the center of the eye, I waited. There was a slight movement as they fused together and then silence.

"What's wrong?" I asked. "What did we miss?"

"The declaration of the prophecy."

"Where?"

"Wait, Sara. Your impatience could quite well be your downfall if you're not careful."

Topetine stepped beside me so that our shoulders were touching and started to utter a phrase in what I assumed was her native language. While I did not know of the Mayan speak, the translation was somehow clear as she spoke.

"By the power given at the hands of the Soltari, I, the guardian of the temple of Kukulkan, bring to the almighty serpent god the Light Carrier to receive the key of understanding and the power contained within it. Her blood has been shed as proof of her existence so that your power may be bestowed upon her, as intended by the all-powerful entity that guides her quest."

We waited, side by side. Nothing but the vague sound of voices could be heard off in the distance, far beyond the walls of the tomb where we were standing. Or were they in my head?

"Damn it. Why isn't anything happening?" I asked. "Do we have to free the beast?"

"No," Topetine answered. "The power to allow your entrance is reserved, separate from the spirit of Kukulkan."

I felt my brows furrow in the center as I desperately tried to think of what was incomplete in the task. *Whatever the power is that allowed me to proceed to this point recognized the ring. I sacrificed my blood. I connected the glyphs. What more? We're running out of time.*

With that thought, I lifted my head to a glow that had caught my attention directly above us. "What does your prophecy say about that?" I asked as I stared at a band of orange and yellow that had lowered to just above my head. The tips of the ring of fire licked closer to the ceiling as the shape began to expand its circumference.

She shook her head. "Nothing is written about a flame like this. You've unlocked a power, to be sure, my dear. But it isn't one I know of."

I took one step back and the flame followed, reminding me of a personal rain cloud that wouldn't leave.

"What do you feel?" Topetine asked.

The truth was I was undecided about what to do or what I felt. "I feel nothing but urgency."

"And that will block energy from entering your spirit. It cannot provide you with the key even if it wanted to. Release the noise that fills your spirit and open it to only the energy around you."

I turned to her. "This is just pissing me off now. There is no getting around the fact that we are bound to be discovered by the dark angel that's watching out there." I pointed in the direction leading outside. The fire above me licked outward, following the extension of my arm. "Any shift in energy could give us away. Meanwhile, someone I love may already be dead and I can't do anything about it."

Her eyes rested calmly upon mine. "You can. And you must. There is only one way and that is through the key."

I threw up my hands and slid them over my face, turning once in a complete circle and resting them on my hips before putting my attention back to the flame above me. "This. This thing is my next step." I looked back to her. "I can't be sure what power is at work. If anything happens, I need to know I can find you."

"I asked you once before if you had faith in what you believe, in the outcome of what will be. You didn't know then and you still don't know. All I can tell you is that I've led you to the key, it has acknowledged your identity, and I'm to follow you into the next location for the third key, Sara. As the guardian on this quest, I'll be here unless your team deems otherwise. And that would only happen if my safety were to be compromised before you obtained what you came here for."

"I've come to learn not to expect anything but the unexpected, and certainly not to have any set plan. I'm not being granted the key or further access to it. That means there is a task that has not been completed to allow its release."

I was measuring every element I was up against. My gaze dropped to the ground in the hopes the answer would be found in the dust beneath our feet.

Kevin, I can't hear you. The sensation of your presence, the closeness of our connection is not with me. Are you alive? Do I risk this mission to find out? Do I attempt to make sure my team is safe before proceeding? Should I go back to the entrance to see if I missed anything? God help me if I overlooked an instruction in the scrolls. There isn't time to go back that far. I cursed under my breath and glanced back to the flame. *It's here. I wouldn't have made it this far if what I needed wasn't already here.* I extended my hand upward toward the dancing glow, as though it were tempting me to challenge it. In one swift motion, the flame expanded, cocooning me. I couldn't move beyond the boundary of the fire, not because of the heat one might expect to feel but because I was caged within the active licks of the flame. The color shifted from the warm glow of yellow-orange to blue-white, while the walls of the tomb began fading from my view, along with Topetine, the one person who could guide me deeper into the realm of the serpent god. As she disappeared, she waited, hands folded together. The evidence of well-practiced patience.

The room went dark for a split second before it began to spin. My stomach swayed into nausea. The world outside my bubble had changed. But as far as I knew, I hadn't moved from the serpent god's tomb. Another jolt of nausea, and this time I did close my eyes. I re-opened them to see a man half dressed, lying on a bed. The raspy sound of labored breathing filled my ears before I had a chance to wonder about why or how I had found myself in his presence.

The sensation of him I'd come to know so well filled me. *Kevin. My God!* I raced to the edge of his bedside. But as I tried to stroke the chiseled jaw of this warrior, my hand fell through it. I was nothing but a mere ghost beside him, unable to touch or console. Did he know I was here? There was no obvious sign of life, with the exception of the sound of his breathing, mechanical as it was, that filled the small room. *Where are you? Why can't I hear your thoughts or feel your emotions?*

"Sara, my love."

My eyes had been studying his face. I was certain his lips hadn't moved. At the words, I spun around but still saw nothing to account for what I'd heard. The hair against my neck shifted to the side and a warm breath could be felt moving up to my ear. Tingles raced from the first location of the sensation and traced a path along my shoulder and down the entire length of my right side. I reached a hand to my neck. The only spirit that sent a chill through me like that when not in Kevin's presence was Cerys.

"Cerys?" I angled my head to the right. "Kevin?" But I couldn't see anyone other than Kevin lying in the bed, and still I knew I wasn't alone.

"Does it matter, love?"

I'd never considered if it did. And I supposed not.

"Let me go." The whisper came into my ear.

I took a split second to be sure of his meaning. "No! I'm not leaving you here to die." I gazed at his form and wondered why he was painted from head to waist.

"You must."

"I won't. Damn you. Don't you leave when I'm so close to the key."

"You must choose."

"Choose?" I felt confused. "You mean the key or you?" I ran a hand through my hair. "That's a hell of a choice."

"If you don't recover the keys, all of them, our bond will be broken."

"Yeah, yeah. I remember." It didn't mean I wanted to. The Soltari or the Alliance. Maybe both. Someone was responsible for implementing the repercussions should I fail this quest. The result would be that I'd never be allowed to remain with Kevin in this world or any other. When this mission was finished, someone, or several souls, would pay for putting me, us, through this. But Kevin was right. I needed to get the keys not only to keep our connection intact and rescue humanity but also to have a tool to bargain with going forward. I'd been granted the power to hold that tool. And as I saw things, I would bargain for more than a small army of Jade's men or the lives of Earth. But how could I abandon the only person I'd ever loved? How could I leave him here alone to face death?

"You mustn't fail, Sara." Another trail of tingles ran along the side of my body. I released a heavy sigh. "For us."

So much was at stake. So much could be lost. And there was only one way to be sure all was secure—the damn key. The burden of it had grown from the minute I became aware of the mission. Choose the only person I'd ever put my complete trust in and allowed myself to love, or leave him to die for the sake of much more. Could that be the reason I had traveled from the tomb to Kevin, to make a choice? To prove my commitment?

"And how can I be certain you will be all right?" I asked. "I don't even know if you will."

"You can only trust what you feel."

Faith. The word echoed through my memory from Topetine as though it were a whisper that could disappear on the mere shift of a light current of air. Unlike so many of the experiences in which I could feel what another felt or know the truth they carried, at this moment I felt nothing about whether Kevin would be all right. My so-called gift was utterly useless in a time when I could use it most. Instead, what remained in my heart, and that I had been keenly aware of since the accident that led me to him, was the fact that if I chose to abandon my mission, there would be nothing left for Kevin and me.

And without the keys, the world could not move beyond the current dark energy consuming it.

I scanned the battered body on the bed and closed my eyes. *I can't. I can't give you up. I can't exist never hearing your voice again, never to feel you again.* Tears dropped one by one into my hands. *Don't you know you're my whole world? You convinced me I needed your love.* The tears fell faster. *And I did need it. I still do.* Kevin's face flashed against my closed eyelids. I dropped my hands and let out a breath to the sky. I felt the tension ease from my distraught face with a sudden realization. *And if I don't let you go now, I'll never have you again.*

"Very well," I said, eyes fixed on his face. I reluctantly surrendered my strength to what I believed should be and what little faith I had ever allowed to guide me. I'd led what I thought was a fulfilling life without Kevin once. He'd made it so much better. I'd connected with him once more in life. Now, he was asking me to leave him, when all I wanted was to stay. Desire had never ruled my heart and mind before I'd met him and it couldn't now. The fact was, keeping what we had created thousands of years ago and what we held in this lifetime was pure necessity. "I'll obtain the key."

And with that, the raspy sound of breath that filled the room was silent. I felt my mouth drop open in a gasp as I stared at his chest, willing it to move up and down. "The key!" I shouted up to the band of fire that still encircled me. "Take me back to the serpent god's tomb."

16

I blinked open my eyes to a darker cave than I remembered leaving. One torch glowed on the farthest wall, where Topetine stood. "Oh, thank the gods," she said, lifting her head to see me.

The blue flame that encircled me faded until it was as though it never existed.

I moved to the jeweled eye in the cave wall. "I saw Kevin, but only for a few minutes." The feeling of having to leave him haunted me with doubt that I'd done the right thing.

I forced myself to press the last image of Kevin to the back of my mind, but I'd be damned if I'd forget. There's no way I could. I swiped my hand over the face of the eye, again, trying to gain access to the key—was it hidden inside?—and remembered the words Eldor, leader of the elves in Ardan, had said. The first key would open the door to the second. Naturally, I thought that meant passage to the realm where each key would be located. But now, as I considered his words, perhaps the first key from the Druids would unlock this one, with the all-important caveat of a sacrifice—the only man I'd ever loved.

I closed my eyes and placed my palms on the center of my abdomen, the location where the Druid priests had left their mark, a scar from the branding of my skin. As my fingers extended across my middle, the palm of my right hand warmed with the same intensity as when I'd received the light. Led by pure instinct, I lifted it to the sky and opened my eyes to see the flame alive. It burned a white glow without any heat. A magic that was calling to the key I sought. The blue lapis in the center of the eye came to life in a sparkling array of shimmer. A fog began to settle around Topetine and me, expanding to fill the cave, until the remaining blue stones of the eye exploded. A shattering of tiny fragments rained down upon us. I ducked my face into my arm, covering my head with my other hand. The flame still burned in my open palm. I lifted my head to a brilliant light streaming out from the iris of the eye, where the stones had been. Its rays stretched to Topetine, then to me, before converging on the fire holding strong in my open hand. As it did, the flame descended, taking with it the blue light as it disappeared beneath my skin, lighting beneath it as my veins lit with the white-blue energy.

My skin prickled into gooseflesh. Every hair follicle lifted as the illumination raced up my arm to my shoulder and across my chest, filling me. What it meant, I could not know. The details of the mission and each encounter had not been provided by the Professors in Ardan. They were a group of wise old men who had reintroduced me to the world I'd forgotten and the importance of the quest. I was now and always at the mercy of the energy of the keys and whatever form it chose to take or whatever space it needed to clear within my body to assume residence within. Was that why I had to let Kevin go? I begged that energy racing through me to hear my plea to keep a place for him. As the light raced down my legs, they gave way and I crumpled in a pool beside Topetine.

The ground shook beneath our feet. A colossal sound rang out as though the world were cracking open in a thunderous and devastating collapse. A shriek could be heard above the sounds, and I knew the call was that of the dark angel that had been keeping watch. Rock began to tumble around us, some in the size of boulders but most in crumbling bits. Dust followed the path to the ground. As Topetine bent down and reached an arm under my shoulders, her eyes went wide and she began backing away. Her eyes, as large as full moons, remained glued open in apparent shock.

"I can't move yet," I called over the sound of falling rock. "Help me." But she continued her retreat. Still confused, I angled my head to the side and lifted my gaze to see an enormous curve of a beast. The head was like that of both snake and dragon. The last breath I'd taken in left in one gasp. My eyes absorbed the form of the creature in its entirety without having to roam, like a sponge placed over a puddle to soak up every detail. Feathers blended with scales from the top of its head down the back. Its body was a mass of curved muscle. No arms. No legs. It was indeed a serpent, a feathered one. The yellow-orange eyes moved with every bit of precision around the room as the muscular form holding it. *Is it angry?* I didn't feel that sensation from the beast. The fight-or-flight response that should have been pressing upon me to pull myself into hiding had decided to abandon me altogether.

Topetine stood glued with fear against the farthest wall, torch in hand. My legs betrayed me as I tried to move out of the way of the approaching beast, leaving my hands grasping at loose gravel. The head of the serpent swung around and narrowed eyes set upon my own. *Will it kill me?* I could try to shift into the hawk…but the thought left me before I could finish the plan of escape. Where could I go in a cave? And as large a bird as I was in that form, this serpent god could simply open his mouth and lunge toward this inexperienced flyer.

So help me, if you aim to kill me, do it quickly. Can the beast hear my thought?

The serpent's face fell close to mine with eyes that pinned me to the ground. My body went rigid and my hands froze in the rubble. I became aware of my breath, coming in and out in quick, shallow gasps. The sheer size of the creature was more than frightening, it was immobilizing. I didn't think the feathered serpent could get any larger until its wings opened, hitting the walls and lifting to the roof of the cave, enclosing me further should I choose to attempt escape. An odd silence fell around us. I was sure if he dropped one of those feathers, I'd hear it graze the floor. All of the energy that held me rigid drained in a single exhale. Every muscle in my body had given up on me. But while the physical sensation of strength left me for putty, there was more. I was in a trance. The hypnotizing eyes of the beast rolled over me in wave after calming wave. I no longer wanted to escape. A warm, steamy breath blew across my face like a gentle breeze in the humid jungle of the Yucatan. I closed my eyes under the penetrating stare and felt my chin drop open further, relaxing into a deep state of calm.

What does the serpent aim to do? Tear my head off? Leave me to the dark side? After losing Kevin, I can't care. Not right now. Even as I wondered, floated, a warm sensation fell over my face and one of the brightest lights lit the insides of my eyelids in a blaze of white. *Dare I open them? The beast should have killed me by now. What is it waiting for?*

I paused on the edge of life, taking in the warmth, the light, and the sudden rush of air that filled my lungs as though I'd been holding my breath and was now free to take in the clean, sweet oxygen that was breath. It was a feeling I experienced once before when I'd returned from Ardan, to the life I'd temporarily departed from following a car accident as I came off the ventilator and breathed for myself that first breath. So effortless and deep, so sweet it had been then, and again now. I opened my eyes and saw the beast lifting away from me, its eyes still upon me. My thoughts were at ease, at complete peace, despite the bitter appearance that upon first sight cut through me with fear. Had this serpent god breathed into me? What other explanation was there for why I had left my panicked state? I was indeed alive and still in a most compromising position. Yes, I should have been fighting for life. Instead, I was wading in some sort of heavenly peace.

A gift for my freedom and your sacrifice.

Confusion set in at hearing the thought I was sure wasn't mine. *My sacrifice? Kevin.* My heart sank again at the recall of him lying in that bed, breathless. I closed my eyes tight, pressing deep sadness into the tiny room in the back of my mind that held my darkest memories. *How can I? How dare I feel such peace when I left him to die. What kind of love is that? I don't deserve to share eternity with anyone. And I sure as hell don't deserve a gift for sacrificing the only love I've ever known.* Only one word filled me with such contrast to that peace—guilt. I felt as though I'd been slapped awake by it.

The beast had spoken in thought to me. But what did it mean? What gift? What about the key?

The two keys have joined and flow within you, as they were intended. Having released the second power to you, I am now free to travel the many realms that exist.

I looked at my arms to see the odd blue energy flowing through my veins.

What is the second power?

The great wings drew up against the beast's muscular form and the walls began to crack further. Topetine stumbled and caught herself against the wall. Finding my strength once again, I pushed myself to stand, holding my balance before making my way toward her and the torch.

"It's coming down," I shouted over the sound of the crumbling wall around us. "We'll be exposed to Tarsamon's forces. Hurry! We have to leave this place." I reached for the torch she held. Her eyes were fixed on the serpent god that stood still and strong against the increasing destruction, his wings acting like a shield of armor. "Hey," I said, shaking her. "Follow me."

I turned in the direction of the entrance where we had slipped past the dark angel. The sound of screeching I had thought I'd heard earlier grew louder. I wondered if my team had made it inside and were battling the dark forces to get to me. If by chance Topetine and I escaped the evil guarding outside the cave walls, there was the very good possibility the villagers would have arrived at the main entrance.

"You'll want to shift," Topetine said as I slipped between the last crevice leading outside the cave, praying it did not collapse the narrow passage as the ground continued to quake. She shifted into her jaguar form.

"There's no room to fly. We're almost—" I was cut off by a loud screech and the sound of sliding above me. As I glanced up, I was met by a crushing force upon my shoulders and a tightening around my neck. The exit into open air was only steps away. And while I couldn't see what was constricting me, there was no mistaking the sensation

I'd felt when I'd stared at the dark angel. It was as if a living statue had fallen upon my shoulders and was trying to strangle me with stone-like legs. She'd been waiting, watching for such a sign, the release of the feathered serpent. The quake itself was like we'd blown a horn directing the dark angel right to us.

Topetine crouched for a lunge, but the passage was too narrow. I started to drag the heavy beast the few steps to my freedom, while struggling to keep her from my airway. With not much room to maneuver and the fact that the angel had landed her target perfectly, preserving my ability to breathe was growing quite difficult.

Separate... when we get out... can't let them kill you. Following a slur of expletives and a struggle for breath, I'd managed to get the thought to Topetine. She had to stay alive to lead us to the guardian of the next key.

"No!" A loud, deep voice sounded like thunder in a canyon. "She is to remain alive. The cat is expendable."

Though I couldn't see him, I knew well enough the sound and the dark feelings that started plaguing my senses. Thoughts of demise and nightmarish images began filling my thoughts. *Tarsamon.*

The clamp around my neck and shoulders lifted, freeing me to call to Topetine. "Get out of here." I stumbled out of the rock crevice into open air. Topetine sunk back out of reach of the angel, her eyes piercing through the darkness at me. But the creature had already abandoned the jaguar. With her primary interest no longer a target, she didn't care about lesser quarry.

"You continue to amaze," Tarsamon said.

My feet had refused to move, locked in the very place they had landed upon stumbling out of the cave. Standing in front of me was the hooded form I'd come to know as the darkest energy that existed in time and space. His black cloak and a face of only beaded eyes that changed color depending on his mood, varying on a scale of annoyance to rage, reminded me of the reaper. A bony hand extended toward me with an index finger aimed near my cheek.

"I wonder," he said.

"I couldn't care less if you do," I answered, hating him more with every passing moment as darkness filled my being and contributed to a feeling of sickness weakening me.

A throaty laugh followed by a growl filled the space between us. As the finger grazed my cheek, an electricity of searing magnitude consumed the area on my forearm that had been marked by the J-man and raced upward toward my cheek. I cried out in pain as the white-blue light exited my cheek and reached for the dark finger. He withdrew his hand.

"So you have indeed obtained the key but have not yet learned to use the power."

Use the dark thoughts. Use them to create the rage.

"You forget I hear your every thought." He shifted to my other side. "Since when does a being of light require rage?"

Block his intrusion.

I could feel him searching to hear my thoughts. While I could block them from being read by C-05 or any number of others with the gift to see into the mind's eye, my ability to block his introspection had been out of reach for me. Not because it wasn't possible, I'd never known if it was, but because I hadn't mastered the ability in all my preparation for the quest. I could see now why Kevin had made it a point to remind me, testing me to do so. I made the attempt anyway, because in his question was the realization he didn't know I could shift. And the less he knew about my abilities the better.

The sound of fighting was getting closer. I couldn't tell if it was my team or the demon dogs at each other's throats.

"Don't go silent on me now. Your thoughts have always interested me. We used to be on the same side, Sara. Has that memory been returned to you?"

The questioning from Tarsamon brought me back from the sounds I was concentrating on, or rather distracting myself with.

"I've heard about it. Can't say that I'd choose to recall anything as ugly as that, though." *Don't antagonize. You're stuck.* "Is what C-05 said true? That you left the Alliance over disagreements?"

"Such a disappointment, C-05," he said, almost in reflection. "As most stories go, there is generally more to them. Now isn't the time to share what brought me to this point, not in the midst of chaos. And not that you're interested."

"That's all your world is, chaos."

I lifted a gaze upward, across the landscape, and back to him. The fire was still burning. More blazes lit the canvas of gray, smoky terrain. The area I needed to get back to was unclear, but I carried a pretty good sense of direction. If I could only move, I'd be able to find my way out with little difficulty.

"I'll discover how to relieve you of this burden you carry, Light Carrier, before you have the chance to die."

It was no favor he was offering. I might be stuck, but so was he. He was stalling, trying to figure out how to get me out of this place if he couldn't touch me. Killing me wasn't an option because he knew he'd risk the release of the existing power I carried in two keys. And something told me he didn't understand fully the magnitude of it. Releasing the keys' light would put his whole plan to consume the energy of humanity into a tailspin. While I might not have the last key in my possession, there was enough stored destruction to cause him a serious multigenerational delay.

Tarsamon's hands reached for either side of my face. The current I'd felt at his first touch stirred again and came to life beneath my skin, traveling upward as if he had summoned the force. The electricity was, I assumed, a sort of protection that prevented his personal brand of poison from sinking into me and making me as weak as it once had, when I'd only held one key. I cringed against the pain and at the same time wondered how it might work with my ability to create a shield of light.

"Perhaps I'll see how much you can take, how strong you really are." He was careful not to touch, but moved his hands above my shoulders, directing the energy as he saw fit. The pain grew with every change in position, as though it dared him to utilize its energy. My legs would have given out had Tarsamon not been holding me up by some invisible force. I tried to bring my hands together to light the spark that would create a shield, but they, too, were pinned by the same force.

"You're growing tired. I can feel your energy not quite as strong as when you first exited the cave."

His words are lies. Don't listen. Don't take them in. See the shield.

A fierce growl came from my left. *Topetine.* "Nooo!" I shouted, as the jaguar lunged. She was no match for the darkest entity known to exist in the realms. A flash that was the same color of the electricity running through my veins filled the dark space and disappeared. Had he managed to manipulate the energy I carried? I felt the look of dread fall over my face, cringing at the sight of the jaguar's crumpled form beside me in a magnificent heap of silky black fur. Her eyes were still lit with life in the bright green irises, but her lids were now at half-mast. An odd green fog floated inches above her form, energy I wasn't familiar with.

A loud hiss filled the firelit sky. I lifted my eyes to the sound to see the serpent god rising from the rubble while its massive wings expanded, preparing for flight. As it took to the sky above me, its tail dipped down and lifted Topetine into the curve of the scaly, feathered body.

I returned my attention to Tarsamon and felt all the hatred I needed and, during his distraction, took that single brief moment to shift into my hawk form. I lifted my wings to fly under the protection of Kukulkan, the feathered serpent, and toward where I thought the cave entrance had been. I ascended only a few feet into the air, every muscle quaking to move with all the force I could muster. I must have managed two smooth strokes of my wings before something grabbed hold of my legs and pulled me close. I flapped wildly, trying to break free. My heart was beating faster than a rabbit on the run. *Why isn't the electricity that flowed from my body once stopping the darkness now? How did he grab me? Jesus.* I opened my mouth to scream but only the screech of a tormented bird rang out. A blast of light ripped across my vision. I continued to fight, to get free of the hold my captor had over me.

Wait. Light? There is no illumination with Tarsamon, ever. Light flees from darkness. "They cannot co-exist." I heard the words of the Professors rattle through my head. *Where am I? What's happened?*

17

The face that stared at me infuriated me more. Jade had traced me from the cave to some unknown place. *But how? How did he know where to find me? How is he able to touch me when Tarsamon can't?*

"The protection you carry works against dark energy, not against light," Jade replied to my thought. "Now will you come down?"

I flew in circles around the room until I landed on a post at the top of a staircase in what seemed like a large barn with several windows. Jade leaned against the wall, arms crossed, watching me. His face was blank as I glowered at him. Both of us knew what the other was thinking. One of the biggest peeves I had was being handled in any way, urged to do something I wasn't prepared to do by someone else taking control. He knew it angered me, regardless if his assistance in escaping Tarsamon had been necessary or not. And he didn't care. By his account, he'd been called to help, a fact I had yet to confirm with the one man Jade said had requested his assistance, Kevin. That is, if Kevin was still alive. Jade adjusted the pack off his back, rifled through it, and tossed a couple of cloth objects in my direction, followed by boots, careful not to approach.

"You'll need those. And I'm not leaving. You'd better hurry because the villagers are on their way back."

I'm not shifting with you staring at me.

He turned to the side, shot a glance over his shoulder, and mumbled something about tanning my hide. "I'm not taking my eyes off you. You get yourself caught in the most dangerous of situations."

"It's the nature of the job." I had Kevin on my mind and that had not only eased my anger but also had left a slight vacancy to fill with guilt. "I thought you knew," I added, dragging a boot on.

"What made you think you could exit the cave knowing the dark angel was standing guard?"

"You mean that...thing...that had been watching on a cliff?" I didn't wait for an answer. "I didn't know of the dark angel. I'd never seen anything like it when I went to Tarsamon's realm," I said. "Besides, I'd slipped by her once already."

"Jesus." He swiped a hand through his hair. "A mere quiver in the energy field would get her attention. You, you caused a major collapse of the energy field when you took the key. You might as well have shouted, 'Hey, here I am. Come and get me.'"

His frustration rose as he spoke. Unlike Kevin, Jade didn't have the same control. He ran on pure instinct. Tell it like it is, do what he wants, and let the pieces fall haphazardly. Clean-up of collateral damage could be done later, if and only if *he* deemed it necessary.

"Like there was any choice in the matter," I said. "It's not like I had a guide book." The man had a way of finding what unnerved me and picking at it. I couldn't let my anger get beyond my control. I didn't want to shift back into a hawk. *Maintain an even keel, Sara.* I took a deep breath to still the rising anger. "Was I expected to tell the serpent to hold on a minute while I asked the dark angel to fly away?" I asked, fluttering my fingers. I turned away from his angered look.

"You could have waited until the serpent took off."

Amidst crumbling rock? Yeah, right.

"Or didn't you get that info from the Alliance?"

I whirled to face him. "What? The Alliance has never given me information on *how* to complete this quest. Why would they share such details with you and not the one who would be slugging her way through it?"

We both stared at each other in silence.

"Because there was always the chance that I would have to back up your boy Kevin if Juno and Matt were unable to take over for him. The question is why the information was never shared with you."

"So it seems," I said under my breath.

"Where's the breakdown in the Alliance?"

"I don't know," I answered. "I haven't had any time to piece that one together. Been a little busy. But thanks for sharing what you know."

He paused. "We never got to finish our conversation about that key."

"The conversation where you need to use it as a bargaining chip for your small army or the one where you tried to take it from me?"

"I believe I apologized for my behavior. But yes, the one regarding my men. What if I can get you information about the Alliance members, maybe even find out why you were not given certain details about the mission, and based on that, you agree to help me."

"As if I trusted you?"

"I just saved your life. You might consider it."

"I was taking advantage of Tarsamon's distraction on my own."

"Because I injected you with a serum to shift."

I couldn't argue with that. "Fine. Get me information about the Alliance and who drives the primary decisions and I'll agree to incorporate help for you in my personal interests for release of the keys.

"Now, where the hell are we? I need to get to Kevin." I glanced around at what was the size and shape of a barn. Stone walls lifted high to a pitched roof and narrow windows were scattered about with one larger square window on one side. We were on a second story that had a wooden bridge running the length from one end to the other.

"You're in the village."

I stopped looking around the place and settled on a blank stare on his face. "Why in God's name would you trace us here? You've landed us right where hell can break out. There are severed bodies hanging from—"

"Relax, before you get your panties in a twist. That hole you and your team ducked into upon arriving leads directly to this village.

I calculated the odds of the residents returning before they found you or your team. The caverns Topetine secured for your arrival are hidden below. They're unknown to the villagers."

"How can you be sure?" I remembered the pool that had flushed me, along with Kevin, far below it. Above us had been open sky. That pool couldn't have remained a secret to all who lived in the area.

"I went checking around when there was nothing more to do but watch your Kevin lying silent on a bed, under the spell of the J-man." He shifted his body and angled a head around a corner. "It looks like they left ventilation holes far enough outside of the village to reach underground. I'm sure the people that Topetine trusted to provide for you wouldn't want anyone getting sick or dying from lack of oxygen."

"I suppose. And just to set the record straight, panties are nothing more than a pain in the ass just like you, and easier done away with." He smirked. "I can't imagine how you and Kevin became friends."

"It's another life-saving adventure. I'd tell it to you but you'd still hate me."

"On that point we agree. I need to get to him. Will you lead me underground?"

"Yes. But we'd best wait for the rest of your team. They managed to keep the villagers away from the cave entrance that led to the serpent god, but the noise outside the primary entrance alerted the dark angel and started a battle." He drew his sword. "It's probably why the demon didn't come looking for you sooner," he added, putting an index finger to his lips.

"What is it?"

"Someone's coming," he whispered.

Without my own weapons, I stepped behind him. "Get us below."

"Sh."

I'd fought without my sword in the past, but only in Ardan. Creating a spark to form a ball of fire would give us away if we were trying to hide.

Jade took one step into the path of the footsteps approaching, stopped, and lowered his sword. Taking the hint that all was safe,

I stepped out from the wall. He slapped a heavy hand on the back of the man I recognized as one of the men who had been with us when we'd found C-05. "Reed," Jade said, angling his head toward me. "My first in command." The man raised an arm toward another person behind him.

"Look," he said to Jade. "The villagers are at the gates and the additional company of the dark forces is not far behind."

"The rest of the men, how many remain?"

"All. Tarsamon's army wasn't interested in anything that doesn't give off the energy she does." He lifted a chin in my direction. "But we believe they've started tracking the team connected to her. They chased after them as though they were pursuing a dog in heat. She's at risk alone and with her team."

"Sara," Aria said, looping an arm around my neck. The rest of the members of my team, who had also become my friends over the last few months, followed her, weary from the fight. She unhooked her arm from my neck and grabbed my face with both hands. "You met with the serpent god, didn't you? Your eyes are different."

"They are? Yeah, I met Kukulkan. But I don't have a clue what I look like." *I imagine a shower is in order at the very least.* "How did you get past the villagers?"

"We're all much faster than average humans. You know that. Even if they are possessed, they don't carry otherworldly abilities."

"Let's get below," Jade said, leading the way toward a back wall and a set of stairs. "Then we're out of here."

"What about Kevin?" Juno asked.

"I didn't touch him, just like you said," Jade replied.

"What do you mean, you're out of here?" I asked.

He turned to me at the bottom of the stairs. "Look, I fulfilled the duty I was asked to by the Soltari and my pal, Kevin. I have no desire to battle with Tarsamon and the demons. I'm trying to save my men, not put them up for grabs, not even for you and your quest. Anyone near you is on the target list. That's what *they* signed up for." He angled his head in the direction of my team.

I stepped closer so that my face was inches from his. "You need some help saving *your men*, if I recall correctly. So the way I see it, you're pretty much stuck on the target list with the rest of us. Or you could appeal to the Soltari alone." While Jade had mentioned the Soltari left his small army to suffer through a series of famines, I had no details to prove the entity was more punishing than I could have imagined. It was a question I was curious about, but also one for another time. I had to play the card and trust what he told me was true. I might not have liked Jade, but I needed him, his militia, for the security of my team. Without Kevin's guidance in moving forward and the protection that came with it, Jade was a safeguard. I would gladly bargain with the Soltari on his behalf for his help.

Jade turned without another word, slid open a wooden panel in the floor exposing a compartment holding hay bales, and jumped in. We followed him to a corner as he lifted another panel in the floor and one more to reveal the dirt path, leaving me to wonder when he had found the time to explore so many levels.

Once we were all inside, he waited as Reed worked quickly to close everything behind us, making the exit appear as though it never existed.

The sudden urgency to reach Kevin drove me past the six other members and race to where I thought I'd seen him while in the dreamlike state that carried me to him in the cave. Maybe there was still a chance he'd be alive. But the thought of his chest not moving was the only vision in my head as I rounded a corner to continue down the hall.

I stopped at the entrance, my breath coming in and out of my lungs fast. Kevin hadn't moved, just as I'd expected. I stepped slowly toward him, my eyes watching for a single twitch of his body. Several cloths dipped in what looked like paint had been placed around him from head to toe, the same colors I had seen marked across his skin. His face was all that was visible.

"Get this stuff off him," I said, reaching for a frayed red square.

A small woman not much taller than four feet moved between me and Kevin, blocking my path to get closer.

"Sara." Juno touched my arm from behind and stepped beside

me. "She's been watching over him," he said. "The J-man was clear he's not to be touched."

"Remove these rags in whatever manner you like or I'll do it. You have ten generous seconds to decide."

Juno nodded to the woman and waved a hand indicating to move. Jade said something in her language and she shook her head.

"She won't be responsible for the undoing of the powers of the medicine the J-man has administered," Jade said.

"Very well." I took another step to move past her. "Step aside, please."

The woman stood firm, unwavering in her guard. "Tell her I appreciate her desire to protect him."

"She's not protecting him, Sara," Jade said. "Her people hold a strong belief that if anyone intervenes or disrupts the workings of a medicine man, it will bring illness upon themselves and their family for years to come."

"I'm sorry she carries a burden like that, but her belief is not going to interfere. For the last time, tell her to step aside."

I moved around her and reached for the cloth near Kevin's neck. The instant I touched it, the woman ran off, for the J-man, I guessed. Fine. It would buy me time, albeit a short amount. Not that I knew why I so desperately needed to get to Kevin and undo any saving magic. It was more than just needing to see him. I was pulled to him as I had been in that vision in the cave, the one where he had asked me to let him go. Only now, I couldn't. I needed to be close to him. I lifted the rest of the rags, until there were none remaining, and tossed the bundle to the floor. I heard a gasp behind me but couldn't care. Nothing, not a few rags, painted magic, a myth, or even the Soltari, was going to stand between us.

His eyes were closed as if he were in a peaceful sleep. My concern deepened. I'd never seen him sleep soundly. His chest was indeed not moving. I leaned in and put an ear to his nose and mouth. The tiniest of breaths, as though they were the quick and shallow breaths of an infant, were present. I eased back and gazed over the face, pale in color. The sexy five-o'clock shadow I loved was fuller in appearance. Something began to stir in me as I took in his appearance and the inkling of life that was with him. That bit of his soul that remained needed to be drawn out to live again. He needed a connection, something to reach for. Sitting by his side, I leaned over him again and rested my lips above his, slightly parted. My hands slid gently along either side of his face.

I'm here. Come back to me, my love.

A warm sensation from my center raced up through my chest and down my arms to my hands, as though I had called the energy forward. I lifted my head and eyes to see the heat from my fingertips radiated the familiar white-blue glow that resonated in my sword—my energy. The heat of that light moved across my hands and extended through my neck to my lips. I lowered them back to his, brushing them gently.

Wake up. Please. Join with me again in this life.

The light began to extend past my lips as I held them close to his. A fraction of an inch between us was enough for the energy to flow to him in an otherworldly exchange. There was warmth, healing, and love in that light, as it quickly started to replace the coolness of his lips and warm the paleness of skin. But would he come back or was the energy just a passing exchange? Could the promise of connection be sealed with this breath into him? As the energy began to slow and fade, I closed the fraction of space with my lips upon his and his face twitched. I lifted my head. He raised his chin and sucked in the deepest breath as though a binding had been freed from his lungs to allow the air to flow into them.

The soft sound of whispering behind me filtered into my ears. "Breath of life. Gift of the serpent god." Could it be? Could that have been what Kukulkan meant by *a gift for his freedom and for my sacrifice?* I'd never felt stronger about putting my lips on a dying man. I'd been asked to release my fear and let go of the only man I ever allowed myself to love. With much regret and a good dose of guilt to follow, I'd done it. Could a centuries-old relic, locked away in a cave, have that kind of power? A god certainly could. Just like the power of the keys for this once-unfathomable mission, the serpent god had proven to be much more than a myth or legend.

Kevin stirred beneath my hands still resting on either side of his face. I lifted them and brushed a hand over his forehead as he opened his eyes to me. The light in them pierced mine and I couldn't help the smile that broke across my cheeks.

"My beautiful love," I said.

"I knew you..." He breathed a heavy sigh. "I knew you would come back. Once you had the key."

"Of course I would. I had to. You're a part of me, and I couldn't finish this without you." A tear, something I worked to hide all my life for fear of appearing weak, fell down my cheek and landed on his chin. I swiped a thumb across it and kissed the spot before moving my lips to his again.

He had known me across so many lifetimes in this realm and others, remembered every tender moment and every battle we had ever fought. The Soltari had stolen those memories from me, still held many of them for fear of me getting distracted on this mission, putting at risk humanity. But I'd proven to be able to handle the complications of this quest. As such, my sights were set on getting every one of those memories back, along with instilling a few changes to the rules in Ardan. But first, I was entitled to an instant lost in a kiss as his lips responded against mine. His strength was returning. He healed quickly as part of his supernatural abilities. But it was something more that had been needed to break the poison of the Dark Lord—a life-giving breath from a god.

"They're here," Jade said, breaking my concentration. A minute more and the sound of footsteps above could be heard thudding in both faint and then heavy pounding.

How were we found?

"We can't stay here," Elise said.

"They've brought the dark angel," Matt added. "It won't be long before she discovers Sara's energy."

"We canna go without Topetine. Sara, she went into the cave with ye. Where is she?" Mac asked.

In my desire to get to Kevin, after Jade had pulled me from Tarsamon's grasp, I'd somehow neglected to consider Topetine's well-being. "She was picked up by the serpent. Rescued, I think."

"Ye think?" Mac's eyes closed and a deep crease filled the center between them.

"Well, I saw..." I paused, trying to find the best way to describe what had happened. "She was struck down," I blurted out. "The serpent god picked her up when I was being held by Tarsamon."

Juno glanced to Matt, who only shook his head.

"Was she alive?" Mac asked.

"I don't know for certain," I said. I remembered the light leaving her eyes but couldn't recall if I'd seen that blank stare that often masks the face once a person passes.

The sounds of footsteps thudded above us. "Trace Sara to the entrance of the realm," Matt said, turning to Jade. "The Aluxes should be able to buy some time before her energy is detected above ground. We've got to find Topetine before we can leave. If we don't, she can't guide us to the guardian of the last key."

"I'll find her," Mac said.

"Wait. If she's with the serpent, both of them know she needs to get back to us to continue the mission."

"He's right," I added, remembering the feathered serpent's remarks to me in the cave. "The serpent god was well aware of the legend. He knew of the freedom I needed to give him to leave the prison of the cave. He'd never take Topetine without the intention of returning her."

Matt turned his attention to Mac. "We'll find Topetine, but we need you here with what is above."

Jade reached for my arm. "Trace us both or not at all," I said, putting a hand on Kevin's arm. "If they find him, they'll kill him."

"Damn, you're the most stubborn woman I've known yet."

"Get out of here," Juno said. "Take Kevin if you have to, but go."

"I can't. Something is preventing movement."

"The dark angel," Matt said.

"Shit," I muttered, wrenching my arm from Jade's grasp. "We're going to have to leave the way we came in." I angled my head to Jade. "My sword. Do you have it?" The last place I recalled having it was when I'd fought with C-05. It had been with me when Jade traced me to his camp.

"Yes. When you shifted into the hawk, we collected it. But it won't do you any good against the dark angel," he said.

"The light from the Druids, Sara," Mac said, "Put the barrier around us now. It will buy us a little time."

Matt moved beside me, sword drawn. "Do it now. Create some fire while you're at it. You should have all of your abilities with the additional protection of the keys."

I closed my hands together, hoping he was right. Faster than ever, they illuminated in the familiar soft white glow. The spark that would light into a ball of fire lit into a scant explosion in the palm of my hand. I shook out one hand, freeing it for creating the defense, while leaving the other balancing the ball of fire, ready for a fight.

"Keep that lit as long as possible," Matt said near my ear. "No telling what power, if any, you will have in the presence of the dark angel."

"We scatter to distract them," Juno said. "Matt and Aria will take the front that blows past the initial force. Elise, you stay with me." She narrowed a gaze at him, preferring to fight as she decided best. She also trusted him as a master at managing tactical teams and ambush. Because Matt hadn't disagreed, Elise eased out of her tense expression.

"Are you out of your mind?" I asked. "Tarsamon has entered the realm. The dark forces have set their sights on my energy. Scattering leaves me open." No reply. I turned my attention from Juno and met Jade's stare. "Your lead man said so himself."

"We need to create a path out of here. We'll all be close enough to you to fight," Juno replied.

You'd better be like a second skin.

"Jade and Mac will stay with Sara at all times. The second you have the ability, Jade, trace to the realm's entrance."

Jade nodded. "My men can help clear a path to exit." He turned and said a few words to Reed, who disappeared down the hallway.

"That'll help." Juno's gaze moved between all of us, looking for a question or challenge in our eyes.

"At least two of us will stay glued to Sara's side at all times. We don't know what effect the demon will have or if she has the power to seep past the protection Sara carries."

I shot a look to Kevin, who appeared somewhat stronger as he tried to sit up, before facing the team. "Someone had better stay with him," I said.

"They won't come for Kevin. They believe he's dead," Juno said.

A touch at my arm had me directing my attention back to Kevin. "They all go with you. I'll find you."

Topetine and now Kevin were being left behind as we tried to find a way out. It wasn't the ideal situation, but there was little choice.

Every instinct this time told me to go, follow the duty I'd been led here to fulfill, and return safely. This time there was no guilt weighing over me.

"To the top then," I said. "I don't suppose we can bypass the barn above?"

"No other way up that I could find." Jade's eyes lifted to the ceiling. "Just more tunnels across." He dragged a hand through the air. "Like some damn rodent house."

"Here," Aria said, leaning over the map she'd opened on the nearby table. "We'll need to go the way Jade led us. It's the closest to where we first encountered the Aluxes." She pointed to a path outlined on the map. Her finger traced the direction to follow. "Head left. That will lead us out. Then run like hell and hope the Aluxes will help slow the dark forces."

"Let's get going," I said. "I don't know how much longer this shield will hold and I don't want to bring the fight into these tight quarters."

We made it up the stairs and above to be met with nothing more than an eerie silence. No dark energy and no villagers. There was something different lingering on the current of the air, however, that I had come to know not to trust. An uneasiness and sense of doom hung as thick as LA smog. Juno motioned two fingers in the direction Matt and Aria should move and indicated for Jade, Mac, and me to hold position. After a brief pause, he then gave the order to move. I could see Aria and Matt steps ahead as their shadows slipped across the moonlight streaming in the large window on my right side. There was only one way across the room, over the footbridge. The shield that had protected our energy from being detected began to fade and I moved faster, closing the distance between our team of three to meet Matt and Aria.

Steps from the door, the stone came to life as the shadow demons lifted from their hidden places against the dark walls. *Jesus, there's no way we're going to make it.* We weren't even out of the damn barn. I threw the two spheres I'd been holding to target either side of Matt and Aria. They took out a couple of approaching shadows in their path forward and cleared a couple more near the door. I watched as Aria turned back to see me only feet behind her. Matt opened the door and they both rushed through. Jade's team was there to greet them as they took on several more of the shadows and what looked like the flesh-colored faceless demons, trampling over bodies of villagers and smaller figures I assumed were perhaps Aluxes. *But how?* I'd seen the little trolls fight, swift and smooth. I lit another flame to clear our approach to the door. As I extended an arm behind my head, I heard a couple of grunts as the flame sputtered and fizzed, dying at its beginning in my hand. A rush of force at my back lifted and sent me sailing into the wall. Jade and Mac were tossed aside like crumpled paper.

I gasped as pain connected with every nerve so alive in my body. *A few seconds more is all we need.* As I tried to move, I saw what had tossed me into the barn wall, the dark angel. She floated the remaining way down from the ceiling and stalked closer. As she moved, a wall of black followed as though she were drawing a curtain of fog behind her. I couldn't see Juno or Elise, who should have been behind us. Jade and Mac were against the wall where the square window was, open to the cold night air, as small moans of pain signaled their injury. My back was pressed against the wall with my feet dangling. *I've gotta get free. Somehow.* I twisted one way and then another, stopping after realizing my efforts were futile. I tried lighting the shield for protection from the negative energy washing over me, but only a faint blue outline began to encircle me. Not enough cover to keep even the wind at bay. As the dark angel drew closer, a flood of images began filling my mind. The corpses of beasts scattered about an open field mingled with human bodies and their parts. Fires burned in different areas around the dead and dying, adding to the obvious destruction of life. *God, is that what they've done on Earth? Has Tarsamon's army already slaughtered a multitude of humans? Am I too late to bring the keys forward?* I struggled against my invisible bonds. *Lies. Negative energy lies. Don't believe.* And yet, because the shadows had already been summoned to Earth and had slipped into the weakest humans before I'd left to fulfill the quest, the image in my mind was likely truth. I couldn't know for certain.

The angel stood only a few feet from me and lifted a long arm, her index finger pointed at me. Her mouth opened to deliver a horrific, ear-piercing scream that closed out all other sounds. The flood of negative thoughts rained upon me in waves. Carnage in multiple forms, from exposed raw muscle to the innocent forms of tiny children, appendages twisted in unnatural positions. I struggled to pull my hands to my head in an attempt to block my eardrums from being shattered but they, too, were pinned with the rest of my body. Blood flowed in rivers from each vision, until I felt wetness leaking from the corners of my eyes.

What does this beast aim to accomplish? To fill the mind of this empath with such horror might just be enough to break me. I wasn't used to the destruction and terror I was viewing against my will. Sure, as a psychiatrist in my practice, I'd heard plenty of horrific stories, but none of them forced me to view the scene as though I was living in it with the victim. I was feeling every death as though it were happening anew. For every life I saw in my vision was one more draped in darkness, layer upon excruciating layer. My body wanted to explode with such intensity that I could not contain it much longer. There would need to be an outlet and soon. Why wasn't I transforming into the hawk? Had all of my strengths been obstructed just like Jade's ability to trace?

"No more!" I called, knowing it would do little to stop the angel's impact. And then I saw a vision Kevin had shared with me. At the time, he had wanted more than anything else for me to trust him, to know that I would be safe with him. He believed by sharing something so personal, so painfully cutting, I would. In that single instance, he'd flashed the memory of his mother's murder at his fragile age of seven. Through telepathy, he had only needed to show me a single image of what he had seen, not the entire experience of his own innermost terror. I couldn't fathom how the dark angel had obtained every sensation, every cry, and all the fear that had consumed Kevin as a small boy that night so long ago.

Dear God, I gasped. *She couldn't know every cry. She's emphasizing the memory, the small piece of what he shared. Don't believe the lies.* But despite how I tried to turn off the sensations, they pounded through, as though I owned each thought. I turned my head away from the angel and closed my eyes as if I could deflect the evil effects of emotion, and this time there was no hiding the tears that chased one after another down my cheeks. *That's not Kevin now. But it was once.* I fought the horror pulsing in waves. *He survived, strong and sure, confident and capable. He's the one man I will love beyond any amount of pain. He's not that child. Block the dark thoughts. Block them.*

Despite my attempts to filter the input crashing into me wave after grueling wave from the dark entity, my abilities had become useless, gone under the attack of energy stronger than mine. I felt my muscles release their fight and go limp with fatigue. *The negative energy is the only source that can weaken you.* The words of the Professors in Ardan somehow found a way through the feeling of helplessness to echo again in my mind. Each of the members joining me on this quest had unique abilities, they had said, that would help us out of any situation. Mine were completely denied at the moment. Every ounce of motivation and defiance squeezed from me, I let myself be at the mercy of the angel, lifting a single eyelid to see her move within inches of me. Her glowing eyes studied my form, tilting a pixie-like head from one side to the other. I couldn't believe I was being held at the command of a creature so delicate in appearance and as vicious as a predator.

"Finally," the creature said. "It's about time you take a rest from your...activities." Her lip curled in disgust.

I wanted to kick, to fight, if I knew it would do any good. All I could do was hang like a puppet under the spell of the puppeteer. *There must be some protection offered by the keys.*

"Not one I can't yet find a way through," the creature answered my thought. With that, I slid the length of the wall to the floor in a crumpled heap, released by the angel. My hair lifted on a breeze that found its way through the window and an icy chill fell over my skin as though the temperature had dropped in an instant to below freezing. I shivered in response. *Movement. I have control again.* A loud hiss came from the angel. I looked up to see something had distracted her from the attention she was showing me. Her sudden retraction had me looking closer. Mac was on the creature's back, his sword stuck into the spine.

"Sara," Jade called from the window. I found all the strength I'd had before the dark angel pulled it from me. I scrambled to my feet and raced to Jade. "Go, out this way, now. She won't be paralyzed long." I looked out at a pulley and a line that led from the barn-like building to another across the village, like a zip line. And what if I missed? It was dark, after all, and I was supposed to leap... "Now." A press at my back had me pushing off my feet and reaching for the pulley. For some unexplainable reason, the thought of Kevin's horror hit me at the same time I eyed the loop and my worst thought became a living nightmare. *I missed the grab.*

18

I was falling straight for the center of the village, to where the battle was being fought with the rest of the demons and shadows and Jade's men. I closed my eyes and waited for the punch of the ground to reach me in the same manner the wall had at my back after being thrown into it by the dark angel.

My eyes flicked open, sharp to the landscape that crossed below, as I glided above it. I might have missed the grab, but either the reminder of Kevin or the fear of dying had caused the transformation that saved my ass from the ground below as I shifted from human into hawk. I cut through the wind that flowed around me with precision wings. And for the first time, I was grateful to Jade for injecting me with his wicked potion. I'd rescued myself for a change, with Mac's assistance. I couldn't help but think of my team still on the ground fighting as I soared over them. I remembered the words Juno had once said to me, that when I leave a situation with the dark shadows, the fight soon ends. Because it was my energy the dark forces were ordered to chase. Wherever I went, they were at my back or would be waiting for me if they could get ahead of the guardian of the key. So far they had not. With my escape, at least those chosen to protect me would have a chance to remain safe. I flapped my long wings in three graceful pumps to lift higher and called to them below as I flew beyond their sight and straight into the night sky.

Would they remain safe? I reconsidered. A dark angel belonging to Tarsamon wouldn't allow anyone to paralyze her and get away with it. Kevin reassured me the team's safety was not my concern. I disagreed with him then, carrying the grief at hearing Elise had died at the hands of C-05 on the last quest. Of course, that had been a lie from C-05 to manipulate a situation between us. Even now, if we were dealing with a force that could penetrate the power, the additional protection provided by the keys, that meant Tarsamon had in fact grown stronger than the Alliance or the Soltari could have predicted. And though I was as vulnerable now without my protection as at any point in this quest, my concern for the members of my team was still a factor. It had to be. My choices, if wrong, would weigh heavily on the outcome of this quest and their futures.

I flew well past the village in the direction opposite the cliffs and the site where we had met with C-05's body tacked to a stake. I wanted no part of anything more that reminded me of the conquest for the second key. All my focus was on getting to safety so that I could somehow travel to Egypt for the final leg of the trip. But where was safe? The J-man? Ardan? *No, neither is possible.* The last time I was in the realm, it had been penetrated by the dark forces. The evil was pushed back to the perimeter dividing the two halves of Ardan by the elves and the wolf leader, Karshan. The realm might no longer be a safe place for me, not when Jade and I suspected a possible infiltration or, at minimum, someone conspiring against the mission. Where could I possibly go where the dark forces would not follow my energy?

The answer was all too clear. *Nowhere.* In Ardan I had more allies. But that meant I'd have to sleep to travel to that world, and I was too revved up to rest. A twinkling in the distance caught my eye, distracting me. The color of the light was what I had learned to trust, to follow. Orange meant evil, whereas white or blue was associated with good. This light was a warm glow of soft white. I aimed straight for it, as though it were a beacon calling to me in the dead of night.

As I drew closer, I landed on a branch in a tree slightly off to the side and away from the still twinkling light and waited to see if there was anyone else who had also witnessed the small, repeating flash.

Several long moments passed before all felt safe. I swooped closer to see the twinkling was coming from beneath a cluster of rocks, camouflaged in vines with brush surrounding. Only someone with eyes as sharp as a hawk could've found such a light. *Maybe it's a trap.* No one knew I would be headed in this direction. But it was unwise to take anything for granted with certain powers in existence, those known and unknown about the dark forces. I shifted into my human form and, under the cover of dark, stepped cautiously closer to the rocks. A sudden weak sensation swam through my muscles as if they were still adjusting. *I must need sleep. And I definitely need clothing.* If I was going to be transforming between hawk and human more often, I'd need to rectify the lack of such necessities. *If anything looks suspicious, I can just shift again and fly away.* A couple more steps and I could see an object dangling in the center of the blinking soft white glow, hanging in midair. Beside the object was what looked like a scroll. I glanced over my shoulder to be sure no one was behind me. *Looks okay.* The light dimmed. My every sensation was finely tuned to hear the crack of a single blade of grass or to feel the presence of energy, whatever form of good or evil that might be lurking nearby. But there was nothing, nothing but me, a scroll, and what appeared to be a ring suspended by the no-longer-twinkling light. My gaze left the ring and wandered to the opposite side as I lifted some fabric. It looked like my size and shape. I hurried to put on the clothing and stopped. The shirt and pants were a perfect fit for my five-foot-ten-inch frame. That meant someone had been expecting me. But who? How could they?

I went to the scroll and unrolled the parchment paper. The edges appeared burned as if it had waited centuries to be discovered or had a rough time on its path here. A simple script had been etched across the surface. The language was one I recognized as that of the elves. While the memory of my long history with Kevin might have been blocked, I carried the necessary tools to decipher, react, strategize, everything that would help me complete the mission.

The ring has been enhanced with the properties of protection you have come to know in your previous encounter with a figure known as Lady Mara.

My gaze left the page, remembering. Lady Mara, a woman I'd met in Europe on a trip with Kevin, was the owner of a unique antique shop. As it turned out, that shop housed a number of weapons she created specific to the warrior by using current DNA to match their gifts. She had given me a second ring that held a power of protection the silver ring did not. England was where I'd discovered my team and the fact that the mission was much more than a figment of my imagination or some construct of a very lucid dream. Lady Mara explained the ring could hide my true energy as the Light Carrier from any evil seeking me. But I'd lost that ring somewhere on my trek through Scotland in search of the first key and after I'd been captured by the dark forces. My eyes skimmed farther down the scroll:

The ring is provided to mask the power of the keys. Take care, as it will conceal your energy as well. One source alone can trace your energy as you move through the realms. The clothing is provided with your recent acquisition of the gift the warrior has bestowed upon you.

Gift. While I could appreciate the benefit of being able to fly, I still considered the giver with such disdain I didn't believe I would ever find myself able to view his injection without contempt. And yet that *gift* had saved my life at least twice already.

I quickly put the clothing on and flipped the scroll over. *Blank.* There was no word on how I would leave this realm unharmed. *My energy and that of the power I carry may be invisible once I put the ring on. But I'm still recognizable.*

"Not as a hawk," a voice said from behind me.

I whirled around to see Jade stepping inside. "What the hell are you doing here?"

"Tracing your energy."

I reached for the ring. My fingers penetrated the light holding it before the illumination faded completely. A glow of green filled the cavern in its place as Jade lit what looked like an oversized glow stick. With the silver band on my right hand, I slid this second ring on a finger of my left hand. When I shifted into the hawk, the silver ring remained fixed on what had changed into my leg, just above my lovely clawed foot. Yeah, that gift was useful, I considered, but I didn't have to like it.

Jade reached for the scroll and set it to fire. "We don't need any-one finding it who shouldn't."

"Doesn't look like anyone else who should will find it, either." I lifted my eyes from the remaining smoke to him. "If *you* traced my energy, then—"

"Don't worry about it. Not yet," he said, anticipating my question as he brushed his hands together. "They aren't looking for me. The dark forces aren't engaged to trace my energy. But it doesn't mean they won't put two and two together eventually."

"My team won't be able to find me. So that means it's just you and me. Have I got this right?"

He laughed. "Lucky you, huh? I gave instructions for Mac to redi-rect the team to Ardan."

"You what? They are all the protection I have from realm to realm, with the exception, maybe, of the wolves in Ardan." Karshan, the great gray wolf I'd met in Ardan, had said he and the pack were able to move between worlds should I need them. I didn't know if there was a limit to how far into the realms they could travel, but with my team removed, I might need to pull another source of protection. "They also need help getting out of the jungle."

"Relax, will you?" Jade said. "The authority guiding this quest has altered the strategy should the dark forces develop a stronger tool to penetrate the keys' power. That tool is the dark angel. Until she had you, we weren't sure if she could maneuver past the elements of the keys. My sources could never confirm for certain. My team will lead yours out of the jungle because my team is not being hunted. They can guide the rest of your team to safety by tracing them out, once we find a safe passage."

"When you say *authority*, are you referring to the Alliance or the Soltari?" With our suspicion that a betrayer existed somewhere in the Alliance, I needed to confirm who wanted to change the strategy.

"Sara, for God's sake. The Soltari. I work for them, just as you and your team do. The Alliance makes decisions based on the order from the Soltari. You know that." He paused from rifling through his pack, looked up at me, and shook his head. "Kevin wouldn't have asked for my help if he thought I was on the wrong side. Is that enough for you to trust me?"

I waited, considering. "Not fully."

"Jesus. Look, I'm not debating with you or wasting precious time trying to convince you. If we don't get out of here soon, there is the possibility they will trace my energy."

"I guess you shouldn't have come then."

He tossed the glowing stick to the ground and leaned back against the cave wall, rubbing both hands over his face. When he was done, he glanced at the ground, his hands gripping the top of his head, mumbling something about friendship and a debt fulfilled. He dropped his hands and lifted his eyes to me. "You may be the most stubborn woman alive, but you and I both know that you're not getting out of here without help. The whole goddamn realm knows it, here and in Ardan, enough for the Soltari to provide multiple sources they deem necessary to aid you. So why don't you forget it's *my* idea and go with the fact that there are others out there with more at stake than just you and your precious love!"

That shut me up. I'd never considered anything else beyond the many human lives to be saved on Earth and my connection with Kevin to be at stake on this quest. I had no idea there were others at risk of losing what might be important to them. Jade had mentioned his army, but only after he'd tried to take the key in a manner compromising any trust. And besides, I'd already remedied that matter by telling him I would make him part of my negotiations with the Soltari. I couldn't do that unless I did get out of here alive.

"There are others with as much to lose as us?" I asked, referring to Jade and myself. The question sounded childlike to my ears.

"They've left you in that much darkness?"

They? The Alliance. I felt my eyes searching for meaning, as if it would be found stuck to the walls of that cave and across the patches of moss and rocks sticking out between my feet.

"I met with the Alliance while on my quest to Scotland in the realm of Randun," I said. "There were a few on the council who argued, were angry at my request to recover the memories of my past lives. I didn't understand at the time, but now..." My voice trailed off as I recalled the distant conversation.

"Look, we have to leave while we can. I want to know the names of the men who were arguing, and as I said, I'll do some checking around."

"Yeah, okay." I nodded, satisfied. "Let's go."

Jade wrapped an arm around me with a look of satisfaction that I'd come to my senses. "I have something for you," he said reaching into his jacket pocket. "You left this when you escaped my tent." He lifted the silver bracelet for me to see. "I'll hold it so you don't drop it again when you shift. But he can find you with it in my possession, when you're near."

"I thought I had to be wearing it for it to work."

"With the ability to trace, I can reflect your energy through a device like this, as long as I'm with you. Trust me now?"

I lifted the corner of my mouth in a small sign of a truce. "A little, yes."

I woke to the sound of familiar voices in hushed tones. *How in the hell did I fall asleep?*

"They'll have the exit that brought you here blocked. Count on it," Jade said.

"Can you trace her past their energy?" Kevin's voice filled my ears in the low and sultry tone that called to me. My heart skipped. I turned to sit upright and felt the pinch in my neck of having slept at the wrong angle against the stone.

"Not if the dark angel is waiting," Jade answered. "She has the power to block my energy. But if she's distracted, she may put down her guard."

"The dark angel is here for one thing, to put Sara out of commission. There's no way she'll allow herself to become distracted. We can't risk that."

"Agreed."

It sounded as though Kevin and Jade were plotting a way out through the main entrance. Was there another way?

"At what point did I fall asleep?" I asked. "I closed my eyes when you traced us..."

"I had to move around a bit," Jade answered as he angled his head toward me. "Took a few minutes."

"Is the team safely out?"

"Out of the barn, yes," Jade said. "They made it out after you left, while the dark angel was temporarily immobile. And they were not happy about the order not to follow us. They only did so after Matt persuaded them it was best. With all of them at your side, they were drawing attention to your location. A multiple source of elevated energy concentrated in one location, you see? Easy to spot. The game has changed and so must our strategy."

"And your men?" I asked, making my way to Kevin.

"They're here in hiding, with your team. Out of danger for now. Tarsamon knows you haven't left the realm and word is the hunt is on. Which reminds me," Jade said, turning to Kevin, "we'll need to trace again to throw them off, in case they have decided to follow us to get to her. I'm thinking we circle back the way we last went. If they aren't after me already, I would expect it to be soon." Jade looked at me. "Demons hunt energy they are ordered to locate. The shadows build their strength by feeding off the fear and weakness of others, which means the shadows will need to leave soon since they've exhausted the villagers. They are lousy at tracking warriors, but still capable."

"I see. And I'm sorry to interrupt." I had felt Kevin's eyes on me the second I spoke. He hadn't tried to send me a thought, but the unforgettable sensations that pulled me to him like a magnet had not faded in our time apart, requiring a brief departure from the current conversation.

"That's the first and only apology I'll probably ever get," Jade muttered as I stepped between the two men.

Kevin's eyes pierced mine in the warm green glow of another of Jade's light-up sticks. The prickles of energy that always chased from my neck and along my arms were followed by heat that caused a muf-fled moan in the center of my chest. I needed to be close, to feel him again. The measure of mere centimeters was all that separated our lips, as I gazed at the full mouth before me. If I allowed myself to taste, I would be lost in the soft, wanting pull of his kiss.

"You okay?" Kevin said, slipping an arm around my waist. I nod-ded and brushed my hand along the side of his cheek.

"How are you feeling?"

"Much better." His palm reached up my back.

"Ahem," came the sound of Jade's voice from behind me. "Hate to break up what you got going there, but if we don't get moving, you'll have nothing."

I stepped back and, in a single blink, broke the gaze and turned to Jade. "I'm going to need to pass through the entrance to the realm alone, under the guise of a hawk."

"We can't risk them identifying you," Kevin said. "That form may be swift but it's not one of the strongest."

"And shifting when you haven't yet mastered it can leave you weak for a certain period," Jade added.

"It allows for speed and agility to maneuver above and beyond any-one blocking the exit," I countered. "Besides, my identity is cloaked with the ring from the elves." I lifted the finger that held the band containing the chiastolite stone.

"There's no time to argue about it now. Jade's right. We'll be back after we try to throw the dark forces off our trail."

"They already think you're dead." *I don't see why you must go.*

With one finger, Kevin lifted my chin so that my eyes met his. "I've missed the moments you wish for me to be near you but are afraid to say so." He placed a single kiss on my lips.

Embarrassed at him exposing my thought and a moment of weakness, I lowered my eyes to avoid further exposure to his keen attention.

"Sara, they've identified my energy once and it wouldn't take long to recognize it again." Kevin stepped past me and put a hand on Jade's shoulder.

"It's a precaution. That's all," Jade said. "Stay here. We won't be long."

I nodded. There was no fight left in me to argue. The choice to remain agreeable had me thinking how ironic that I would give in to a command from a man I wasn't yet sure I could trust.

The silence in what was left of the green glow was blending more into darkness as each moment passed. Time crawled at the heels of desperation. How would I get out if I couldn't fly past the demons that were assuredly guarding us from passing? My mind raced to think of other possible solutions for returning to our world or to Egypt, where the next key could be found. Did the J-man have magic that was powerful enough to move me from one realm to another? Was there another port of entry, perhaps? The questions were endless. I was sure I could hear each second ticking by without my thoughts to fill the blanket of silence as my only companion.

The dark brought with it the risk of overthinking. I didn't like that I overanalyzed almost everything, but it had served me well in my practice as a psychiatrist. The path to this place had been unfathomable until my life had been interrupted, forcing me to explore Ardan and the mysteries of being immortal, as a spirit. My body would die one day and my soul would continue on for eternity. Kevin and Cerys were proof of that. I felt the door to the darkest corner of my mind, where I kept hidden the deepest pain in this life, unlock. There was a time when the worst thoughts were the cruel behavior of my parents. But now, it was having watched Kevin dying.

I didn't need minutes to consider the thought or how it had seeped through my body to pierce every emotion and nerve with such pain before I could feel the heat creeping through my center and following the familiar path across my skin. *Cool it.* But it was too late. I'd shifted, even faster than I had falling out of that barn window to the fight below. The weight of the additional ring was present on the ankle of my left foot, now a claw. The elves must have enhanced it in a similar manner to remain in place, like the silver ring on my right hand. Thankfully, I could shift and still keep my energy hidden.

I tried to shift back to my human form but was unable. The

memory I'd used to change into a hawk was still too fresh. Perhaps another of happier times could replace it. But each time I tried to reach for a loving or kind thought, the horror of the memory fell over it like a dense cloud. I was growing tired of the effort. The light had gone out and nothing of a million twinkling stars or moonlight in the vast sky filtered into the cave. The darkness was as though the Powers That Be intended on aiding us in concealment. With that thought, I eased my feathered body into the corner between a jutting rock and the wall to drift to sleep and into the passage that might take me to Ardan to ride out what was left of the darkness. Hopefully Jade and Kevin would make it back before I was discovered by someone else.

Trust in the power the elves have provided. I am concealed.

I must have said the phrase a dozen times. But in the back of my mind, I still heard Jade's words echo about the uncertainty of the dark angel's ability after she broke through the power of the keys to reach my weakest point. If that were possible, what other unknowns were we gambling with?

19

The depths of night were ever present in the realm of Ardan, making me wonder if that had anything to do with visiting only when I slept. With the soft illumination from an unknown source to light my way, I glanced at my feet and realized I was human again and thankfully clothed.

The Soltari resided somewhere in this realm, though didn't gather their white shadowed faces to show themselves unless it was deemed necessary by them. And while I had business with the Soltari, I hadn't yet formulated how I would approach the subjects of not only changing the rules that governed the forces of good and evil, but also potential punishments of those who sought to aid the entity on a mission, should it fail. I was not yet prepared to meet with them until I had all of the bargaining chips in hand, namely all three keys. That begged the question as to why I'd arrived in Ardan with no specific intention to do so. Who had summoned me? I strode ahead only a few paces, getting comfortable in the flexible yet snug-fitting black pants and matching long-sleeved shirt, noting the material was stronger than a jersey-type material but moved like it.

I wonder if I can take this back with me? Will I wake wearing it?

A small chuckle nearby had me peering deeper into the darkness to where I'd heard it. "Anything that aids you can be taken with you. Remember?" The voice was familiar but I had yet to see the face to match. A few more steps and the leader of the elves appeared as though he were some sort of magician.

"Eldor," I said. "I have you to thank for the ring and the clothing."

"We keep eyes on you and try to provide as much as possible where we can."

"You seem different," I said. "What's wrong?" His eyes had lost some of their shine and the tone of his voice was a fraction off. In place was a hollow and distant gaze set on one thing I had yet to discover.

"You have done well in acquiring the second key."

"But?"

"War has been declared upon Ardan as well as on Earth." He reached for my hands and brought my fingers to his lips, kissing them. "My dear, what you see is fatigue. The armies have been fighting nonstop for the last several days." He released my hands.

"Tarsamon has set his sights on obtaining Ardan as well as taking over Earth to grow his forces?"

He released a breath to the sky. "To extinguish the rule of balance over good and evil and have one force, his, lead Earth, as well as all of the realms. While he was banished to the darker side of Ardan, he built the forces he needed to unleash a power we could never have imagined. He's been working on a plan to seek vengeance since being expelled from the Alliance." He paused. "He doesn't need more forces to win a war. But if he attacks you and Ardan, he will win his claim over Earth."

"Can the powers that exist here not stop the forces? I mean, the Soltari with their strength..."

"The guiding powers have been infiltrated."

"So it's true."

His eyes moved toward the ground and back to mine. "We aren't sure how. Members of the Alliance are chosen for their loyalty to the Soltari. So many years of dedication to the rule. Tarsamon could only have managed to slip dark energy through someone who was unhappy or angry. Which means the amount of discord in the Alliance must have been growing but hidden for some time. More and more relies on the last key and holding on to the two you have. More importantly, that you stay out of the grasp of the darkness. We heard rumor of a possible demon that could penetrate the power the keys but believed it nothing more than that, a rumor. The powers were built to be indestructible."

"They can't touch them," I said. "The dark angel only knows how to filter past the power to reach my mind, my thoughts. She was able to interfere with my abilities, but I don't yet think she has determined how to inactivate the actual power of the keys."

"Good." He nodded. "But given enough time in your thoughts, massaging your mind, the angel might be able to unlock the power of them, weakening you and destroying the keys. You can't allow yourself to be caught, to end up in their hands. You are the only hope for Earth, but now also for Ardan."

I felt the weight of the additional responsibility heaped on my shoulders. I lowered my head, considering, and nodded my understanding.

"We will guide you," he said. "But one of your biggest weaknesses is trust and it will be tested consistently on this quest. Know who you can rely on."

"The ability to shift has created an additional challenge. C-05 and his knack for grazing the energy of any living creature by merely brushing against them and shifting into that animal, human, bird"—I flung my hand in the air—"whatever he chooses. The point is, I can't be sure of anyone who can change their form. The energy of my opponent is no longer identifiable. I can't feel their ill intentions until they are beside me. That's too risky."

"Agreed."

"C-05 might be dead after my last visit with him, but there have to be others like him."

Eldor was silent. Too silent, I thought. "What? There's more, isn't there?"

"C-05's fate was to roam the realms without form, a lost soul, for treason against the Soltari. They won't take him back."

"Nor should they." I reflected on the body I'd seen pinned to the stake. "He's tried to return?"

Eldor's gaze dropped and then lifted to meet my stare, the answer reflected in his eyes.

"No. No, no, no. He may live." *God only knew how.* "But there is no way I'll have him on my...no way I will ever trust him. He will never be part of this quest. And further, if I suspect his energy is around me in any form, I'll be sure he's good and dead without a single other soul around for him to brush energy with. I won't leave him pinned to anything with mystical markings that condemn him."

"We know." His calm and steady gaze eased me a little. "He's under continuous protective guard now."

"He's so damn lucky," I said under my breath as I walked off the rest of my irritation in a self-made circle. "Guy is luckier than anyone I've ever met," I added.

"Sara."

"What?" My tone still held the frustration I carried and would never otherwise have directed toward Eldor. "I'm sorry." I turned to him.

"You'll need to trust Kevin and Jade."

Kevin I could trust. It had taken a little time, but I had learned to. Jade was another story.

"We have to keep you in hiding from the dark forces." He rubbed his forehead with his index and middle fingers. "This provides for some difficulty in moving you from realm to realm as the forces have increased their strength and aptitude for gaining access to you. Listen carefully. The way out is with the ring, to hide your energy. But it can't be through the same cave opening that brought you into the realm. The dark forces know you can shift into a hawk, because they've seen it."

The barn.

"They'll be looking for this form, even if your energy is undetectable. And because your location underground has been discovered, you'll need to follow a path through the jungle around the caves."

"I trust you. You gave us passage from Scotland undetected and led us to the Yucatan under the guise of the cloaked ship."

"That ship cannot be relied upon in the realm you are in. You will be led out. Do not deviate by trying to exit the realm the same way you came in. The details of how are being finalized."

"How will I know where to go?"

"The J-man will lead you. You'll know. I must get back," he said. I nodded.

"The task you're faced with is wrought with more danger than we could have anticipated, not only for Earth but now for Ardan." He started to turn.

"Wait," I said, remembering one last item that had crossed my mind only a couple of times. "Can you tell me why I haven't seen Cerys?"

Eldor smiled. "My dear, he is Kevin's spiritual guide. And while you are bound to both, he works to aid Kevin."

"And where is my spiritual equivalent?" I had wondered that for some time.

"She is at work for you, ensuring all the contacts are in place once you arrive in Egypt to recover the last key."

I reflected on how that might work. One entity. One human. Both part of the same whole. Was that the parallel existence theory I'd once read about? I thought I'd seen this spirit of myself, once, talking with Kevin in the recent past, when I'd come upon him in conversation in Ardan. I hadn't been spying, per se. I'd been called to Ardan and the path had led me to him. The moment I'd been detected, she had sped away like a shooting star. In retrospect, perhaps I was meant to see, to know there was indeed something to be trusted that was working beyond my limited beliefs.

I should have left following my conversation with Eldor. There had been no other reason to stay. As I stepped through the forest, expecting to wake at any moment, my route was intercepted by a paved path of stones.

I know this. I've seen it before.

I followed the cluster of smooth rock and found a cheery bunch of red yarrow. The gold centers of the flowers were as though lights had been landscaped into the darkened forest floor, illuminated by the soft glow that guided me.

Cerys. It was a calling card that he was near. I stepped along the path, found another cluster of yarrow, and stopped where the stones ended. As I looked up, a glittering array of twinkling white lights filled a small circle in front of me that I could swear hadn't been there earlier. I'd never known Ardan as anything more than a place of learning, or where the Alliance met to decide the fates of the immortals in the deepest hollow of a large tree. This was new to me. I stepped into the circle and the warm, tingling feeling of his presence swept over me in such a way I couldn't help the small gasp that escaped from between my lips. I closed my eyes and felt it again. And when I opened them, it wasn't Cerys standing in front of me but Kevin.

"Oh." A single word, choked off by the unexpectedness of seeing him, was all I could manage. The sensations I'd come to know from the spirit I had loved across lifetimes filled my soul with as much light as the darkest energy that had once pinned me to a wall.

"Surprised, my love?" he said.

"A little. Though I suppose I shouldn't be. You and Cerys are one and the same. It makes sense that I would feel these sensations from both of you."

"Perfect sense." He stroked a finger along my cheekbone.

"They are much stronger in Ardan than when I'm with you when I'm awake."

"You aren't encumbered by the 'noise' of your human form here, all the bothering thoughts, the random sounds scattered all about."

"So it seems." I lifted my hand to his cheek. "I have missed you."

"And I you."

"How did you find me in Ardan?"

"I had business to attend to and sensed your presence."

"How? The ring from the elves. They said it would hide my energy." *Is it possible I'm only protected on Earth and not also in Ardan?* Maybe Kevin was just especially sensitive to my presence. After all, no one else, none of the other team members, had tracked me down in Ardan since I'd received the enhanced ring.

"It's possible the additional security the ring provides isn't needed in Ardan," Kevin said. "Tarsamon would be hunting for you in the jungle, where your body holds the power of the keys, not your spirit." He brushed a few strands of hair from my forehead. "Tarsamon would never consider approaching you where you have the elves' protection."

"I'm sure you're right." I sighed, wanting to believe him. While the likelihood of the evil coming after me in Ardan was slim, I also recalled that no one had expected Tarsamon to cross over the border separating the dark side from the rest of the immortals. Preferring to lean on the small comfort found in Kevin's reassurance, I switched gears. "I needed the rest, anyway. I wasn't able to shift into my human—"

He placed an index finger to my lips, effectively quieting me. "I found you, there and here."

"I hate that you had to return and see me in that form," I said.

"Why do you say it with disgust?"

"It's not who I am, not what I chose."

"Your shifted form is a graceful creature, with skill and agility. *That* is who you are." He paused. "Besides, I never saw you as a hawk. Your body had shifted by the time I found you, curled into a ball as tight as you could get into, wedged against the wall. I have a request of you," he said. I held my gaze with his and waited. "Let go of your worry for me. It will not serve your purpose. Understand?"

"As an empath, I can't help but feel your pain and want to ease it for you."

"It's not yours to carry."

As true as that statement might have been, I couldn't forget what I had experienced through whatever spell the dark angel had cast over me. *I will make this right for you. I will ease your pain.*

"You returned my life. You owe me nothing. All I want is right now, right here, with you." He stepped so that we were no more than a breath apart. "Don't you see? Time with you is precious. Not only could it be taken from us, but it restores my soul. Do you understand that I'm not complete without you?"

"Yes, because I feel that way, too."

I was beginning to understand the feeling of emptiness without him all too well. But only because time with him had gifted me the love I'd never allowed to seep into my heart. That void was a feeling I'd fought so hard never to know, and why I didn't allow people I could care for close to me. Love, to me, was a weakness that had no place in my life, despite the reward that assuredly came from it. That is, until now. I couldn't ignore our connection. Nor could I repress the desire for what my body and soul needed in order to feel joined with him. He had woven a mystical tapestry through me that had become a thread of life, and one I couldn't deny any longer. And that thread was anything but weak.

He bent his head toward mine and placed a kiss on my lips so softly, as though sensing me for the first time. His warm breath and delicate touch had me leaning into him. I wanted to feel the scratch of the facial hair that had come in over the past couple of days, the weight of his strong frame against my breasts, and the arms that said *mine* as they enclosed me to him. Time had indeed stopped and allowed me to feel as though we had eternity, even if only for a few minutes. The very contrasts of his strength and softness, confidence and need were the key to conquering the rigid wall of stubbornness. He'd known it from the moment he met me. His kiss deepened and pressed harder, claiming.

He eased back, breaking the kiss with only a fraction of space between us. "My God, it never ceases to amaze me how the pull to you is stronger than the last time we were together."

"For me, too. I can't explain it." I slid my fingers through his hair and drew him back to me.

"There isn't much time," he mumbled against my lips. "I need to feel you."

The tingling sensations and heat flooded my body in waves. I closed my eyes as a faint breath escaped against his ear. He swept me up and began walking. But to where? Ardan was an open forest with vacant areas set aside for discussion or practice of our skills. I opened my eyes to see a pagoda a few feet ahead of us, the flowing panels of which were carried on a current of air that lifted them in waves of white.

That wasn't there when I arrived. The twinkling of white lights is what I remember.

It was all I could dream up without more time. With his mouth pressed upon mine, his answer floated through my mind. *I'll make love to you in our bed, the place we've kept together in Ardan, when this mission is over. For now, will this do?*

I might have had a family and a lifestyle with a lot of money, but I was in no way high maintenance. "You've bedded me on a cold forest floor with tree trunks and scattered ferns as our only concealment, and that did just fine. This"—I lifted my eyes to the top of the canopy as he lowered me to a mass of pillows scattered about and returned my gaze to the smoldering eyes in front of me—"is lovely."

The whites of the lights blurred around us as his eyes skimmed over me. All I wanted, all I needed was his touch. His fingers stroked my jawline, my neck, and moved over my breast, answering my desire. But I needed to feel skin against skin. The muscles of his back, the pectorals that pressed against me, and his smooth, rhythmic stroke were going to be more than a memory from days past. I arched up to meet him and slipped my arm beneath his and, with a little coaxing, sent him onto his back to enjoy what pleasure I had to give him. I stripped the black shirt from my body and proceeded to unfasten his pants. He reached a hand to my neck and guided me down toward him. As I opened my lips to him, his hand grew tighter. In a protective embrace, he pressed my cheek against his.

"Don't move until I tell you, understand?" he said into my ear.

Those weren't the words I'd expected to hear. And while I'd entertained fantasies of play with him that involved mild control and submission, this didn't have the feel of such a scenario set in the trusted hands of Kevin Scott. My eyes drifted to his, not answering him. The lights that twinkled in welcome of our presumed encounter had grown darker, as though a filter had been placed over them.

And I knew what had made its way to us. Despite his warning, I whirled off Kevin and pulled my shirt over my head. With his otherworldly ability of speed, he was already buttoned and sword drawn. The soft, pillowed world vanished, as though someone had blown out a candle along with the wish of solace and reconnection.

"Together at last." The deep sound that was only Tarsamon's unmistakable voice filled our quiet retreat.

"He's mine," I said to Kevin. "Don't even try to argue it with me."

"No, Sara."

"How did you find your way into this area of the realm?" I asked, seeing the red eyes ahead in the distance. There was no body visible, not even the cloak. Tarsamon blended with darkness as if he was the night itself.

"Really. It's surprising how you underestimate me. There is no reason you should still be alive."

"Except that, by killing me, you'd release the keys and destroy your plan of consuming Earth."

"Otherwise, I'd have to kill you simply because I don't care for the overbearing strength you carry. It annoyed me when we were in the Alliance together, and that in and of itself is enough to rid the realms of you."

A flash of memory blazed across my vision of his fists pounding on the table and of me leaning forward into that anger, more adamant that he was wrong about what direction to take a mission from another time and place. We had been equals back then, high-level members of the Alliance, set to direct a war that had been taking place in a realm far from Ardan or Earth. He'd been known by many names on several quests he had taken on in various realms, but acting as part of the Alliance, we remained true to our spiritual identities as Tarsamon and Arwyn. Over time, I'd grown to despise his name more and more.

"Sara, don't taunt him. Just back away," Kevin said, interrupting further recollection. *At least until reinforcements arrive. You can't win a fight with him.*

Without moving my head, I flicked a look at Kevin and returned my attention to Tarsamon. *Trust me for once. Will you?*

Kevin was not unjustified in directing me to back away. I had lost in battle to Tarsamon's forces in the past and been carried to the darker side of the realm, trapped, and implanted with illness. But something had happened since that occurrence that I couldn't explain. I no longer felt weak or fearful in Tarsamon's presence. Maybe it was the last quest and the fact that I'd had to kill a man. That had been my first killing of a man in this lifetime and I wasn't comfortable with it. Or maybe the additional confidence in my ability was from freeing the serpent god. Whatever the reason, I was much stronger following my entrance to the Yucatan. I'd been given the knowledge once when some of my memories had been returned that I was as strong as the evil that would hunt me. I was young in my development then, not really believing the message or much of anything concerning the quest. But now, I knew who I was. The strength I carried was fit to engage with a power as strong as one that ruled the dark realm of Ardan. The key to that strength, I believed, was in the release of my fear, the fear that I would fail.

"Why wait for another chance?" I said, stalking toward the red lights of the eyes that glowed a short distance away.

"Jesus H. Christ," Kevin mumbled beside me.

The figure that looked like the grim reaper revealed its outline in the darkness but remained unmoving. How could he resist the temptation to take out the Soltari's leading weapon against him? And would he, knowing how it could interfere with all that he'd planned for his expansion?

"A fight is what you desire. I shall give it to you, and there will be no mercy for you to find in death. But one condition. None of your otherworldly powers can be used."

"The power of the keys cannot be set aside for a mere fight."

"Of course not. Weapons only," he said as a glimmering blade of steel appeared in the skeleton-like hand. Several others lined up in midair for the choosing, including the dual blades Eldor had once given me but that had long been lost somewhere after I'd dove into the underground caverns.

"No, Sara," Kevin said. "This was never part of the Alliance's plan. Just get the keys and stop him that way."

"That can't happen," I said to Kevin, keeping my eyes on the target in front of me. I stopped a few feet from Tarsamon. "There's a personal vendetta here, in addition to the agenda to consume the energy. He will never stop hunting me, in this realm or any other. Wouldn't you agree?" I asked of Tarsamon.

"Your perception has not diminished," Tarsamon replied. "You've become stronger than I anticipated."

He transformed his appearance from the dark entity into the man I had met with months earlier, prior to the onset of the quest. At that time, I was being introduced to my role as the Light Carrier and what it would entail. He had appeared as any ordinary man, attempting to appeal to my rational state of mind by asking me to see clearly what the human race had created and how their carelessness would eventually result in their undoing. He would hasten the process, for his own means, but claimed to be putting humanity out of its slow pain. He was then as civil and clean-cut as the image standing before us now, and still every bit a killer.

"While it wouldn't help me to end your life, now that you've acquired two of the keys"—he tapped the sword on the ground twice before lifting it to the level of my waist but still beyond my immediate reach—"I will enjoy watching your pain, again and again. You see," he said, raising a palm to the sky, "you can't hide, not even in Ardan. Not anymore."

It was true, for a time, that Ardan had been sealed from evil, guarded by the elves. But at some point between being born to my predetermined life on Earth and obtaining the first key, Tarsamon had not only been growing his forces and the dark energy but also figuring out how to break past the barrier put in place by the Soltari to keep him away from the rest of the immortal souls. And using C-05, a former member of the Alliance, he had received key information allowing penetration of the realm, I had no doubt.

"Weapons it will be." I uttered the words before I had the chance to give the idea a second thought. *Am I crazy? I'm about to fight the strongest evil that's been banned by the most powerful entity governing the immortals. I may feel strong, but am I strong enough?*

Don't do this. Kevin sent the warning in thought to me.

I don't see that I have a choice.

You always have a choice.

"A moment, please," I said to Tarsamon. He waved a hand to proceed with all the manners of the prim and proper human he reflected.

I turned to Kevin. "There isn't a choice in this case. Tarsamon has grown his forces and crossed boundaries never expected by the Soltari."

"And what do you think you'll accomplish by fighting him, other than getting yourself seriously injured? It's not a delay we can afford."

"I know. I know how it seems, how it sounds."

"How it is, Sara," Kevin corrected.

"There is a draw here. One that I don't believe I have a choice to turn away from. Despite what appears irrational on the surface, I have to do this. I can't explain it further."

He huffed out a breath and held my gaze. "I'll stand beside you no matter what. You must know that by now. And I'll fight with you despite disagreeing."

I flashed a smile. "I know you will. But I'm going to have to ask you not to this time."

"Absolutely not. I have one job here, and that is to protect you so that we can remain together. If you care anything about that, you won't ask me to idly stand by."

I let the silence pass between us, growing strength in my persistence for this request as each second passed. Kevin shook his head, either in disbelief or conceding to my desire to fight alone. I wasn't sure. The feelings coming from him were mixed in frustration, pain, strong will, and a desire to allow me to follow what guided me on this mission. The battle within was a fight all its own for him.

"I won't disappoint you, or those who have put their lives on the line for me with the Soltari," I said.

"You never have. One condition." He paused. "If I can no longer feel your energy, we intervene."

We?

"He won't kill me."

"He thinks he can put you out of commission, to stall your quest until he has fulfilled his mission to bring a reign of darkness over Earth. If he succeeds, you may never get to that final key."

"I know."

"Then I don't get this." His tone was growing less tolerant.

"Nor do I. Like I said, it's something I have to do."

"Give me the option to intervene."

"If you no longer feel my energy and only then."

He nodded his acceptance. I shifted my attention to my opponent to see what I guessed were two-dozen elves standing several feet behind him, bows drawn and aiming for the harmless-looking man in front of me, Tarsamon. I turned my gaze in the opposite direction and saw the rest of my team standing a few feet behind me. Why were they here? How much time had actually passed since I'd fallen asleep?

Juno approached Kevin with a look that could kill. "What the hell do you think you're about to allow here? You're going against every rule we agreed to in coming on this quest."

"Hey," I said, pinching at Juno's sleeve. "He's mine, okay?" I said, referring to Tarsamon. "You want to go after someone over it, then it's me, not Kevin."

Juno looked back at Kevin. It had been everyone's understanding, until now, that Kevin was in charge of the final call when it came to defending my life. Kevin only shook his head.

Juno pierced me with a glare. "You don't know what you're doing, what unrest you'll cause with the forces guiding this mission," Juno said to me.

"I actually have a good idea about it. And I know that coming on this mission meant a large sacrifice in some way for you. I'm not going to let anyone take something precious from you or anyone else here."

He shook his head, a bitter look plastered across his face. "You don't have the means to control that. Goddammit." He turned on his heel and went back to join the rest of the team.

Everything was on the line for a fight. I couldn't explain why it needed to happen, instigated by the evil that waited patiently with a smug look on his face, as though he'd already won. Tarsamon must have found such pleasure in seeing the fracture of the team that stood by me. If there was any truth to the "unrest" in the forces caused by this interruption, then so be it. I needed to root out a traitor, maybe two, in the Alliance anyway. The Soltari was just another matter I needed to address. I'd come pretty far without any real effort in separating my forces and had managed to add to my list of tasks a slew of fixer-uppers.

Kevin shot a look to *our* opponent and gave me one final stoic glance before joining the others. I turned to see my team had moved to the edge of the field. A vacancy opened up in my soul. I hoped this driving force I carried to fight was enough to repair what I'd just undone.

20

"Just what the hell do you think you're doing?" Juno pulled at Kevin's arm as he exited the field and stood with the elves to watch. "Did nearly dying screw with your head?"

Kevin gave Juno's hand a long glance before he looked into his eyes. "Sara leads this quest. She knows what she's doing."

"You'd better damn well hope so. Because the Alliance and the Soltari would never have pitted her against the one force with the strength Tarsamon has. This goes against everything we—"

"Don't you think I know it?" Kevin barked. "I don't have to like it, but I need to follow where she's led."

"And what if she's being led by a hidden dark force?" Aria said as she leaned against a tree trunk, twirling the tip of the long red mane of hair at her shoulder. "And before you say you somehow know she isn't, just remember Tarsamon found a way into this side of the realm that had held him at bay for as long as a century."

"I believe in her."

"Pathetic," Juno muttered, shaking his head. "You're letting your feelings get in the way. That's the very reason the Alliance didn't want you to be part of this mission."

Kevin grabbed Juno by the shirt. "If my feelings were in the way, she wouldn't be out there right now." He pulled the shirt tighter in his fist. "Back off. If you had an ounce of trust in her position on this team, you might give her the chance to show you her strength." Kevin let his hand drop.

"It is no' about her strength, ye understand," Mac chimed in, stepping closer so that each man stood on either side of him. "It's about her survival." He tilted his head toward Kevin. "Ye've got faith enough to leave all that ye care for beside the one person who could end forever for both of ye. What this man is askin' is if ye know that she'll survive it. And because we all have a hefty stake in this, I believe the answer is deserved."

"What if he beats the shit out of her and delivers a blow of another illness to keep her down?" Juno asked. "One the elves don't have a remedy for."

Kevin scanned the faces of the team members, all eyes on him, waiting, and shot a look to Sara, who had just selected her weapon to engage in the fight. "Everything you're thinking, all of you, has run through my head a hundred times before now." He turned his back to Sara. "I don't want to leave her alone. Yes, she will survive because he wouldn't kill her. And the only faith I have that he won't pass her an illness to keep her down is his word that they would not use anything other than weapons, no otherworldly abilities."

"Your putting trust in our enemy's word? That alone could kill this mission," Juno said, shaking his head as he turned away.

"I trust *her*. If her energy begins to weaken, then we go forward." She would understand, he thought, if he intervened before he no longer felt her energy. She might never speak to him again, but eventually she'd soften. Maybe.

"It might be too late by then."

"Kevin has never led us down a path that would risk any of our lives, not on any mission," Matt added.

"He's never trusted a single word from our nemesis, either," Juno countered.

"I think we should trust him."

"If Sara has a chip on her shoulder she's begging to be knocked off by Tarsamon, why not wait until the third key is obtained?" Juno asked. "That way, if she's burdened by some evil curse, nothing is lost. She will have fulfilled the mission."

"And you would be safe," Kevin said.

"Everyone would be safe from repercussions from the Soltari for not finishing the mission." Juno paused. "It makes no sense that she's out there to face him without us to protect her."

"Maybe it does and maybe it doesn't." Kevin eyed Juno, daring him to challenge him. He whirled around to face Aria and Elise. "Don't even think about creating a storm to disrupt either of their vision." Kevin had heard their thought. His abilities were stronger in some areas than the members selected for the team and one reason he was chosen to direct them.

Aria and Elise had the power to manipulate the forces of nature. Not that Ardan was considered natural in the general understanding of a windstorm like the type one might find on Earth. Ardan was a realm where there were familiar aspects of scenery to Earth, like the forest or water that flowed into falls over cliffs. But the air with its ionized scent, like purified water, and the lack of birds or the sound of a breeze were just enough to remind anyone who inhabited both realms that Ardan was anything but a typical natural environment. Despite the differences, nothing would stop Aria and Elise from creating such nuances to intervene as necessary. They'd practiced such creative endeavors countless times in Ardan and even used them in other realms when the situation called for their skills. At this point, anything was on the table for consideration to get Sara out of the direct path of the Dark Lord.

"This needs to be handled in the manner Sara decides is best, and right now that means letting her get close to the evil," Kevin added.

"You must know something you aren't sharing, something we can't detect coming," Juno said. "Because it also makes no sense that you'd protect her so vehemently and yet allow her out there alone."

"She isn't alone. Just give her a little time. That's all I'm asking. If it even begins to look bad, we've got the elves and we can be beside her in an instant."

Juno waited, contemplating what to do. "I'll go along with you on this, but only because Matt is right that you've never risked our lives on any mission. But if you're wrong..."

"I'll owe you the price of the sacrifice you would have had to make to the Soltari if we failed."

"You can't pay out that expense. You know that. Just be sure this choice is right for her and for us."

"Well, now," Mac said in a jovial fashion, "it looks like we've come to an agreement, for the time being."

The clang of steel upon steel rang out from behind the team, drawing attention back to the field as the duel engaged. Sara had come a long way from when Kevin had taken her out to that open field near his home to test her agility, show her a few moves, and more or less help her remember the fighter she was. As he watched her speed and the angles she chose now, he felt a sense of pride at the woman he loved again in yet another lifetime. He'd grown with her time after time, year after year, in every life they'd shared. With any luck, this mission would be their last and he could finally rest not having to worry for her and an eternal future together. Sure, he felt the lust to kill from Tarsamon, as he felt every sensation from any soul. There was passion in every swing from the Dark Lord, and as much in the defensive block Sara held him with. He noticed that his feet had moved a few steps in Sara's direction without any conscious intent. Just beyond the fight and at the opposite border of the field, Eldor stood with his arms folded. His eyes moved past the fight to meet Kevin's. But there was no thought shared. All was quiet, as it should be, with the focus on the two strongest powers in the realm.

Kevin's concentration was broken as a figure flashed beside Tarsamon. In the time it took for him to wonder what had appeared, a wall of gray slipped between Tarsamon and Sara. *Jade.* In all his thought about Sara, he'd forgotten about the one man who had abilities the rest of them didn't.

Sara began beating on the curtain of dark separating her from Tarsamon. "Shit," Kevin said aloud as he ran to catch up with Jade.

"Jade," Kevin said, arriving at his side where he was now standing on the edge of the field, deciding what to do next.

"Why the hell is everyone watching this?" Jade asked. "The shield won't last long. Get her out of here."

"Put the shield down, now."

"Have you, has everyone lost their minds?"

"Just do it. Do it now! Explanation later," Kevin added, sensing his friend's confusion and indecision.

Jade raced across the field. The curtain chased after him, allowing the dark and light forces to face one another again.

Kevin watched for any sign of distress from Sara, relaxing a fraction of a second when he noticed she'd wasted no time reaching a hand toward the neck of her enemy, and before he could shift from a man to his invisible energy hidden inside the cloak as black as his soul. As her fingers clutched his throat, his head lifted but his eyes remained fixed in a deadly stare with hers. A promise, Kevin thought, for Tarsamon to return the challenge. But only if she wasn't powerful enough to kill him. Even so, would she?

The energy that flowed through her veins in white-blue streaks exited her fingertips and raced down Tarsamon's neck and across his chest, illuminating him from beneath the black sweater he wore. The powerful demon held firm in her grasp as he shook from the energy. What sort of strength must it take to command the forces of darkness and light to hold a demon with a poison as potent as Tarsamon's at bay? They'd hardly begun to fight. An instant, one as quick as the blink of an eye, was all she'd needed to—

"How is she doing that?" a voice asked behind him, interrupting his focus on the very same wonderment.

"I'm not sure," he heard himself reply in a distant voice, his eyes fixed upon her. He couldn't feel the usual energy from her, what defined her mood, her personality, or if she felt well. And that was putting him on edge. If he felt her fatigue, a slip of the strength in her hand, anything, he could be beside her in a heartbeat. But he'd made a promise to her. Besides, from this angle, she was doing quite well.

He wondered if the effect was a potion to remedy the evil, if it could. He didn't know what the outcome would be if Tarsamon continued to receive what looked to be so painful. Would it kill him? At the thought, he swore he saw her fingers tighten.

Kevin watched in awe as the Dark Lord caved to her mercy. The words *do it* flitted through his head. He wanted her to be the one to bring Tarsamon's rule and consummation of energy to an end by killing him. If she did, the Soltari would have no reason to call upon them, unless another powerful entity swung the balance into an uneven kilter on the side of evil. The souls of Ardan could live in peace, as they once had for countless millennia. And the worlds they protected could have their lives play out as they were intended, without the need for rescue.

Tarsamon's struggle to hold on to his energy had him turning color, as his head angled back in distress, turning from one side to the other. The eyes that had been dark changed to red, an indication of his mood and obvious fight for breath in the human form. He struggled against the apparent agony as her fingertips indeed sank deeper into his flesh, dispensing a constant flow of energy into him.

A rustle from the large foliage at the edge of where they fought had Kevin's attention shifting. The flick of his eyes to the border told him the elves had shifted, angling their bows on a target he couldn't see. It was no more than a long blink before the sensation of the evil that was present was rushing him as though a torrent of water was about to shake his footing and sweep him away. He turned from the elves to see the dark angel had appeared like a flash nightmare out of the darkness. Her tail wrapped around Sara's legs.

"No!" Mac shouted. A look of desperation plastered his face. "They could kill her."

They? Kevin thought.

"The elves. Call off the strike," Mac shouted. "Not while the energy is exiting her." He ran toward the elves, his palm extended upward as if he alone would stop them. "She could be killed by the very energy she carries."

The elves held their target in sight while the energy continued to flow from Sara into Tarsamon, as if it were its only purpose.

The dark angel scooped Sara from her stable footing on the ground, causing the firm grip she held to be ripped away from the throat of the man she held captive. A long shriek of pain tore from Tarsamon's bare throat and carried into the darkness. That scream was followed by another from Sara. *She'll let me help her now, right?* Kevin thought. It was a far cry from what he'd hoped to hear in the passionate embrace of his lover only minutes earlier. Everything was unpredictable, and that was expected at this stage of the quest. Sara hanging from the tail of the enemy was not. The bows went flying in perfect unison, aiming past Sara and straight into the gathering of shadows and faceless flesh-colored demons that had congregated behind the dark angel, who had assumed command in Tarsamon's place. All that were struck by an arrow lost their form and shifted into a black fog that spun in an upward cloud before disappearing into the sky.

Free of Sara's grip and the energy that had kept him locked in her grasp, Tarsamon collapsed in a pool of black as he returned to his shadowed form to regain energy. The white-blue light that had flowed through Sara's veins into him retracted. Matt waved an arm over his head, indicating the rest of the team move forward into the fight. Juno was already steps ahead of them while Kevin raced for Sara, who had begun to fold herself over to grasp the tail of her assailant but couldn't manage with the slight movements the angel made to keep her well out of reach.

Seconds and I can have her to safety, he thought. His body slammed into the emptiness of air as an invisible wall severed his path to Sara. The dark angel had blocked his attempt to get to her and was now pulling her tail close to her body. He sensed the intention of the creature and hoped he was wrong. The tail whipped out, sending Sara hurling into the trees that lined the border of the field. Kevin struggled to find the opening that would allow him past the wall that held him at bay, his hands frantically searching for a break in the barrier. *Jade.*

"Jade," Kevin called. "Get me to her."

"I can't break through the force," he replied.

Maybe the elves will pull her to safety. But as he ran along the perimeter, he could see ahead that even they didn't have access beyond the shield that kept them separated.

With the dark angel free of Sara and any chance of death to her from the energy Sara carried, the elves fired their arrows high and low, to no avail. The spears hit the invisible wall and fell to the ground like stunned soldiers.

Kevin spotted Sara, crumpled at the base of two trees, motionless. A fine line of the energy encircled her form. Was it protecting her or was it still seeking a negative force to feed into? From what he could see, a trickle of blood ran a path down the side of her face and neck. He shifted his attention across to Tarsamon, whose form was being lifted by the dark angel. The demon dogs snarled, ravenous for the fight as the rest of the team stood blocked from defending Sara's lifeless form. A few of the dogs broke from the pack and cautiously approached her body. Kevin clawed at the boundary, stopping at the sound of electricity crackling and in time to see the dog closest take a charge for the effort, as the white-blue light lunged from the circle and struck the dog. It collapsed, unmoving. The other two beasts ran back to the pack. The dark angel cradled Tarsamon's black form as the army of darkness began moving in retreat.

They must not know how to stop the power of the energy Sara carries.

With his heart in his throat and the pulse driving him forward, Kevin fought to gain access to where Sara lay, until he noticed one of the elves emerging from one end of the forest. His hands were folded in front of him as he chanted into the darkness. Kevin felt a gentle pull at his arm from another elf, as an indication to stand back. He waited, but only for a couple of seconds, as the drive to get to her continued to pull at him.

A soft glow began to light in the hands of the murmuring elf. Steps from where Sara lay in a heap, jade-green eyes beamed in the darkness, like two polished gems under a jeweler's magnifying lamp. The sound of several footsteps behind him had him turning to see the team giving up the search for a way in to join him.

"Can you take down this wall?" Kevin said, turning his attention to the elf that had pulled him back.

"It will be done. Like picking a lock, it requires just the right element of magic to penetrate the strength of what holds this energy in place."

The green eyes grew larger as they approached Sara. The body that owned those eyes could not be seen. It was as black as the night that cloaked its form. Kevin sensed no evil, even though all other darkness had fully retreated to the depths of Ardan from which it had come. He knew nothing should be trusted anymore. The dark forces might be retreating for the time being, but they'd be back as soon as they figured out how to dismantle the energy that protected her. They weren't going to give up. Too much was at stake for them.

Like Tarsamon, is the dark angel also impacted by the effects of the energy Sara carries?

"You're probably right," Jade said, listening to Kevin's thoughts. "The dark angel used an invisible force, just like she did with that barrier, to immobilize her in the barn. She never touched Sara." He let out a breath. "But that demon creature is made with the intent to find ways into the most defensive of places, even the power of the keys. Won't take them long to figure out how, now that they've felt the power of the energy from Sara."

"Maybe that angel is already figuring it out. She lifted Sara with her tail but never actually touched her skin."

The green eyes approaching in the dark had stopped moving closer. *It won't hurt her.*

"The beast is of good energy," the elf said, confirming Kevin's thought.

"Can we be sure?" Juno asked, staring deep into the forest.

"Yes," Jade said. "It's Topetine."

"We thought she might be dead," Juno said, looking at Matt. "Sara's memory...We saw the vision she had of her being carried off, limp as a rag doll, by the serpent god."

"Is she just a spirit or does she exist in flesh and blood?" Aria asked.

"Her energy is—"

"Sh," Kevin interrupted. "You'll break his concentration." Kevin angled his head toward the elf still chanting.

"In the flesh," Jade said.

Sara moved from her crumpled position on her side to flat on her back with the help of the enormous black paw that had pressed upon one shoulder. Mac stepped beside Kevin. Sara's left arm was twisted back in a most unnatural position.

How much longer? Kevin twitched to get to her.

Impatient for the chanting to stop and the barrier to be removed, he reached for the elf but hesitated before yanking his hand back. The sound of crackling followed by orange sparks fell in a linear pattern from high above. The barrier began to dissolve, at the fracture of the spell that held the invisible wall in place.

Sara's eyes flew open and her head lifted inches from the ground, but there was no sign of intentional movement from her. Kevin leaped over what was remaining of the orangey electric current that outlined the wall and caught himself before falling onto Sara. The jaguar warned against further continuance with a fierce growl, protecting her quarry.

"What's wrong with you?" Kevin asked. "I need to know if she's alive, if she's okay." The reply was met with another growl and a step over Sara, forcing Kevin to angle backward. Sara's energy was undetectable, which had him nervous. There had never been a time when he couldn't sense her or feel everything that she did, until now. And yet something other than the animal's energy pulsed within him.

"I don't think she wants you near her," Juno said.

"I'm sure as hell not leaving here without her."

Another loud growl, followed by one more and a fine set of sharp teeth had Kevin reconsidering.

"Damn cat," Kevin said under his breath.

"She knows what's best for Sara," Mac added.

A grunt of dissatisfaction erupted from Kevin's throat.

"That man behind her, just over there"—he pointed diagonally over Topetine's shoulder—"should be of some comfort to you." Jade patted Kevin's shoulder.

Kevin lifted his head. *A J-man.* His face was painted in black, red, and white. He wore the plumed headdress signifying his connection to the serpent god. In one hand he held a feather. The other palm was open, faceup, with smoke rising from it. He lifted that palm and blew across it in Kevin's direction, creating a white veil that held fast in front of Kevin as he drew the feather through it. Kevin had no idea what it meant or what he was supposed to do. All he knew was he needed to get to Sara. Frustration was going to pour out of him. He lifted a hand to clear the air and move again toward the woman he was to watch over. The J-man spoke in tongues that had the effect of locking Kevin's feet in place as the smoke twisted and turned into an image of a scroll. As it unrolled in front of him in the mist of white, he could see a series of equations he recognized as algorithms. Below the smoke was Topetine, resting beside Sara. Kevin took one step back, then another, farther away from the jaguar and Sara until he bumped into Mac.

"What is it?" Mac said. "What's got ye scared?"

"Not scared," Kevin mumbled. "I've forgotten something. I've got to get back. We have to leave the jungle. All of us."

The misty scroll, meant only for his eyes, was a number of steps to unlock passages. It was also a reminder of certain algorithms that needed to be passed to Sara to move forward in the next phase of the mission. That couldn't be done as long as they were in the jungle. Kevin had to get back, to wake up from Ardan.

What happened to a body in dream state, while the spirit was in Ardan, carried over to Earth. Kevin wasn't sure if Sara would be responsive when he woke next to her.

"You're no' worried about her then?" Mac asked.

"She's in good hands." The knowledge and assurance of the fact had come to him as clear as seeing Sara lying on the ground. From behind the dissipating white smoke and farther still behind the J-man, the image of a snake with colored feathers on the top of its head, trailing down the length of the visible body, lifted high above. "He's free. The serpent god. We've completed this quest. Got to move on."

"The man has put him in a trance," Juno said. "He's not thinking straight. Do we go get her? Matt and I can hold Topetine."

"No," Mac said. "He's been given an order to follow from the J-man, a messenger of the serpent god." A low growl in approval came from the jaguar beside Sara.

"How the hell are we getting out of the Mayan jungle with Tarsamon blocking the exit?" Elise asked, watching as Kevin disappeared from beside her.

A slight wrinkle between Jade's brows was the only sign that he'd taken notice of Kevin leaving the realm. "Sara is protected by that." He pointed to the ring provided by the elves. "It will conceal her energy but not yours. As far as we know, my army isn't being targeted yet. That means all of you will need to stay with my men to help you escape. There's a better chance of distracting our enemy if you're with a group that isn't being tracked. Sara, Kevin, and I will arrive at the realm exit ahead of you."

"They thought Kevin was dead," Aria said. "Now they know he isn't. They'll track him to get to her."

"It's a risk we have to take, unless I can trace them separately. As it stands, Sara will not leave his side."

"That can be good and bad," Matt said. "If she's feeling strong enough to try to kill Tarsamon, being with you two is best."

"She might've been successful if the dark angel wasn't watching over. It would've changed everything," Elise said, considering.

"Jade's right. The less company the three of them have, the less dark energy will be drawn to them. We hope," Juno said.

Jade turned to Reed. "Give the order to the men that Sara's team is to travel with them out of the realm, fifteen minutes behind us. You know where I am in the jungle. If you detect any—and I mean any— dark forces, adjust the formation every seven minutes by threes with the men tracing two miles and fifteen degrees in the opposite direction. With each trace, one of Sara's team members goes with each man. That should throw them off for a bit and, with any luck, long enough to get to the exit." He paused before turning his attention back to the team. "I'll track Kevin if he hasn't returned to our hideout," he added.

"All agreed? If you have a better suggestion, speak now." With no reply, he looked at Reed. "I'll await the signal from you that everyone is ready to move. Make it fast. Aria's right. With the dark forces aware Kevin is alive, they'll set their sights on him next."

When Jade awoke back at the cave, he found Kevin cradling Sara in his arms and his head tucked against her cheek.

Of course he would return.

"Hey," he whispered, not wanting to startle him. "You awake?"

Kevin lifted his head. "Yeah."

Jade paused, stunned by the remnants of tears that tracked down Kevin's cheeks. He'd never seen the man, known by all in the realms as the Last Great Warrior, in so much pain. All of the warriors had suffered loss at one point or another, but most kept it to themselves. And, he supposed, Kevin had been alone. The lack of privacy so that the man he called his friend could cope couldn't be helped.

"I can't wake her," Kevin said. "And I think her arm is broken. But her pulse is steady and strong."

Relieved, Jade let out a breath. Having Sara alive would make getting them all out of the jungle easier. Jade searched Sara's face. The blood he'd seen trailing down her cheek and neck in Ardan was still present. For the first time, he thought, the strong-willed fighter actually looked quite weak. "We'll set the arm and I'll trace her with us. You can hold her." Jade turned around to look for a stick to set the arm and to busy himself enough to allow his friend a moment to pull himself together. "You have to trust that they wouldn't let her die, not the dark forces or the Soltari."

Jade wasn't sure if even he believed the statement that rolled off his lips. He probably wouldn't buy it if roles were reversed. But it was all he could offer as he stood and stepped several feet beyond the cave walls to relieve himself and find a sturdy branch suitable for setting an arm. He waited a couple of minutes more, until he couldn't wait any longer.

"We've got to go. Tarsamon's forces will be wanting to recover their lost package here." He lifted his chin to Sara. Jade ripped a strip of cloth from his bag, placed the stick he'd picked up against Sara's arm.

"I'll do it," Kevin said, placing his hand over the stick. As the former head of the ER department at a top New York hospital, he began setting the arm and wrapping it in a makeshift splint. "Do you know the way to get out of here or where we go from here?"

"Not exactly. I've got a way back to the underground cavern. From there, you can get us back to the exit, right?"

"It'll be overrun with Tarsamon's forces, but yeah. If Sara is protected, you and I will have to find a way through. But I'd need her awake first." Kevin tied off the last knot for the splint.

"I gave it some thought when the J-man had you under his spell," Jade said. "I think Tarsamon wanted to battle with her to weaken her enough to have the dark angel get her back to their territory. I don't think he expected the power she carried to overcome him."

"I don't think she planned it, either." He paused as Sara began to awaken. "But she was going to kill him."

"Too bad she didn't. Because the wrath he'll unleash now is going to feel like jumping from the frying pan into the fire."

"You okay, love?" Kevin asked. "How do you feel?"

I moved carefully. "Sore but okay, I think."

"Wait," Kevin said, angling his head toward Jade. "What did you say about the J-man's spell?"

"Don't you remember? You mumbled something about algorithms. I'm taking over directing this team if you don't—"

"Oh, God. The codes."

"What codes?"

"Never mind. We have to get out of here," Kevin said as he stirred over Sara. "Don't worry," he said to her. "We're on our way."

Jade shook his head. "Like I was sayin'. But we're going to have to wait for the signal from Reed, which should be coming any time now." Jade looked at his watch. "Your team is going to join with my men and follow us because they're on the demon target list." He took his pack and slung it over his shoulders. "My men are not on the hit list yet, so the plan is to hide your team while we keep moving."

"She needs a few minutes," Kevin said as Sara started to sit up. "While you wait for your signal." His attention went back to Sara. "Is it your arm that hurts most?" He could usually feel her pain, but for some reason it wasn't resonating with him.

"No. Why is it in a splint?"

"It's broken."

"I don't think so."

"Of course it is. Joints don't twist in the manner I found yours, and I felt it broken when I set the bone."

"Could you check again? If it were broken, I'm sure it would hurt."

"Sara, it couldn't have been more than a couple of minutes since I set it and you woke."

"All I know is it doesn't hurt. I kept dreaming about the J-man. Everything was black for the longest time until I opened my eyes to see Topetine and Mac standing over me. Can you take this stick off my arm, please?"

Kevin's fingers started to work at the knots that he'd tied with every intention to hold for days rather than minutes. Frustration at his tidy work and concern the bones had not mended set in quickly. His fingers fumbled with the well-tied material and just in time for Jade's knife to flash in front of his eyes.

"Here," Jade said, "this'll make quick work of that constructive mess."

"When we arrive at the cavern, we'll get as close as we can to the exit and send Sara through first," Jade said to Kevin.

"We won't need to go there," I said. "There's another way. Topetine and Mac will meet up with us."

"What other way?" Kevin asked.

"The J-man." I paused, trying to recall the words I'd heard in my ear. "He said the way out would be to follow the water, the falls." *Is that right? Was it a dream?* "Yes, the falls," I said again, as if trying to convince myself the instruction I received was indeed real. My recollection was that we hadn't seen any falls except the one that had emptied us into the cenote.

"Careful," Kevin said, pulling away the last scrap of knotting.

I held my bent arm as he pulled the makeshift splint away and eased it into a straightened position.

"It might still be weak. Take care with it."

Kevin shot a look to Jade. "Do you know the area she's talking about?"

"My men and I crossed a few cliffs. One had a small fall when we first arrived, not too far from here."

The sound of footsteps behind us had Jade whirling, gun angled at the cave opening. He lowered his hands at the sight of Juno, Matt, and Reed.

The demon shadows would have made no noise, but the sounds of the dogs or the beasts that ruled them would have. Jade was accustomed to taking no chances.

"We're ready," Reed said. "The men and the rest of her team are just over there." He waved two fingers to indicate where they were waiting.

"Good. Set the time on my mark," Jade said, pressing a thumb and forefinger on the two buttons on his watch. "Now." Each of the men followed suit.

"You're all right?" Juno asked. His brown eyes searched mine.

"Yeah. Sore but otherwise okay. Thanks."

He let out a breath.

"We're heading toward the falls," Jade said. With a nod in response, the men disappeared into the dark.

I turned to Kevin. "What were you saying about codes?"

"It'll have to wait. You won't need them to get out of here." His eyes held mine. "Thank God you're okay. I want to know what made you want to try to kill Tarsamon."

I shrugged a shoulder. "Just a really strong feeling, almost as though this key had a motive all its own in that moment."

"Let's go," Jade said, ducking under the top of the entrance. "Time's literally a-tickin'."

When is it not?

21

"That," Jade said, "is our escape out of this jungle? It looks more like a trap." He angled his head in multiple directions, looking for any sign of unwelcome followers.

I stopped my hike on the opposite side of a rather large pool of water to get a better look at the entire ruin. The front set of steps was crawling with arms of dusty green moss. The walls not covered in green revealed the rough nature of time that had taken an obvious toll on the somewhat crooked but sturdy features. Who knew how long it had actually been here? The whole place would easily be considered eerie, even if the day had been beaming with sunshine. As it was, a fog had settled low over the top of the building, giving the image a more ominous appearance, like it had been plucked from a ghost story. The entrance was blocked by stacked stone and not a glimmer of light could be seen from the cracks beyond. On either side of the building were what might've passed as a group of headstones, had it not been that they were almost as tall as the building itself. Many of them were still standing beside several that had fallen. Beyond the ruin, the sun was beginning to crest in the sky, beaming rays through a thick haze of mist that crawled over the stones.

My senses had guided us here. Now, as I stared at the ruins as a whole, I agreed with Jade that it had the makings of a possible trap. I could only see a way in, not out. After the brief hike across a ridge to the base of the pit in the jungle, I wondered what lay beyond the other side of the blocked doorway. *Is it a gateway similar to the portal we entered that landed us in this earlier Mayan culture? One way to find out.* I stepped up the slippery path leading to the entrance.

"It's part of the Forbidden City. I recall it from the scrolls, but I didn't know what it meant at the time, or if I'd even need to find it."

I scanned the walls before peeling away the greenery that covered the edge of the framework around what should have held a door. A gap in the pattern of the moss revealed a square with a cutout in the center for four fingers.

"Check the other side," I said.

Jade stood guard while Kevin began pulling at the moss covering the opposite side of the doorway.

"There's another one of those markings here," he said. "Looks like the right hand from the direction of the fingers."

"Same here." I put my hand in the first square. Nothing. I put my hand in the second square. Again, nothing. "Shit," I said under my breath. "I hate these riddles."

Kevin's hands were at my shoulders. "What can you remember?"

I felt my gaze fall slowly to the ground in thought as I started drifting into a daydream state of mind.

The love of one for another can open any blocked passage in the Forbidden City.

"There was a saying," I replied. Each of the squares to this ruin had the hands in the same position. "Two right hands." I paused. "Put your hand on the one over there," I said, pointing to the area he had cleared. As he did, I placed my right hand in the square closest to me.

The imprinted block fell back, turned once to the right, and came forward to be flush with the rest of the stone, as if a key had just been inserted into a lock.

"That's it?" Jade said. His voice was a little closer now. I glanced over my shoulder at him. He was indeed closer but had taken the position of watchman with gun in hand.

As if in answer, the ground shook with a single violent rumble that almost set me off-balance. I placed a hand against the frame of the door, as the squared stones blocking our entrance tumbled backward, allowing a rough passage into the ruin.

I started to climb over them but was stopped from progressing farther with a pull at my back. I looked over my shoulder to see Kevin had a grasp of my shirt.

"What are you supposed to find in there?" he asked, releasing his hold.

"I'm not sure. With any luck, a way out. Like most anything on this quest, I'll know it when I find it." *I sure as hell hope so, anyway.*

I stumbled over the last few blocks of stone and stood up, brushing the remaining debris from my hands. Kevin was right beside me and Jade had made it halfway in.

The sound of air passing through a tunnel had me turning to see how we were going to find an exit in the dark. Jade was right. Without being able to see the back of the ruins, it did feel like a trap. But my senses were telling me this was the way.

Two steps into what I thought would be a search in the dark, the crackling sound of electricity rang out in open air and, along with it, sparks. *This is it.*

"This is the portal that should lead us out of here," I said. The sounds of snapping and buzzing grew louder as a pipeline alive with electric current expanded and curved into a similar size hole as the one in Scotland when I had the three medallions clutched in my palm, deep in the bottom of my coat pocket. Eldor said one door would open the passage to another. But he didn't say where they would lead.

"Are Mac and Topetine with your men and the rest of our team?" Kevin asked, turning to Jade.

"They weren't the last—"

A flash blew across my vision, fully lighting the darkened ruins as though daylight had blazed in. "We have to hurry. I have to pass through."

"We can't leave without Topetine."

"We can't stand here and wait, either. Once I open the gateway, it will remain open for passage," I shouted over the current. "But if I don't go through it, I don't know how long the path will stay open."

My eyes darted to the left at a movement that caught my eye. Jade whirled around and lowered his weapon seeing Aria beside one of his men. *Fifteen minutes can't have passed since we entered. Something's wrong.*

"There's trouble," Reed said, confirming my suspicion. "The rest of Sara's team is on their way here." His phrases came out in bursts as he fought to catch his breath. "The dark forces were stationed at multiple points in the realm. Every fifteen-degree location we traced had a shadow, sometimes several approaching within seconds. Her team isn't safe with us."

"How far are you from—"

A shriek from the ridge outside the ruins sailed over the crackling electricity waiting for us, interrupting Jade, as another one of his men arrived, delivering Elise. There was no mistaking the sound of the dark angel.

"Five minutes, maybe, is all we have before they are here."

"Sara, go through," Kevin said. "That ring should protect you on the other side. I can't be sure if it will with the angel."

I was reluctant to leave without my team. But I'd been in a similar position before and had gone against his direction. That had been a grave mistake that almost ended the quest.

I turned to Reed, "Is the jaguar woman with you, Topetine?"

"The little woman?"

I nodded.

"Yeah. Mac brought her with him, after my men found her hiding just outside the cave with the glyphs. She'd been trying to get back to you, she said, after the serpent god was freed."

"Sara, go," Kevin urged, placing a hand at my back. "I'll wait for you and the others."

"As long as it's safe. Otherwise, we'll find you."

I reached a hand toward the electric current, still buzzing, and felt the unmistakable pull of its energy like a magnet. The silver ring was its connection, the key to open the transport. As I stepped forward, the fall grabbed me and sent me sailing through what looked like a wormhole. In my past travels through the passages, I'd blacked out. Headaches had swirled me into darkness just before nothingness swept me to another place and time, only to wake wondering exactly what year I'd arrived. This time was different. I was still awake. The tumbling had me wishing that I'd blacked out. Falling into the unknown had my stomach threatening to revolt. I swallowed hard and closed my eyes tight, wanting nothing more than to hold on to something, as my head started swimming in dizziness, until the wormhole disappeared and blackness curtained across my vision.

I woke to the sound of a rhythmic squeak and the scent of dead, damp leaves to see a homeless man pushing a cart with a loose wheel along a sidewalk. I was also wearing different clothing, a skinny jean this time with knee-high boots, always boots, and a loose-fitting black shirt with a long black coat. The sky was darker than the one I'd left. *Central Park? In the middle of the night?*

The feel of cold, sharp steel against my temple that couldn't be mistaken for anything other than the pointed blade of a knife had me frozen and far from further reflection on my location. I'd just received confirmation of my guess. The man wielding the blade crouched beside me and lifted my right hand. He could try, but there was no way he was going to swipe the ring from my finger unless he cut the finger off. Even I hadn't been able to get the shiny band to budge since it had been put there.

"Sara Forrester?" a voice said over my head. "Or is it Arwyn?"

I rolled my eyes in the direction of the man's voice and tilted my head ever so slowly. Not feeling the pressure of the blade, I took in a breath as he lowered the knife.

"Either will do," I replied. "But most people refer to me as Sara."

"One good jab in the right place is all it would take to end your quest and keep things as they are," he said, offering me his free hand to help me up.

Good thing you know who I am.

"Of course, you wouldn't know about what's been taking place because you've been away. Go on." He pointed at random with the tip of the blade before stashing it. "Get a good look. That evildoer you're trying to stop isn't going to wait to see if you succeed."

With the realization I wasn't going to die immediately, I stepped to the side and set some distance between us. The stout man, who had crept up on me, was wearing jeans, a basic black T-shirt, and a tan trench coat that, on his stature, looked like an open dress. He looked as though he'd walked out of a rerun of an investigator-type sitcom from the 1980s. His hair was in thick waves of white framing a bulbous face. I blinked once and again, shifting my gaze in another direction. When I'd last left New York, the shadows had begun consuming the weaker people, those who carried fear and anger. To me and the members of the team who were fighting Tarsamon's effort, they had looked like nothing more than small children attached to their hosts. I doubted if the person that carried one even knew it was there. But now, they were full-sized and heavy with the life of the person they'd taken, and the shell of several bodies walked aimlessly across the grass.

"And what side are you on?" I asked.

"Well, you're still alive, aren't ya?"

"That makes little difference to the evil that hunts me," I said, remembering that Tarsamon didn't want to kill me for fear of releasing the keys I already held.

"I suppose it doesn't."

"How did you know where you could find me?"

"I'm one of the good guys, a member of the Inner Society."

"What are you talking about? What society?

"It's a sleeper cell of people who have held the belief that this day, your quest, that is, would come. They know a lot about you and your mission. You'll have to come with me to stay safe." He gaze darted right, then left. "This is no place to talk."

He was right about that. "If you are in fact one of the 'good guys,' you'll know I'm not going anywhere with you, and especially not without my team."

"I anticipated that might be the case. Your team will be directed where to find you. Besides, Mary Ann would be happy to see you."

"Mary Ann?" I tried to hide my surprise. "How do you know her? What've you done?" When I'd left New York, she didn't know anything about the actual mission, only that I was following Kevin to the

Yucatan for research. I was fairly certain she wouldn't follow anyone she didn't know, unless she'd been tricked. My adoptive mom was to me like a real mother, and the only person besides Kevin I loved. "So help me if you've hurt her."

The man lifted the corner of his mouth and turned, heading off in the opposite direction.

22

Sleeper cell? Inner Society? My team should be passing through the same portal I'd come through within the next few minutes. But then, so would the evil chasing them, if the passage worked like the last one. I watched as the man strode farther away. *Mary Ann or the team?*

"Hey," I called. "What's your name, anyway?" *I can track him down later.* There was no reply as the man kept walking. "Damn it," I said under my breath, knowing I'd have to follow. *Kevin said he would find me.* I jogged a few paces to catch up with the man. Just as I was about to ask him about the Inner Society, the sound of thunder rolling across the sky interrupted any attempt. I stopped in my tracks and turned back to see several people fall a few feet to the ground out of thin air and tumble like laundry across the grass. *One, two, Juno, Kevin, flaming red hair—Aria—Topetine, and the rest of them.* I breathed a sigh of relief.

"Now you've done it," a voice said behind me. I shifted my attention to see the man who had been walking away was inches behind me.

Done what?

"You should have come with me when I told you to. We can't stay hidden with that many of you walking about in a world mostly consumed by the shadows." The man reached into his coat and pulled out a radio. "No go. Expect near thirty. Assistance at the gate."

Thirty?

The answer became clear as Jade's men arrived behind my team. *Okay, that might attract attention.*

My gaze locked on Kevin. His head turned and our eyes met. Behind him, in the space they had fallen through, a window formed of the electricity that had opened the portal, and in that window was a light similar to the glow of white I'd seen in the wormhole. Was it a signal more people were coming? What if they were the shadows?

"Hurry," I called. "The portal is still open." The answer to my question became clear, filling the light and turning it black to match the night sky. Jade's men and my team jumped up and headed in my direction. A single crack was all I heard before the electricity fell to one scorching seam in the sky, pressing the window closed and, with it, whatever was inside the portal.

"Someone's got our back," Aria said. "That was too close."

"Who's this?" Juno asked, referring to the man behind me.

I turned to him. "Now you've got to give up a name."

"Later," he said. "You can't be out here. Follow me, and hurry."

"He belongs to a group known as the Inner Society," I said.

"Is that true?" Kevin asked the man.

"Yeah, it's true. Now can we get going?"

"He's got something we need, Sara," Kevin said, "to help us in accessing the next key."

The man led us past a few store windows, one of which I noted to be a sushi shop and next to it a bakery, reminding me that I'd stuffed my need for nourishment somewhere between a cave opening and an old ruin. At the glimpse of food in the lit windows, I realized I was famished. *I've missed this city, even if it's been overtaken by evil.*

We passed the shops and turned into an alley. The man stopped at a dumpster, flattened both palms, and pushed it a short distance to reveal a cutout in the shape of a five-by-five square in the pavement. He bent down and placed a thumb in the corner, causing a thin glass box to extend a few inches upward, transforming the space into an elevator.

"Get in," he said to me.

"Take Jade with you," Kevin said. "He can trace the others to the location faster than this can move if he knows where he's going."

"You go, too," the man said, waving a finger between Kevin and Topetine. "Someone else is on their way up to meet the others and carry them down behind us." And with that, the five of us piled into the small compartment. With the push of a button, the glass shield lifted to its full extension, encasing us, just before it descended below ground.

"Can you tell us your name yet?" I asked, breaking the silence.

"Carl," he replied. "But it's not important. I'm only the delivery-man, assigned to find you and get you to safety. The people you need to meet with have the piece you're in need of."

"What piece?" I asked.

"The piece that unlocks the codes I'm carrying from the J-man," Kevin said.

"Ah," I replied. "And is it still—?"

"Current year, yes."

Which means cell phones, Internet, TV, assuming I can get TV or a connection this far below ground, and food.

"Do you know where we might be able to scrounge up some food?"

"Arrangements have been made."

I hope the arrangements include…Oh, who could care? I'd settle for a handful of Peanut M&Ms. After what we'd been through and how so much of the bright, busy world of New York had been sucked dry of most of the energy in it, my expectations were pretty low. But that didn't stop a fantasy of delectable food from forcing its way through my head, whether in the shop windows or a vending machine.

"This is quite far beneath the surface, isn't it?" I asked, seeking to avoid the awkwardness of silence in a tight space and a distraction from the nagging pangs of hunger. The elevator passed quickly through a channel that was as transparent as the glass that held us, with layers of rock changing at varying levels. Within the tunnel that carried the elevator were tubes I assumed to be some sort of air filtration. It felt very much as though I were looking into an oversized ant farm, minus the ants.

"Yes. We'll be close enough to the outer core but safe from the heat. The energy increases in intensity the farther down we get, or the closer to the core, disperses all other energy, even yours, making it as safe a haven as possible from someone hunting you or your team. This city has been under construction for many years in preparation for your quest."

City? How do the people Carl is leading us to know about me? Are they connected to the Alliance? Can they be trusted?

"Who belongs to this Inner Society?" I asked.

"The Inner Society is made up of what you would call introverts, the silent type, meditators, spiritualists, and the like."

Which might explain how they lured Mary Ann to follow them. She was the type to gravitate toward peace and a bit of the supernatural to escape the desperation often found in the faces that presented to the shelter she volunteered with.

"Here we are," he said.

The walls of the elevator retracted into the base of the floor. We stepped off the asphalt platform to shiny marble floors and a large open room crafted in modern décor. Any sign of dirt and rock was neatly tucked away behind white textured panels, with varying shades of gray and blue accents. Several sconces of clean burning flame floated within glass cylinders attached to the walls.

"Wait here," Carl said.

Jade's eyes had not stopped searching every corner of the immaculate room in an effort to justify such a place underground or a potential surprise that might jump out from a corner.

"Ten seconds and I'm going on my own to search for Mary Ann," I said.

Kevin stopped his casual gaze across the room and stared at me. "Mary Ann?"

"The guy said he had her. He wanted me to follow him before you came through the portal."

"I'm going back up to get the rest of my men, your team, whoever is left," Jade said. "If we were being set up, I'd have to believe someone would have approached us by now."

"If being this close to the outer core disperses all energy, how will you trace back to us?" I asked.

"I can follow the path of that." He gestured to the square, where the elevator had disappeared into the floor. "Its energy can be tracked." I watched as his image gradually faded from view.

"Sara, Kevin, and of course, Topetine. So pleased to finally meet you," a woman said, stepping forward with her hand extended. She was dressed in a long, loose-fitting, multicolored dress. Her eyes said more than the words flowing from her lips. Within them beamed depth and understanding. They held a kind of all-knowing wisdom. "My name is Leahnan. I head the operation to keep what light is left on Earth protected from the dark forces. But we can talk about that later. I'm sure you'd like to see Mary Ann."

"I would. Thank you. Is she hurt at all? From the activity I saw above, it looked like very few people were functioning with their own mind-set." But what I really wanted to know, too, was if Leahnan and the others in this secluded place had tricked or possibly threatened Mary Ann.

"My goodness, no." We stepped in beside the woman, who turned and started heading down a hallway. "She's here of her own accord, unharmed. I assure you. Your adoptive father, Robert, however, was not able to be persuaded."

No surprise there. Never had there been a time when Robert wasn't more concerned with work and the resulting money that came from multimillion-dollar deals. The last I'd heard, he was on business in England, ensuring the acquisition of a company. Who knew if London looked anything like New York did with the shadows and shells of bodies walking about, but I was certain it would take a catastrophic event to get him to come home. He wasn't one to leave a deal on the table under mere persuasion.

I cast my gaze through a window opposite from where we were and saw daylight. *How is that possible?*

"We wanted to create a world with all the comforts we found above ground but without the noise and irritation," Leahnan replied. "Holograms, enhanced lighting features, and other images are used to simulate those tranquilities people tend to enjoy, in place of the real thing."

"You're telepathic?" I asked.

"We all are. The difference between this little city, if you will, and the one above us"—her eyes lifted upward—"is that we've honed the ability, made a conscious choice to utilize it."

Leahnan opened a door and invited us to step through. I spotted Mary Ann and wasted no time closing the distance, throwing my arms around her. "Are you okay?"

"Of course," she said, pulling back. "Can you believe what has happened?"

I shook my head. I hadn't had much more than a glimpse of Central Park, but if everything looked at all like what I'd seen, then no, I couldn't believe Tarsamon would have infiltrated humanity so quickly. His plan seemed to be moving at a relatively slow pace when I'd left to find the first key, but clearly he hadn't let his chase after me interfere with his mission. In the span of a month and a half, he'd made good on his promise to end the "suffering," as he had once described to me, of the humans and his intent on consuming that energy for the purpose of growing his forces.

"We'll let you two catch up for a few minutes, but then we must move on," Leahnan said. "There are light refreshments to tide you over until dinner this evening. Kevin, if you'll follow me, I believe we have a matter to attend to while Sara and Mary Ann reconnect."

"You have a connection here?" I asked him.

"The algorithms," Leahnan replied, smiling. "If you'll follow me," she said to Kevin.

After Leahnan and Kevin left, I pulled Mary Ann to one of three plush sofas angled in a U pattern.

"How did they find you?" I asked, eyeing her. She appeared healthy, well rested.

"Who? Leahnan?"

"Yes," I said with a tinge of impatience in my tone.

"She and her assistant showed up at the center where I was doing some work. They said they knew you and that you were on a trip, but didn't say how they knew, only that they had important information and that I should come with them." She paused and reached for my free hand. "What happened to your wrists?"

"Just a few scratches...on a hike." *From a few tight bindings.* The previous red bands left from the vines C-05 had wrapped around my wrists had lightened into a darker shade of pink but hadn't faded fast enough to go unnoticed. She eyed me speculatively. "I didn't tell anyone, except you, about my trip with Kevin."

"How did they know?"

"I'm not sure." *Is Leahnan's telepathy focused enough to know such detail?* "But I assure you I aim to find out. How long have you been here?"

"Only a few days."

"And they've been treating you well?"

"Yes, Sara. They even let me bring your dogs with me. They're in a nice area. I don't think you have to worry."

For Mary Ann, I always worried. No one had cared for me like she did, and it was my minimum responsibility to be sure she remained safe and happy if possible. I patted her knee. "You're probably right." I stood up and wandered over to the table of refreshments, unable to deny my hunger any longer and not wanting to worry Mary Ann about my doubts. I downed a bottle of water and eyed the finger food, mini pizzas with a fresh basil leaf on top of each, slightly wilted from the heat, avocado bruschetta, mini Italian grinder sandwiches, and a host of other carefully prepared items. I selected a few pieces while my stomach signaled it wanted much more than the small collection on my plate.

"What information did your hosts say they had?" I asked casually, eyeing a salad. *Wait until Jade and his men get here. There won't be a crumb left to be found.*

"A mission of some sort. They said you were responsible for helping to stop the chaos."

"They said that?" It surprised me that anyone tied to this mission would provide that much information to someone not involved. I sat beside Mary Ann.

"Yes, but they wouldn't say how you are supposed to do this or why you were asked to do it. Is it true?"

Should tell her all that I knew or just what she asked? I'd never lied to her before and I wasn't going to start now. Mary Ann was a tough woman. She'd stared into the eyes of battered wives and their children and handled it with all the strength and finesse required.

"Yes, it's true. Kevin is part of this mission, too, as are a few other friends. But I think I mentioned some of this when we last had dinner together."

"I remember you were going with Kevin on a research mission. You told me if I ever felt scared to get somewhere safe like your house. But as I mentioned when we last spoke, that's been ransacked."

I frowned. The mansion had ancient artifacts I'd recovered over the last ten years. I'd just begun adding to the collection recently. And the cars. I hoped the garage full of exotics was untouched. What bothered me most, however, was that in her own way, she'd just admitted she had been afraid and had nowhere to go. At Mary Ann's touch, I looked at her and pressed a smile through the thought. "It's all stuff, right?" I said, hoping to shift my discomfort aside.

"Sara, nothing appears to have been stolen, just broken." I wasn't sure which was worse. "Mainly the floors, walls. Looks like a wildcat used your interior as a scratching post."

"Insurance will cover the damage," I said, hoping such a thing still existed.

"Tell me," I said, "Is everything, I mean are *all* the people stumbling around like those I saw when I arrived earlier this evening?"

"Evening? Good God, it's nearly three in the afternoon," she said, eyeing her watch. "The people here say it's not safe to venture above. The clouds never part and the day shifts from light gray to dark gray. Yes, I've heard that people aren't the same. But I only saw a few that made me wonder. I think a lot has changed in the last several days," she added.

"It certainly seems so. Are you comfortable here for a little while longer?"

"I'd like to get back to helping the people that need the services the center offers and my gardening." Her eyes drifted in another direction. "My life, you know?" she added, glancing back to me. "But I understand if that's not possible right now. Besides, if it's always dark, there isn't much gardening I can do."

I could feel her understanding. Her patience, however, was on its own ticking timer. It wouldn't be long before she'd demand to get back to what life she thought she still had. Maybe it did exist. But from the little I saw, not likely, and certainly not in any manner she'd expect.

"Look," she said, pulling me from my reflection on the matter. "If what they say is true, that you're responsible for resolving the conflict that is occurring, whatever that is exactly, I'll stay if you say that's best."

So they hadn't told her everything.

"I do, for the time being. What about Robert? Does he know where you are?"

She waved a hand in dismissal. "The last I spoke with him, day before yesterday, I believe it was, he was tying up the last few ends of that deal he'd been working on and was planning on coming back from London. I told him I was visiting with a few friends and to take his time. I mean, as nice a place as this is, there's no way anyone is going to keep him here, even if you say so, Sara. You know that."

I nodded. "That's probably better, anyway."

"I think so."

"He didn't mention the darker skies or strange behavior of people?"

"Nothing more than it's been cloudy for days and there was no sign of it letting up. When his head is in a deal, he doesn't notice much around him, has dinner with only the people he needs to, and the rest of the time keeps his nose in the news, reading. That may be the only way he does know what's going on, but he didn't mention anything to me."

"Okay. I'm glad at least you spoke with him and that you're well."

"What's left for this mission of yours? How much longer?"

"I wish I knew exactly. I have to go to Egypt. That's the last leg."

She let out a heavy sigh.

"Try not to worry. I think you're safest if you stay with the people who brought you here, and I'll do what I can to finish this mission as quickly as possible. Maybe then we can look back on this adventure as nothing more than one realistic bad dream, over a few drinks and dinner."

"I'd like that," she said. "You look so tired." She brushed a hand over my arm.

"I haven't had time to think about it. But now that you mention it, yes. I believe I am. And I'm in desperate need of a shower. Do you think they have that way the hell and gone down here?"

She tossed out a small laugh, reminding me how I'd missed our chats over dinner, usually consisting of my favorite, her home-cooked Italian. "They do. Let me show you. Your room is next to mine."

I didn't know anything about Leahnan or the other people of this city beneath the city, but one thing I was grateful for was that they told Mary Ann the truth and had kept her safe. That wouldn't grant them my full trust, not yet, anyway, but it was a good start. Now, I thought, for a shower and some information from my new hosts.

23

The water pulsed steaming hot streams onto the crown of my head. It didn't matter that the shower stall was smaller than the elevator bringing me to this underground haven. A haven because I'd stepped from mud, moss, and humidity of the jungle to what might be considered a high-end resort with its amenities. After not properly bathing for days, my muscles began to soften like butter at the feel of the jets pulsing the near-scalding water across my skin.

The relaxation I felt now was a brief respite from the business I'd have to get back to very soon. Time was less and less on our side as Tarsamon was growing more desperate with only one key remaining. *What will he do now that the power that protects me could cause him to lose his own?* Fascinating how he was so depleted of his own energy that he'd had to retreat. I hadn't expected that outcome, but instead for him to somehow restrain the energy clearly causing him pain. I'd finally become stronger than he. *How will he try to intercept my path this time?* I'd better expect him in Egypt. The glimpse I'd gotten of C-05's secret 'think-tank,' before setting out on the path for the first key, held the secrets of this mission. *Is that why I wasn't given certain key information I need to get through the mission? Is it possible the Alliance gave that task to C-05 and why I've been left in the dark?* Something still wasn't adding up. The Alliance would have known C-05's decision to abandon the quest almost as soon as he'd made it.

Tarsamon had taken everything he needed from C-05 and left him for dead, a lost soul left to wander. If C-05 lived and was indeed under protective guard as Eldor had said, there's no way he would go back to Tarsamon. He'd burned a bridge with the Soltari. Where could he go? "He's probably thrilled to be under protective guard," I said under my breath. *But under whose order was that done? Who would take him?* My thoughts skipped over the Soltari and Eldor.

As I turned off the water, the sound of a small thud outside the bathroom door I'd left open partway caused all thought of C-05 to depart. I reached for the towel, wrapping it around me quickly as I stepped onto the less slippery flooring of a tiny bathmat. *Mary Ann? She would have said something by now. Jade?* I felt my eyes narrow. *He'll be a bloody pulp when I finish with him.* There was no place to go but through the door. My hair dripped in beads across my shoulders and back, sending a slight chill over my skin. *One of us is going to have to move.* I peeked across the slit between the door and the frame, giving me only a partial view of one side of the room. *Nothing. Damn it. Do something. What do I care if I lose a towel and end up standing naked before an aggressor? At least I'll still have my life.* I pulled open the door and smacked head on into the six-foot-two-inch rigid, disrobed form of Kevin. There were still remnants of the J-man's paint across his chest, making him appear as a warrior who had come to stake his claim.

"God," I gasped, "I almost killed you."

He laughed. "What? With terry cloth?" His index finger slipped under the edge that held the construct in place. One small tug and the towel was pooled at my ankles.

"I think you missed a spot," he said, raking a gaze over my length.

"And you"—I paused—"have yet to address a single one."

"A minor oversight I aim to rectify right now." He stepped through the door, forcing me backward toward the shower. He pressed the buttons on the wall and dialed in the digital temperature next to the shower with his left hand, while his right hand remained solidly in place at my hip.

I've become used to the feeling that I'll need to fight at any moment. Can I really take time without the worry of interruption, the worry we aren't alone?

"You will," he said, hearing the thought. "We've nothing but time, for now, anyway. The door to the room is locked, we aren't expected for a few hours, and I've missed you terribly." His eyes clouded.

My hand slipped along his cheek, still scruffy with the formation of a beard over the last few days. My fingers extended into his hair and pulled him to me. His eyes closed to half-mast as his lips brushed across mine once and returned to taste, delve, and reclaim. I met each sweep of his tongue across mine as the water pulsed between us. I felt his intensity rise to heights neither of us had experienced since we'd had that fight in the cabin that seemed so long ago. Because while there had been plenty of pent-up frustration then, as there was now, no anger remained, no fear, no taking for granted the love between us. Raw, carnal lust joined with eternal devotion in a way I'd never known, not in this life. He pressed himself against me, pulling me to him.

He turned so that the water bounced off his shoulder. "I can't have you the way I want to in here," he said, evidently feeling the pinch of the size of the shower.

I smiled, breaking the embrace. "I'll wait for you." I stepped back and out of the shower, scooping up my towel and wrapping it around me.

"Thirty seconds," he said. "A minute tops." As I closed the door to let him enjoy the comfort of the warm pulse, I heard him mumbling, "Bloody shower...ruining a good thing."

Wondering if I'd have to dress in the same attire I'd been clothed in since coming through the passage into Central Park, and more out of curiosity, I opened the small closet to find a pair of black heels in my size with a pair of Italian leather dress shoes for Kevin. A black dress and a man's tailored suit hung beside each other. I flipped the tag on the dress. *My size. How did they know? Mary Ann? Who fed them all the other information they have? Got to get to the bottom of this.*

I stepped away from the closet, turned back the covers of the bed, and sat down, pressing my back into the pillows. Someone had gone to some lengths in considering the cozy ambience of the room. Aside from the small shower, the area was spacious enough, holding a king-sized bed easily, with plenty of room for two chairs against a wall and in front of what was a good replica of a window gleaming a bright yellow hue of a late-afternoon sun against a radiant blue sky. I picked up the remote beside the bed and pressed the button marked *shade* and the light from the make-believe window grayed, dimming the room. I debated lighting the cozy space and, with the press of another button, settled on a single small lamp on a table between the chairs.

The trickling sound of water, the dim lighting, and the soft feel of the pillows had me tilting my head back and closing my eyes. How I'd missed such basic comfort. "The door is locked," I said to myself, remembering Mary Ann was only steps away on the other side of the wall. I opened my eyes and stared at a couple of speakers on the ceiling, picked up the remote to find TV and music available. *Entertainment. God, how I've missed the present day and getting lost in a program or the individual notes of a good composition.* Pressing the latter caused a flow of soft music to fill the quiet and mask any curious ears. The door to the bathroom opened.

"Well now," Kevin said, towel wrapped around his waist. He'd shaved in the short time I'd been waiting, revealing the angular cheekbone and jawline I'd first fallen in love with. My favorite look was a toss-up between the clean-shaven face before me and the three-day-old scruff. The wry little smile that edged out across that masculine face was more than a bit sexy. "An angel sitting alone."

As if on cue, Paula Cole's "Feelin' Love" started to play softly over the speakers. I stood from the bed and closed the distance between us.

"Hardly," I replied, letting the towel I'd held tight fall. I slid my hand across his side, skimming the deep scar left by a wound he'd received in the dark world long ago, and placed a kiss on the side of his neck, with a tiny play bite before pulling back to meet his eyes.

"Warrior angel is more suitable," he said. "We're never going in there"—he angled his head back toward the bathroom—"together again." The back of his hand stroked across my cheek. He scooped me up. "Pity, too."

Placing me gently on the bed, he stood over me. His index finger skimmed across my bottom lip, full and eager to taste him again, while the long, slender fingers of his other hand slipped across my neckline and over my breast. A flat palm drifted down my abdomen, causing a slight quiver at his touch.

The familiar warming sensation that presented when he was near began to heat, first at my left side, then up and across my chest. The tingling that followed raced down the left side of my arm.

I gently grasped his wrist. "What is this overwhelming sensation across my skin?" I asked.

He dropped the towel, revealing himself to me. His eyes were again at half-mast. "It's our bond. I feel it, too, every time I'm around you." He lowered himself onto the bed, settling above me. His lips were at my cheek, and I felt the heat of his breath brush across my skin. "Every sensation with you is stronger than any other I've known in my life before you came into it. There's no comparison." His lips came back to mine.

"I've missed this," I said. "You. Us. Alone."

"When this mission is all over—"

"No," I interrupted, placing one finger against his lips. "Don't finish that thought. I'm happy with right here, right now. No plans."

I'd come a long way, having never wanted the burden of a relationship and its demands. Over time, the careful approach, right touch, and delicate patience that Kevin utilized to shift that desire had worked. It wasn't that I didn't want a future with him after this quest was over but that I didn't know what would happen when it was, or if we'd finish it alive, either of us. Mac had suggested only once that, to release the keys I carried, it might mean having to give up my life. I, of course, hoped he was wrong. The truth was I didn't know how the power I carried would be transferred from me to aid Earth. And after nearly losing Kevin, I didn't want any promises of together to haunt me.

The look of confusion that had skimmed across his eyes was replaced by understanding. The slight furrow of his brow eased.

My hands glided into his hair and I lifted my head, pressing my lips to his, giving him my unspoken promise. I was his now, as I'd always been and would forever be. Taking the kiss deeper, I rose up and leaned into him, rolling him to his back.

He broke the kiss. "I can give you so much more," he began. I positioned myself over him as he spoke, my eyes locked with his, and with one swift motion, he slipped inside me. "God," he gasped. "You're pure fire."

"Stoked by you," I said. The heat from his body lit the flame, had me turning over in desire for all of him. His want, his need, the fuel that burned us both. Feeling his thrusts as I held on, this time riding the wave as it threatened to crash to shore too soon. The music over the speakers only added to the intensity and rhythmic thrum that was calling for our release.

A guttural sound came from him, interrupting my silent gasps for more, as he flipped me to my back and pressed his palms into mine. He drove me deeper, harder than I remembered him ever doing. He eased back, slowing his pace, all the control he demanded contained but on the brink of release. The sensations of love and lust, his and mine, pulsed through my veins, before the waves of protectiveness and control followed. A sparkle of gold flashed across the eyes I stared into as we remained joined in that slow pattern that held me in his clutches, on the brink. And he knew it as much as I did. I closed my eyes in a long blink and took in a deep breath.

"Look at me, my love." He waited for me to open my eyes. "I want to connect with you in every way."

"I'm yours." The words spilled across my lips in a single gasp.

He increased his thrusts, faster, deeper. The exchange of emotion, the sensation of skin, muscle, and movement, the pulsing of my own heartbeat in my ears. The music faded behind the rush. The wave was cresting, and this time I couldn't stop it from breaking against the solid form of the man holding me. As I gripped him, my fingers tightened against his back, never to let go. He clutched me tight against him and drove me into the soft bedding with each press of his body, claiming his peak with mine in a quiet melody of moans and gasps.

Several minutes passed, locked in our embrace as our breaths fell back to a rested state. The air cooled around us, and the music continued to play the soft notes of a light classical selection.

I lifted my hands to my face and brushed my hair back. Kevin shifted to the side. I turned to face him and placed a hand on his heart.

"Your eyes. They're different," he said, reminding me Aria had mentioned noticing a similar change.

"In what way?"

"A sparkle. A glimmer of blue across the jade green I fell in love with," he said, studying them. He stroked a hand through my hair. "It's not constant but shines like a flash of light across a dark room every so often."

"How…distracting, probably annoying as well."

"Light from the Light Carrier."

"I never like to draw attention, you know?"

"You don't get a choice this time," he said, kissing me on the forehead. "Come here." He snaked an arm around my waist and gently pulled me into him. "We have a couple of hours before we need to meet for dinner with the Inner Society. Let's enjoy the alone time while we have it, shall we?"

I smiled and placed a light kiss on his lips. "This society, can we trust them?"

"There you go, not letting yourself rest." He pulled back slightly and angled his head at me. "Yes. And that's all I'm going to say on the matter. Sleep. You'll need it."

Rest wasn't something I could allow myself with questions rushing through my mind. *If he says we can trust them, then it must be so.* More questions pried their way through the comforting thought as I settled against his chest and breathed in his masculine scent, thanking the Powers That Be and the magic of the J-man for returning him to me. Within minutes, I gave in to the trust I'd been practicing to have in others, especially in the one person I'd learned to put my faith in. The one content, breathing deeply beside me. Of course, only time would prove him right…or wrong.

24

The hearty laughter of a woman carried over the sounds of conversation, lifting me away from the daydream I'd departed to. I shifted my attention and smiled in her direction, pleased to hear the happiness while everyone talked over a dinner of ribeye or butternut squash enchiladas, for those individuals not partial to meat. The taste of the vegetable dish was so much better than it sounded. I took another long sip of Chardonnay, peeking over the rim of my glass at the number of guests mingling with my team and Jade's men.

"Are you all right?" Kevin asked. "You're awfully quiet." He leaned in closer so that his lips were at my ear. "I can't hear a single thought from you."

"Yes," Mary Ann said, sitting to my left. "I can't remember another time when you've been so quiet."

I nodded, setting my glass on the table. "I'm fine. I'm absorbing the atmosphere, lost in thought. Not sure yet about the Inner Society."

"Darling, you worry too much," Mary Ann said.

"You have nothing to worry about." Kevin dabbed a napkin at his mouth. "I spoke at length with Leahnan while you were with Mary Ann."

"I don't understand what they bring to this equation, to the quest."

"I assure you, Leahnan would be happy to provide you with an answer."

I didn't doubt it, but I was growing impatient. The world was being sucked clean of the life it carried while I dined. That annoyance was growing into anger and quickly.

"I can't sit here any longer."

"One moment, okay?" Kevin said. He stood, tossed his napkin on his chair, and made his way toward our host. I downed the last sip of wine, more for my nerves than the enjoyment of it.

"Everyone looks about done, or close to it," Kevin said, returning to his seat after a few minutes.

"I don't want to rush anyone. Why don't I just go and—"

"Ladies and gentlemen," Leahnan said, cancelling my plan of escape. "I'd like to thank you for sharing your time with us this evening. A few of us will be departing, but don't let that interrupt your evening. Feel free to continue enjoying dessert and discussion as long as you'd like. Thank you for sharing time with us this evening, and thank you to Sara and her team for risking so much to rid our world of this darkness."

Leahnan held up a glass as applause rippled across the room. I couldn't have felt more awkward. By the look on Aria's and Elise's faces, they felt the same discomfort. I'd only grown slightly comfortable with being the center of attention when asked to provide a speech for one of the many Forrester charity events. Otherwise, Mary Ann had done a good job of absorbing any spotlight with her grace and charm. I kissed Mary Ann on the cheek and leaned in for a hug.

As if the chairs were suddenly set afire, the team and I stood and quickly gave our pleasantries before sailing out of the room behind Leahnan.

"Feel better?" Kevin asked, scooping up my hand and lifting it to his lips.

"Yes, thank you. I couldn't sit any longer."

"I'm so very sorry," Leahnan said, angling her head in my direction. "We'd hoped you would've found the dinner a nice respite."

Damn it. The comment wasn't meant for anyone other than Kevin's ears. "It was, indeed. And thank you for your kindness and hospitality. What I meant was I feel an urgency to continue with the quest and it doesn't allow me time to enjoy such luxuries." *That's the truth. Luxuries can wait until time allows.*

"Well, I certainly do understand."

Leahnan stopped at one of the squares in the floor, not unlike the one Carl had delivered us to via the elevator. The only difference was this one was larger and had a guard on duty.

"We'll be taking two transports to block D, section 444," she said to the man.

"Yes, ma'am." The guard stepped to the wall, inserted a card, and punched in a code followed by a fingerprint identification. Leahnan pressed a thumb to the same screen and the outline of two squares lit up in yellow. "The transports are ready at your command."

"Thank you." She turned to the rest of us. "Please, step inside the lit outline and we'll be on our way." Just like our transport with Carl, a box of glass lifted and enclosed us before lowering into the floor.

This material can't be as fragile as glass. I resisted the urge to put a finger out to touch it.

"It's stronger than glass," Leahnan replied. "It's a material that looks like glass but has been remanufactured. Which means it won't crack under any force. It's been tested with everything from boulders to lasers and even bullets before we decided to utilize it for the building of this underground fortress."

"Fortress?" Aria asked, echoing my thought.

"Yeah, locked down like Fort Knox," Elise said.

"You'll see why in a minute. We're protecting something very sacred to the existence of man. Nothing but the best materials went into the creation."

The elevator came to a halt in front of another guard standing in a tiny room. The man whispered something to Leahnan, who nodded and provided her fingerprint once more. "Your right hand, please," she said, turning to me.

I held out my hand to the guard, who pressed a palm-sized screen against it. A green light flashed and the guard nodded, as another set of doors behind him opened, allowing us passage from the elevator to a large, comfortable space. Sconces were lit in each of four corners of the room, revealing a tailored leather U-shaped sofa in the color of alabaster. Two people had arrived before us and were seated facing us. One I recognized as a member of the Alliance, Aren, and another I couldn't recall the name but looked familiar, likely from the Alliance as well. I met their eager stares before my gaze fell to the center of the room, where an orb, the size and shape of a bowling ball, swayed gently forward and back, suspended in air as though held by an invisible string. A single white-blue light illuminated in its center.

"Please, make yourselves comfortable," Leahnan said. Her eyes scanned the group of us.

Jade and Reed stepped toward Aren and the other man. "Good to see you again, my friend." Jade shook Aren's hand and squeezed his shoulder with the other.

"It's okay," Kevin said at my ear. "You can trust this."

Maybe I can. But what are two members of the Alliance doing here?

As I walked past the orb to take an open seat beside Aren, the light in the center grew brighter and bluer.

"Sara, this is Jandar and Aren." Leahnan extended and an open palm in their direction. "You may recall them from the Alliance."

"Hello," I said to Aren, nodding to Jandar. "Pleased to see you again." Of the seven members of the Alliance, why were only two here? The last I'd seen of either was after I'd received the first key. Aren had been arguing with the Alliance for me to remember my past with Kevin, while others disagreed vehemently with him.

"My followers and I are keepers of the light," Leahnan said. "This orb is connected to your energy, Sara, and was created at the moment of your birth into this world. It holds a fraction of the life energy of human beings. It's a fail-safe, if you will, should all light be extinguished above ground.

"Fail-safe?" I said. "Meaning, if I fail to obtain the key, a new world could be created?"

"That's a consideration," she said. "If it were to be used for that, however, it would take a very long time to reestablish a fully populated planet. The orb has two functions—the one you eluded to and a tool to aid you and your team."

"Has that happened yet? The complete elimination of the energy on Earth, that is?"

"Not yet, but the time is drawing closer."

I turned to Aren. "This orb is something created by the Soltari?"

"Yes," he answered. "It wasn't thought that you would need to know of it until the last key had been recovered and it could be destroyed."

"And yet here I am."

"The orb not only holds the remaining existence of man, it will also help you to access elements in Egypt," Leahnan explained. "What you should understand is this location is unlike any idea you might hold of Egypt. You'll be stepping into a world more advanced than history could ever have taught. The orb has been uploaded with algorithms Kevin received from the J-man that will be provided to you."

"It's a computer that can access points in the realm?"

"In a matter of speaking. Specifically, you will hold the codes to access elements that are otherwise locked."

"I need to back up a minute. How did you and your followers become keepers of the light?"

"Just as you were chosen to hold the power of the keys, there are specific people who were chosen to keep the light protected, to be on Earth at the same time you are. It's now and has been our task to find peace in an often chaotic world, to never seek harm or revenge or hold on to pain. This was the way of the Inner Society before Tarsamon carved a path into Earth and deposited his shadows of evil."

"Chosen by whom?" The Soltari I trusted. Although, I didn't agree with the means of punishment should an immortal fail an assignment. But I had yet to fully determine if that was indeed a punishment by the Soltari or handed down by the Alliance. Given the suspicion Jade and I held that members of the governing order might be working against this mission, I couldn't trust the decisions coming from them.

"The Soltari, of course," Leahnan replied.

"Is this true?" I asked, angling my head again to Aren.

"It is."

"And why wouldn't I have needed to know of this orb until I'd found the final key?"

"As Leahnan said, it was initially created for two purposes—to hold a portion of the life energy of man, something you never would have needed to know about. And"—he paused—"to release all three keys from you."

I resisted asking if that meant my death, as had once been suggested by Mac. Instead, silence filled the room as I reflected on the information.

"Why are you here?" I asked, lifting my gaze back to Aren and Jandar.

"To be sure the passage to Egypt, which only this orb can provide, is opened for you."

"As a means of protection to you and the others to get to the next realm without the dark forces at your back," Leahnan added. "But understand, you won't be able to return here, to this location, through the portal on the other side. The orb will close passage to protect the energy it holds. However, your return from Egypt will land you in New York."

"So here, but not underground here."

"Exactly. We'll keep tabs on your location and recover you as we did earlier."

Assuming we survive. I looked away from the two men and to the rest of the team. "Where's Jade and—"

"He and Reed have stepped away briefly to see if they can identify the members of the Alliance working against you and your team."

He must have left right after I was introduced to Aren and Jandar, the only time my focus was off the entire group. He'd slipped away without so much as the sound of the brush of leather he wore or even a few whispered words.

"Jade traced to the Alliance, using your energy to shift into your identities?" I asked, motioning a finger between Aren and Jandar. I was surprised he would risk being caught by any of the other members of the council who were advanced in their skill set to read thoughts and sense energy and, more specifically, to sense the presence of a change in energy.

"Yes," Aren said. "His assistant, Reed, is utilizing Jandar's energy."

"You suspected the Alliance was infiltrated by evil, too? For how long?"

"Just recently, in fact," Jandar replied. "There's been too much disagreement among the Alliance members for reasons that could not be justified. In thousands of years together, even with new members, we've never had such discord. We suspected a problem might exist after Tarsamon extended his reach into Ardan, past Eldor's guards at the border." He paused, shifted his eyes to Aren and back to me.

I nodded.

Soon after receiving the first key, I discovered Tarsamon had broken through the boundary dividing him from the rest of Ardan. It was a message to the immortals that he would not be held by any rule set by the Soltari.

"In time, you'll remember how things worked while you were with the Order," Aren added.

My memory was a sensitive topic of discussion. The fact that I'd had some parts of my history with Kevin returned to me only reduced my temper from the point of rolling boil to simmer in recent days. Knowing I had two people who were open to allowing Jade to slip undercover into the Alliance to confirm suspicions gave me great relief in believing we had at least two Alliance members we could trust. *Make that three,* I thought, remembering Eldor. Perhaps the infiltration had been going on since the onset of the mission. If so, how many decisions by the Alliance had been made that compromised our outcome?

"There is one more thing I need to know," I said, locking my gaze with Aren. "Who decided to implement a punishment to separate any member on a quest, on this quest, for eternity should we fail?" I thought of C-05 and the loss of his partner, knowing the punishment had been implemented before my quest had begun.

"Do all the members of my team stand to lose the same thing?"

Aren waited. "You put it up for a vote. And yes, each one of you"—his eyes moved past me to the rest of my team—"is at risk of losing your eternal connection."

"Impossible!" I felt my eyes scan the ground in search of an explanation. "I-I would never suggest an action, a *retaliation*, so cruel."

"It's why C-05 wanted you dead."

"Why? What would have caused me to put such a thing up for consideration by the Alliance?"

"You knew he was weak, even then. And you were right. He fell under the Dark Lord's control, leaving your team in this life."

"He felt he had nothing left after he'd lost his partner. That made it easier for him to fall."

"Regardless of why, Sara, you needed him removed from the Alliance before he made the entire force weak. One can weaken others, like a disease passing between each other. That was your argument and many of us agreed."

"I reject that. I have absolutely no recollection or even the slightest sensation that kind of decision would come from me."

"You wouldn't," Aren said. "Not with your memories blocked."

"No," I said again, more firmly. "Give me those memories, and I'll show you I'm not capable of that level of cruelty." In my heart of hearts I knew I was compassionate. My entire life as a psychiatrist, philanthropist, was based on helping people who would otherwise be considered weak, less fortunate. I wouldn't have come into this life, into that role, with the ability to punish severely and yet have such compassion for people.

Jandar's eyes went to Kevin, and I turned to him. "Eldor said you're a member of the Alliance. Is what Aren says true?"

Kevin stared blankly, the answer clear as a summer's day in his eyes. I felt my mouth drop open, shocked at his unspoken confirmation.

"Undo it," I said, turning to Aren. "Undo it right now."

"None of it, not the decision, the separation for C-05, or the risk all of you share can be undone by me alone. When the decision was approved, it was approved by the majority and held for all."

"Take it to the Alliance. Hell, take it to the Soltari. Overturn it. It's wrong."

A whisper of a sound as though someone had sucked in air came from behind me. I continued to stare at Aren, whose eyes lifted from mine.

"It's done," Jade's voice broke the silence. I turned to see he and Reed had returned. Both were breathing as though they'd run a marathon. "Jesus, the air is thin down here," he said, gasping for breath. *Takes so much energy to shift for that long.* He lifted a finger in Leahnan's direction. "You might want to consider oxygen supplementation, you know, for shifters." He lifted his gaze to me, then to Aren and Jandar. "What?"

"Sara has discovered she is responsible for the punishment of her team should this quest fail."

Jade's brows lifted. "I don't think so. Not after what I've finished witnessing."

I felt my breath escape in a rush. I closed my eyes with a sense of relief.

"Two. That's how many members were suspected of infiltrating the Alliance because of the failure at the border." He shook his head. "Almost half of the Alliance members have been compromised. There apparently had been discussion at different points for the last few months regarding when the best time to alter the power in the group would be. There has been a plan to shift the power and gradually turn it over, breaking up the balance of good and evil that had been maintained well before this mission. It's why decisions are being put up for vote that work against Sara and the team as the quest continues. If she fails, she will be gone from the Alliance and so will Kevin."

"How were you able to determine that much information so quickly?" I asked.

"Jade possesses a unique gift, Sara," Kevin said. "Not only is he able to track an individual's energy, but he also has an excellent ability to recover conversations, spoken or in thought. He's one of the best trackers that exist. Because everything is energy, including communication, once a word or phrase is produced, it can be picked up by those sensitive enough to hear and locate who said it. He only needs to be careful that he's not detected in a group of people who know of his ability."

Is that how Jade could make himself sound like Kevin in that dream in Ardan, when he'd wanted the key?

Jade winked at me and a slight sense of irritation skimmed across my face.

"I see," I said. "The knowledge is ever so helpful."

"Does that satisfy my end of the bargain to get you information about the Alliance?" Jade asked.

"I suppose. But we still don't know which members have turned against the Soltari, only that half of them have."

"You'll know when you get the third key. It provides the power to accept everything as it is. Truth will come from that power. After all, how can you have acceptance for all things as they are without truth?"

"What bargain?" Kevin asked, referring to Jade's earlier question.

"We made a deal that once I obtain the keys, I would bargain for the lives of Jade's men and that the Soltari will never impart punishment, such as the four famines, upon him and his men again. Which reminds me." I turned to Aren. "What can we do about stopping such punishments that separate eternal partners, effective with this mission?"

"You put the decision for the separation of eternal connections up for vote," Aren explained, looking at the rest of the group. "It's already been approved."

"That's the thing," Jade said. "She didn't. What I did by shifting into your form to meet with the Alliance had been done to Sara."

"By whom?" Aren and Jandar said at the same time.

"Taro. He's the only one who can split energy." Jade shook his head. "I had no idea anyone, even a member of the Alliance, had the strength to pull that off."

"Where was I when he was playing substitute for me?" I asked. "There's no way I would have let that happen."

"On a mission," Kevin said, after a gap of silence. "I remember a time on our last quest when you felt a shift in the energy. You described it like being hit by a wave that rocked you so hard your head felt as though it would explode."

"I've felt that pressure and dizziness when we went through the portals, though."

"I've been with you through those, with the exception of this last one. It's not the same. You were in tears, like you were almost going mad. It lasted a good part of one day and then nothing." He paused. "That happened right before your return to Ardan, to the Alliance. Back then, you asked what had happened to C-05, why he was no longer in the Order. That's proof she didn't know."

"I don't remember," I said.

"I do," Kevin said.

"I remember you asking where C-05 was," Jandar said. "I wondered what you meant, why you cared when you wanted him out. I dismissed the question, assuming you only meant to know where C-05 had gone to keep tabs on him."

"Jesus," I said, shifting my gaze to Aren. "The plan was to weed people out of the Alliance." *How long has that been going on?* "Can you take the issue of separating eternal partners to the Alliance now, based on the fact that *I* never put the matter up for vote?"

"Not with half of the members working against you," Aren said. "The only way to set things right is to stay alive to recover the third key. There's a way we can reverse the rule through the Soltari. Until then, you have my word, our word," he said, glancing at Jandar, "we won't allow any decisions to be passed or handed down to your team until the balance in the realm is returned."

"That's good. Because we wouldn't take any guidance now, anyway," Aria said.

"That leaves us without any governing force, no assistance," Elise added.

Without direction from the source responsible for our missions, we might have our hands tied from being able to access certain tools, certain connections.

"You have us," Leahnan said. "My group has a connection to the Soltari. It may be safer to send your requests through us and we'll take them to the Soltari directly, bypassing the Alliance."

"How?"

"Using the orb, we can track you. With the connection you will make with it to access the algorithms, we should be able to connect with you in dream state, as you would if you went into Ardan to communicate with the Alliance or the Soltari yourself."

"I think it would be best for you to stay out of Ardan, Sara," Matt said.

"Matt's right. Topetine, you have the information leading to the next guardian of the key, yes?" Kevin asked.

"Of course."

"With Topetine, the Inner Society's connection to the Soltari, and the algorithms here"—Kevin pointed to the orb—"we should be able to find our way to the third key. We also have Eldor. He can provide any additional weapons we might need."

"What we don't know is how much damage the Alliance members working against us have already done on our path into Egypt," Juno said.

"True," I replied. "But Eldor mentioned certain assurances were being made." I turned to Kevin. "You don't think Eldor is involved in a plot against us, do you?"

"Never," Kevin answered. "I know him too well. That said, no one can be trusted."

There's a position I'm comfortable with.

"Somehow, word needs to get to Eldor," Juno said. "If he's aware of what's happened, he'll instruct the elves not to act on behalf of any Alliance member's direction."

"We'll have to go through Karshan. No one will think to pass information to him before Eldor," I said.

"I'll go," Kevin said, "and meet up with you."

"I'm the only one Karshan will believe with this information," I said.

"We don't have time for you to drift into Ardan, and it isn't safe for you there," Matt said.

"Jade, do you have the strength for one more trace with me?" I asked.

"I can do that." He looked to Matt. "She's safe with me. But tracing without being discovered is riding on borrowed time. We can move quickly, but this is the last time I trace her to Ardan and back."

With Jade's ability to follow the energy of another individual, one didn't need to wait for sleep to get to Ardan, the way the rest of the immortals on the team did, providing a more efficient route. What he was concerned about, and with good cause, was the shift in energy that was detected by even a novice immortal in the realm. A repeat of entering and leaving would draw attention to him.

In a matter of minutes, I'd given up any and all fight to trust. The people in this room were everything to me and the outcome of our future existence. There was no room for my ego, my fear, or my doubt. *All in or go home.* And the latter wasn't an option.

25

"The instant you touch it, the orb will become liquid. Anti-gravity will remain in its form," Leahnan said. The orb sparkled blue, silver, and gold on the inside of a palette of black. I couldn't guess its composition. Yet I was mesmerized by the twinkling light that had come to life after I'd held my finger with the silver ring close to it. *The ring, the orb, and my life energy must all be connected.*

After I'd received Karshan's assurance that no order from an Alliance member would be fulfilled, that the borders would continue to be secured as they had always been, Jade and I returned quickly to the small group waiting for our return. I looked on as the mysterious illuminated orb continued its comfortable sway back and forth as if all the time in the world existed to rescue Earth from the clutches of darkness. If that evil was able to find us now...

You must not think like that, Sara. Thoughts become reality, eventually. Set your mind to the vision that you hold the last key. In fact, you hold all three of them.

My gaze lifted to Leahnan, telepath, spiritualist, and who knew what else.

"When you're ready," she said, "place both hands on the orb."

I stood and did as she suggested, effectively stopping the hypnotic sway, and started to lift my hands from the sphere. Faster than I could shift away, two streams of mist as black as the center of the orb lifted and wrapped around my wrists in a tight grip. I gasped and tried to pull away. Juno, Matt, and Jade jumped up, ready to make a forceful attempt to release the restraints.

"It's okay," Kevin said, extending an arm out to stop them.

I glanced at him, knowing the look of panic was assuredly plastered across my face. "How is this okay?"

"It is," he said. "It happened to me when I was asked to touch the orb, when you were meeting with Mary Ann."

I relaxed a tiny bit at hearing Kevin had already experienced the same, but didn't understand why the grasp had to be utilized at all.

"Everything is energy," Leahnan said. "Your thoughts and a choice to react or not."

I'd heard that same phrase from the Professors that had provided information at the onset of this mission.

"What you know, what you create from that knowledge, and what you share," she added, "that energy creates a physical outcome."

"Look at the orb," Kevin said.

As I did, the image of gold numbers, formulas, code streamed across the black palette, mesmerizing me into a trance.

"Her eyes," I heard Juno say.

He must be seeing the blue light Kevin mentioned.

The color of the code changed to silver, followed by blue. And with each color change, more and more of the black space in the orb filled with the language of physics, individual keys to unlock a component, or several. But what, specifically? The information blasting across my vision wasn't sharing the meaning. I felt my eyes moving back and forth over the orb, as though I were speed-reading codes to a story I couldn't put down. *When will it stop?* And then it did.

The mist recoiled from my wrists. I pulled my arms close against my chest while the edges of the sphere fell away. What remained was a floating pool of black energy with sparkling flecks of gold, silver, and blue.

"Step back a bit," Leahnan said.

As I did, the pool expanded, lifting upward until it was about the height of an average adult.

"This will take us to the location of the third key?" I asked.

"Yes," Leahnan said. "But you will have to find the guardian."

I looked at Topetine. "You're sure about this? Did you know this transport was available?"

"The text in the scrolls I studied to prepare said that another realm of enlightenment exists that holds the key I am to lead you to. The only mention of anything related to what we are experiencing is of a *society* of evolutionists that would use the mind to connect with energy."

"Okay. Leahnan is the representative of the society of evolutionists, the Inner Society, and this orb is the energy that we must connect with," I said, more to myself as I worked out an understanding that would allow me to enter the enlarged, floating pool in front of me.

"Now?" I asked, looking at Leahnan.

"When you're ready."

I angled my head in Jade's direction. "There's no need for you to send your men through. Let them remain safe. Besides, we can hide better with fewer of us."

"Never leave a man behind, Sara." His gaze pierced through me. "You'll never see my men."

"But their energy is still detectable. They may be identified before they are seen. If you won't leave a man behind, much less twenty or so, then I must ask that you stay behind." I waited for him to protest. "With the entire structure of the Alliance compromised, we have to be more careful, watchful. I won't forget the request for your men, my end of the bargain, or how you've helped us."

His eyes softened. "Tell the men to take leave in any manner that is safe for them," he said to Reed. "I'll connect at a later date in Ardan."

"Thank you," I said.

My attention went back to the portal. With Kevin standing behind me, I extended a hand toward it and was stunned to see the blackness reach out, encompassing my hand, my wrist, and my arm. With one glance at Kevin, I stepped into the center of darkness, a complete unknown, and trusted that all Leahnan had said would be true.

Like the path back to Central Park, this travel was different from the other passages. I wasn't dizzy. I had no throbbing in my head. To my surprise, I dreaded the perfect clarity and feel of the seemingly never-ending fall into oblivion that centered only on the trust of a group of mindful introverts of the Inner Society. The sound of white noise filtered across my ears, closing out further thought of anyone. It was soon replaced by the music of a simple melody in slow, singular notes. I wanted the blackout, the pounding in my head that would block all of this unusual sensation. Reality was too clear and uncomfortable in more ways than one.

The world that I'd seen when I returned to New York had changed so much that it had begun to resemble the area of Ardan where Tarsamon resided. The dark skies choked out the light, halting the progression of life. Depression had to have set in much like a seasonal affective disorder might in places clouded like Seattle, except this shade had no intention of parting. Without the renewal of the sun and life-giving energy, people would grow increasingly more depressed. Oxygen and food sources would be depleted, leading to inevitable death. Had it been two months, possibly three since I'd set off on the path for the first key? However long it had been, it hadn't taken much time for Tarsamon to increase his hold on Earth. Which meant to save lives, and not just provide a place for them to exist, I had no time to waste.

The fall began to slow as though the coaster I was on was coming to a stop. In front of me appeared pillars, reminiscent of an ancient Roman empire. *Not Egyptian.* As the tunnel I'd traveled through came to a complete halt, the blackness that carried me to this unknown place expanded until it was level with the ground. I stepped from the platform, knowing that if what Leahnan had said was true, the passage would indeed close and would not return me to the safety of the underground city.

So, this is Egypt. Leahnan was right. It doesn't look anything like what history taught me. Would an "advanced Egypt" reflect traits of a Roman empire?

The crackle of energy from the open portal behind me brought some comfort that there still remained a choice to leave if something didn't feel right or, at minimum, the rest of my team was on its way to join me. With that thought in the back of my mind, I stepped closer to get a better look at my surroundings and ended up between two enormous stone-carved faces. I lifted a hand toward one. Maybe I could pick up some sensation that would tell me if where I'd landed was good or bad, safe or unsafe.

"Careful, Sara," a male voice said behind me. Before I could turn around to see who had spoken, my neck was locked in the firm grip of the unidentified assailant. "You don't want to wake them yet."

My hand slipped through one of the figures. *An illusion?*

Just above the grip, I felt another object press against the lower part of the back of my skull. There was no mistaking the barrel of the gun.

"Just. Like. That," the voice said. "It could all be over."

The device shifted to an open area against my neck, as the person stepped within view.

C-05. Caution and calculated movement were my only thoughts.

"You're lucky I found you," he said.

"I seriously doubt it. Any minute—"

A click and a searing sensation burned against my neck. "It's necessary. You'll forgive me, one day."

I fell to the ground, though still awake and in his grasp. *No pain?* My body was incapable of exercising control over the ability to move. But I was still conscious. With his arms under my shoulders, he dragged me to the edge of the path I'd stepped onto from the portal and into the shade of a low-hanging tree.

I freed him, sure, to dissolve into the realms and possibly seek out his lost partner. Is that how to repay someone who helped you, by hitting them with a stun gun? Besides, Eldor said he was being "held." How did he break free of the protective guard? Was it a lie? No, no. He wouldn't. He must've made a deal. But who would deal with a dead man, a man who betrayed both sides?

"Shh. You need to remain quiet, for a little while longer, including your thoughts, or I'll have to hit you with this again." He flashed what looked like a gun in front of my eyes.

"By the way," he whispered. "Thank you for cutting my bindings. You saved me."

Except now I wished I hadn't.

"I'm pleased to return the favor this time around."

And look for the next installment of the Three Keys Series...
Dana Alexander's
Winter's Labyrinth

1

T he point of the gun jabbed into the side of my neck, proof that the man holding it was serious about pulling the trigger. Again. Shallow puffs of air were all I could manage. It might have only been a stun as opposed to a bullet, but given the chance, I'd be drawing my breath and his blood at the next opportunity.

"I'll explain everything later, Sara." C-05's familiar voice filled my ears, causing my blood to boil well beyond a low simmer. The rage I was feeling would likely cause me to shift into the hawk, as a means of protection. That was the result since I'd been injected against my will with a serum to alter my DNA. While I didn't like the result, it had been useful on more than one occasion. "It must be hard to believe I'm here to protect you this time around, given our last few encounters." He moved beside me.

Or because you're holding a weapon against my neck?

"I don't blame you," he said at my ear. "I'd have a hard time believing me, too. And that I'm no longer working against your effort to recover the last key." He placed a hand on the top of my head. Rage melded with a new sickening sensation.

Did the stun affect the ability to shift? Can't move equates to not being able to fly.

"The evil that hunts you has already arrived." He angled his head so I could see him. "I can't have them find you. Not now. You didn't have to open the gateway to this realm like you did in Scotland and in the Yucatan. I gave the dark forces the location this time." He stood and looked right and left before ducking down again beside me, returning the gun to its original position at my neck. "Oh, it's true that, given the proper coordinates for the initial passage, it opened an entry point from one realm to another. This one, with its *advancements,* shall we say, took a bit more effort to track. It didn't take long for you to find the path leading to the temple." He glanced around at the trees above. "Egypt. Strange how it resembles more of a jungle instead of a desert, huh?" My stare answered him with imaginary daggers, as the gun slipped down my neck an inch. "It was only a matter of time before the dark forces homed in on your energy and our immediate location." His gaze flicked back up to the sky.

How exactly are you helping me?

C-05, a man who'd once been sided with me, had put me on my back one too many times and never with my approval. Over the short time I'd come to know him in this life, I'd given him a fair show of strength that ended up drawing blood. A single chance was all I needed to put him down for a good long while. He was, after all, a man who'd turned against the mission to rescue Earth and keep Ardan, the world where immortals resided, safe.

Enemy number one to the immortals, the Dark Lord, Tarsamon, had used every bit of information C-05 held before pinning him to a wall and leaving him for dead. He'd marked his body so his soul would be forced to wander the realms, unable to reincarnate or find solace. On our last quest in the Mayan jungle, I had cut C-05 free from the necromancer spirit drifting over his immobile body, waiting to take his soul. I never thought granting him one last act of mercy would haunt me. The man should be grateful, not repaying me with the element of surprise and a weapon pressed against my neck.

"Where's that team of yours? They'd never leave you alone for long." His eyes swept across the landscape and back to the area where the portal had opened up.

Should be here any second to string you back to that wall. For good this time.

"Now, now. Don't let our past get in the way of me trying to hide you from the evil that hunts you. Both of us now, I suppose," he said, hearing my thought. "Better keep that mind quiet, too. Can't risk any of your energy being detected."

ABOUT THE AUTHOR

Dana Alexander is a summa cum laude graduate of Arizona State University who spent her career in Medicare policy, education and audit before being compelled to write the story of two souls connected across countless millennia and held together by their duty to the Alliance. When she isn't creating scenes, dialogue, and realms for the series, her time is spent with family keeping cool in the ridiculously hot desert with their two huge, swim loving Labs, Ryley and Brodie.

Connect with Dana at her website:
www.danaalexander.net